Larrah Thomas

Chad's Choice

Book Two of the Chosen Saga

Larrah Thomas Books
10120 Two Notch Road
Suite 2, Unit 126
Columbia, SC 29223

https://www.larrahthomas.com

Copyright

Copyright © Larrah Thomas.

This book is an original publication of Larrah Thomas. This is a work of fiction. Names, characters, places, and incidents either are the product of the author's imagination or are used fictitiously, and any resemblance to actual persons, living or dead, business establishments, events, or locals is entirely coincidental. The publisher does not assume any responsibility for third-party websites or their content.

All Rights Reserved. No part of this book may be reproduced, scanned, or distributed in any format or by any means, including photocopying, recording, or other electronic or mechanical methods, without the prior written permission of the publisher, except in the case of brief quotations embodied in critical reviews and certain other noncommercial uses permitted by copyright law. Please do not participate in or encourage piracy of copyrighted materials in violation of the author's rights. Purchase only authorized editions. For permission requests, write to the publisher, addressed "Attention: Permissions Coordinator," at the address below.

ISBN: 978-1-64945-312-9 (Ebook) (EPUB)
ISBN: 978-1-64945-313-6 (Hardback)
ISBN: 978-1-64945-314-3 (Paperback)
ISBN: 978-1-64945-315-0 (Ebook) (Mobi)
ISBN: 978-1-64945-316-7 (Ebook) (Audiobook)

Library of Congress Number: 2020912658
Cover Photograph By: Fotoandrius/Shutterstock.com
Image used under license from Shutterstock.com.
First printing edition 2021.
Larrah Thomas Books
10120 Two Notch Road
Suite 2, Unit 126
Columbia, SC 29223
https://www.larrahthomas.com

Contents

About the Author
368

"Was it hard?" I ask. "Letting go?"
"Not as hard as holding on to something
that wasn't real."
— Lisa Schroeder

Prologue

Chad Greene and Angelina Simpson have been sweethearts since the sixth grade. They have both recently learned of their true heritage. Their parents were waiting for the right time to tell them. The *urge* is putting pressure on their relationship. Now eighteen, Chad and Angelina have witnessed their friends, Molly and Toby, as their connection awakened and grew, while theirs lies dormant. Doubt blooms as they wonder if they are meant to be together or find love with someone else.

Chad is also facing a great responsibility, while a "beast" inside him threatens to take over. There is a threat looming over him and his friends. A group of rebels will stop at nothing to accomplish their agenda. Chad must do everything in his power to protect the ones he loves.

Paisley O'Riley and Max Brody's relationship is still new and beginning to bloom. Neither of them truly knows what to expect in their relationship, but are starting to fall in love. Only fate will decide if or when their connection will awaken and with whom.

Preface

July 5, 2019

Chad

The Demolition Derby is underway. Cars are smashing and crashing into one another and slinging mud all over the patrons in the stands. One car revved its engine and shot into motion, aiming at another vehicle on the opposite side of the arena. Its target moved out of the way just in the nick of time. The car went through the barrier wall and hit the announcer's stand. Paisley O'Riley, the Derby Queen, was knocked off and had fallen to the ground. Toby, Max, Molly, and I jumped up and ran as fast as we could. I got to her first and knelt beside her.

"Paisley, are you all right, are you hurt? Look at me. Talk to me."

"Chad? Is that you?"

"Yes, it's me. I'm here. I think you hit your head. Try to keep your eyes open, okay?"

"Okay. My arm hurts—a lot. Please don't leave me. Will you hold my hand until the medics get here?"

"Of course, I will." I reached out and held the hand of her uninjured arm so I didn't jar the other one. Static electricity shocked my hand. I hope it didn't hurt her. The poor thing is hurt badly enough without my clumsy self shocking the hell out of her with static electricity. "I'm not going anywhere. Just don't close your eyes. I don't want you passing out if you've got a concussion."

"Chad, is she hurt?" I heard Toby ask.

"She said her arm hurts, and she might have hit her head."

"Let's get her out of here so her injuries can be seen to," Toby said.

"Okay. Do you think you can stand?"

"Yeah, I think so," Paisley said and winced. "Ow, my arm."

"Easy now. I've got you. Hold your arm steady, okay," I said.

"Okay, folks," Max said. "Nothing to see here. She's going to be just fine. We're going to get her seen to. Go back to your seats. The real show will be starting up again really soon."

"Thanks, guys. I appreciate you helping me."

"Anytime. It's what friends do," Toby said. "Let's get her to the girls' bathroom. I just saw Molly motion to us to bring her in there. She can heal her in there if no one else is in there with them."

"Whoah, she can do that?" Paisley asked.

"Yeah, she can do a lot of cool stuff," Max said.

We handed her over to Molly and watched the bathroom to make sure no one else went in. Remembering the car striking the announcer's stand was like I was watching it happen all over again but in slow motion. I'll never forget the fear I saw in Paisley's eyes as she fell over the edge. My heart stopped when I saw her body fall and hit the ground. She wasn't moving. My only thought was, God, please let her be okay. I heard her whimpering in pain as I knelt beside her. I hardly know her, but I hated seeing her in pain. I felt useless, knowing I couldn't do anything to help her. Then, I looked up to see Molly and Paisley coming out of the bathroom.

"Let's get back to the Derby," Molly said. "The Derby Queen needs to get back to her throne."

We all laughed, and Paisley went back to her post as the Derby Queen, while we went back to our seats with Angelina. On our way back to our seats, Molly touched my arm and stopped me in my tracks.

"Hey, are you okay?" she asked.

"Yeah. I mean, I think so."

"Something is off about you. What's wrong?"

"It's just—." I took a deep breath, blew it out, and nervously ran my fingers through my hair. "Paisley. I've never actually seen someone hurt like that before. I mean, I've seen a few sports injuries, twisted ankles, and sprains, but never witnessed anyone involved in an accident like that before my eyes. It's like it happened in slow motion, and I couldn't do anything to stop it. I've never seen broken bones like that either. How did you fix it?"

"It's just one of the things I can do. She's one of us, Chad. She's going to be just fine now."

"Yeah. I guess you're right."

"Is that all that's bothering you, or is there something else?"

"Yes, no, well, I suppose so."

Molly's eyes widened as she looked at me and speculatively asked, "You felt something, didn't you?"

"I don't know what I felt. I was scared, like terrifyingly scared. I'm still shaking. She was in pain, and there was nothing I could do to help her. She asked me to hold her hand and not to leave her until help arrived. You showed up and healed her. Thank you, Molly. You truly are amazing."

"I just did all I knew how to do. You did great by keeping Paisley calm. I'm sure she was scared too."

"True." I kept my gaze on my shoes. "I think I'm okay now, Molly. Thanks again, by the way."

"Sure. Let's get back up there to our seats. I think they just about have everything ready to go again."

"Ladies first." I offered her my hand to help her up onto the bleachers.

"Why thank you," she said with a sweet smile.

We all hung out in the bleachers a while after the Derby ended and let the crowd thin out a bit before heading to Toby's truck. Paisley saw us and walked toward our group.

"Ugh, what does she want?" Angelina huffed under her breath.

I elbowed her. "Enough, Angie. She's had a rough enough night without you adding to it."

"Hey, guys," Paisley said. "What are y'all up to?"

"Not much, just waiting on the crowd to thin out," Molly said. "What about you?"

"I just wanted to say thank you again for helping me tonight. You guys are pretty incredible."

"You're very welcome, and thank you," Molly said.

"Do y'all have any plans or anything to do next? It's still pretty early, and I don't have to be home until midnight."

"Us either. We haven't made any other plans as of yet. What did you have in mind?" Molly asked.

"Would y'all want to go bowling? The Alley in Asheboro is open until 1:00 a.m. on Friday nights. We could bowl a game before we have to start heading our separate ways."

"Sounds good to me," Molly said. "What about you? Are y'all up for a game?"

"I still owe you for kicking my butt in ski ball," Toby said and winked at Molly.

"You're on! What about you guys, are you in?"

"Sure. I'm in," Max said.

"Me too," I said.

"Fine, let's go." Angelina rolled her eyes.

"I'm afraid there's no more room in Toby's truck," Molly said. "I do have an idea, though. I can transport a few of us at a time and leave Toby's truck here. We can come back for it later. It'll give us more time to play."

"Transport, how exactly?" Paisley asked.

"I can pop us anywhere I've already been or seen a picture of where to go. It just has to be somewhere that no one can see us do it. It's riskier with it being a public place, though."

"Let's not risk it, darlin'," Toby said. "I'd rather not take the chance of being seen by humans."

"I can drive my car. It's no big deal," Paisley said. "Y'all can follow me. Anyone want to come and keep me company?"

"I will," Max said. "Where's your car?"

"Follow me. I have a red convertible MINI Cooper."

We followed Paisley to The Alley. I noticed that Angelina didn't seem all too happy about Paisley joining our crew.

"What's got your panties in a wad?" I asked her under my breath.

"Like you care," she huffed. "You're practically drooling over *her*."

"No, I'm not, Angie. You need to lighten up. Who knows, maybe she and Max will hit it off, and he won't feel like a fifth wheel anymore."

"You don't get it, do you? She doesn't want *Max*! She wants *you*!"

"Angie, *you* are my girlfriend, but I'm not going to put up with you being mean and nasty to everyone anymore. I mean it. You'd better start being nicer to people, and you'd better start now."

Chapter 1

Chad

Angelina, Paisley, and Molly have gotten closer since the night of the Demolition Derby. Max and Paisley have gotten closer, too—much closer. We had all started going out on triple dates and enjoyed spending time together. Max seems to be happy with Paisley. Thank goodness, because I was starting to get worried about him. He was always kind of left out when Angelina and I would double date with Toby and Molly. I had even joked about him being an unhappy camper, a fifth-wheel one. While I'd thought it was funny at the time, looking back now, I realize I was an ass to a good friend who was feeling down in the dumps.

Molly and Toby are so in love that it makes me wish that Angelina and I could feel our connection the way they do. We are all eighteen now. The *urge* to find our chosen mates and complete the bond should be hitting us like it has for them. They can hardly keep their hands to themselves. I love Angelina with all my heart, but she's been a bit on the jealous side since the other girls joined our group of friends. If our connection would just spark, she'd see how much I love her and not worry about other girls. I think she and I need some alone time, especially since school starts on Monday. Maybe that'll spark something up between us. I'm going to call her right now, while I'm on my morning break, and ask her out tonight.

"Hey, baby! I was just thinking about you."

"Hey, beautiful. I've been thinking about getting some alone time with you. What do you think about going out tonight—just you and me? We can have a nice candlelight dinner and see a movie, maybe?"

"Awe, I'd love to. You are so sweet."

"Anything for my girl. Can you be ready by 6:00 p.m.?"

"Absolutely. I can't wait to spend some alone time with you. Triple dating is fun, but I need some one-on-one cuddle time."

"I figured you did. I do too. I miss our alone time too."

"May I make a request?"

"Sure, baby. What's up?"

"Instead of a movie out somewhere, can we come back to my place? Mom and Dad are going to one of their friend's houses for a get-together. They'll be out late, and I'd rather just cuddle with you and watch a movie here."

"Even better. No one to scold us or tell us to get a room when I can't keep my hands to myself."

"Oh, you're so bad! Hahaha!"

"What? It's true. Angie, you are gorgeous. That body and those plump lips of yours are bad influences on me."

"Good. The feeling's mutual then."

"I really can't wait to see you tonight, baby. I've been missing you these last few days. I'm sorry I've been so busy with school starting soon." Helping Dad around the house and working at the marina keeps me pretty occupied these days. People always go crazy during the summer. So, Dad gets called out a lot more during the summer months. The marina has been busy, too, with everyone filling up their jet skis and boats for fun on the water.

"Yeah, I know. I just miss you."

"I'm going to make it up to you tonight. I promise."

"I'm looking forward to it. Well, as much as I hate to, I should get going. I need to call Stacy. I need a shopping day to get ready for my hot date tonight."

"Okay, beautiful. Have fun. I'll see you at six. I love you, Angie."

"Thank you, baby. We will. I love you too, Chad."

Well, back to work. There are boats lined up at the boat slips, waiting to fill up with gas. I see all kinds of lake comers here at the marina. The early bird fishermen are gearing up to go striper fishing before the speed boaters, jet skiers, and pontoon partiers find their way to the lake. They cause a lot of wake that can disturb fishermen once they come out. Not to mention, it gets hot sitting still on the open water. They've usually got their catch for the day by then and are ready to head home to fillet it all.

The fun seekers come to the marina to fill their gas tanks and coolers with ice, drinks, and snacks before they head out for a full day on the water. Some are families just spending the day together, while others are groups of friends hanging out and having fun. Then, there are the flirts. Single guys and girls alike come to the marina to check out the scantily-clad opposite sex, showing off and trying to get a date. Some people will do anything to be noticed by the opposite sex. They make me laugh and shake my head. So many of them are desperate for attention.

I've never been part of the single crowd. I've always had Angelina—my beautiful Angelina, the voluptuous, golden-haired goddess with silvery-blue eyes and plump lips. No other woman has ever held my attention as she does. Just thinking about her makes me smile and remember just how fortunate I am. I love holding her gorgeous body in my arms. I can't wait until I can call her mine for eternity. If only our connection would just spark up already. I have loved her for so long. She has to be the one. I've got to find a way to awaken our connection. I'll have to talk to Toby. Maybe he'll know what I should do. He's the only one of *us* I know my age that has an active connection with his chosen mate. I still don't know how all of this works.

Everyone keeps saying, "fate will step in when it's time," "leave it up to fate," and "just enjoy one another and make memories together." Ordinary guys my age, don't worry about this stuff. They just date whoever they want, and if it leads to more, then so be it.

We are different. *We* mate for life. *We* don't have sex with just anyone. *We* choose to wait for our chosen mates. Now that I'm eighteen, the *urge* to bond is getting stronger and stronger. I remember Toby and Molly talking about how hard the *urge* makes it for them to wait to complete their bond. I already want to jump Angie's bones every time we make out. I honestly don't know if I'll be able to resist making love to her if the connection makes the *urge* any harder to resist.

Thank goodness a boat just pulled in for service. I have to get my mind off of Angie and the *urge* to bond for a little while. The boat's owner is having trouble with the engine. That'll give me something to focus on for a few hours, at least. I have a feeling this one is going to take a while. The four-stroke outboard engine needs to be taken apart and cleaned out well. The owner took his freshwater fishing boat in saltwater. The corrosion from the salt is causing some issues. It's not a challenging task, just a tedious one, but it's just the distraction I need at the moment.

Before I knew it, it was quitting time. The boat engine is free of corrosion and ready to go. I went to the service desk and called the owner. He said he'd be picking it up in the morning. I hung up the phone and clocked out. I hopped on my jet ski and headed home. Living on the lake makes it pretty easy to travel this way, which saves on fuel. The jet ski gets much better gas mileage than my truck.

I still can't help thinking about Angie and our date tonight. I'm taking her to an authentic Italian restaurant in Concord, North Carolina. We've never been there, but we've wanted to go for a while now. I want to show Angie how special she is to me, sparked connection or not. I haven't told her where we're going, but she always dresses classy and sexy as hell for our dates. Tonight won't likely be any different.

I showered, dressed, and headed to Angie's house. I pulled into her drive at 5:50 p.m. I parked, got out, walked to her door, and rang the doorbell. Her dad, Andrew, answered, wearing a very sharp suit and tie.

"Chad! It's always a pleasure to see you! Come on inside. Angelina will be down shortly. She's told us you two have a date tonight."

"Yes, sir, we do. It's been a while since we went on a date with just the two of us. We've been going out with all of our friends here lately. I want to show her how special she still is to me."

"Good for you. Just have fun and be safe. Deirdre and I will be out late tonight. I trust you with my baby girl. I know exactly where to find you if something happens to her."

"She's in good hands, Mr. Simpson."

"Just keep those hands to yourself, will you?"

"Yes, Mr. Simpson. Of course. I've always respected Angelina and always will."

"That's my boy. You two have an excellent time tonight, and we will see you later. Deirdre, honey, how much longer? We are going to be late if we don't leave in the next fifteen minutes."

"I'm coming, sweetheart." She came downstairs quickly and grabbed her purse. "Hello, Chad. It's always so lovely to see you. Angelina is on her way down now. Have fun and be safe. See you soon, dear!"

Angie began walking down the stairs, and my heart nearly stopped. Her golden hair is draped over her shoulders in soft curls. Her luscious red lips turned up in a sexy smile meant just for me. Her red, knee-length dress is hugging her curvy body like a second skin. Her shapely, tanned legs seem to glide down the stairs as though she is walking on air. My God, she is beautiful.

"Hey, handsome. I've missed you," Angie cooed as she wrapped her arms around my neck, pressing her amazing body against me.

"Hello, beautiful. I've missed you too. Wow! Look at you." I took her hand and twirled her around slowly, so I could get a good look at her. "You are truly stunning, Angie."

"Thank you, baby! You look rather dashing yourself. What's the occasion?"

"I just want to treat my beautiful girl to a romantic night out. I don't need an occasion for that, do I?"

"Mmmmm," she purred. "I love you, Chad."

"I love you, too, Angie." I offered her my arm and asked, "Shall we?"

She took my arm with a huge smile. "Yes, we shall."

Angelina

Chad hasn't said where we are going for dinner, but I don't mind where we go. I just love that he wanted to spend the evening together without our friends this time. I enjoy going out with them, but I have missed my alone time with Chad. I fully intend to push as far as he's willing to go tonight. Our connection is bound to spark, with what I've got in mind, for sure.

Chad and I talked and held hands the whole way to the restaurant. To my surprise, he brought me to an upscale Italian place that we've been talking about coming to for a while now. I'm so excited! Authentic Italian cuisine is my ultimate favorite! A romantic candlelight dinner is just what we need to get the evening started and set the mood. Chad called ahead and made a reservation. Our table was ready and waiting for us when we arrived.

Everything on the menu looks fantastic! We placed our orders and nibbled on the freshly baked bread and spiced olive oil. This place is exquisite! There are other couples here, enjoying their dates, but when I'm with Chad, he makes me feel like we are the only ones in the room. He makes me feel special—as though I'm his whole world.

On top of everything else, he is so handsome and incredibly sexy! His hazel eyes seem to glow in the candlelight against his olive complexion and black hair. He laid his hand across the table, palm up, for me to place my hand in his. My heart began to flutter as he brought my hand to his lips. His eyes never left mine. The heat within them seared me to my very core. My breath caught in my chest. He must have noticed. His lips turned up on one side in a sly grin as he removed them from my hand. His thumb rubbed gently over my knuckles. I love making out with Chad, but it's the little things he does like this that get to me

in ways that send heat surging through my
body.

"Are you okay, beautiful?"

"Yes, I'm more than just okay. I'm enjoying
this extremely romantic evening with the
sexiest man on the planet. How could I not
be?"

"You just seem a little jittery."

"You have no idea how the little things you
do affect me, do you?"

"I think I have a pretty good idea" he says as
he waggles his eyebrows and winks at me.

"Oh, you are so bad. I love it."

He chuckled and said, "Good because I don't
intend to be good anytime soon unless I'm
good at it." I felt the heat rise within me and
flush my cheeks. "Even after all this time, I can
still make you blush."

"You do more than that."

"Oh? I may have to see that for myself later.
Angie, I want you so much, but I love you so
much more. You are by far the sexiest woman
I've ever met." His voice dropped to a low
whisper. "If I am your chosen mate, I'll be the
luckiest man on the planet."

I dropped my voice to a low whisper too. "I
truly hope you are, Chad because I love you. I
want you to be my chosen mate more than I've
ever wanted anything else in my entire life."

"I know you do. It sucks, but we just have to
be patient. Everything will happen as it is fated
to in due time. In the meantime, I'm going to

enjoy you as long and as much as I possibly can."

I smiled and nodded in agreement, but my heart sank a little. Why is it taking so long for our connection to spark? It didn't take but one touch of Toby and Molly's hands for their connection to spark. Why not us?

Our beautifully plated meal selections were brought to our table and placed in front of us. Everything was perfect. We chatted and laughed together while we enjoyed our dinner. The evening couldn't have been more perfect if it were written in a fairy tale, but still, no spark awakened our connection. This cold hard fact weighs on my mind and pains my heart. How can I love Chad so much and not feel the spark? *I* choose him. Why can't the rest of me do so too?

We headed back to my house after our incredibly romantic dinner together. My parents were still out with their friends and likely wouldn't be back until sometime after midnight. Chad and I would have a few more hours of alone time to watch a movie or something on television and cuddle. Maybe if I'm lucky, we'll do more than just cuddle.

We walked in, and I led Chad up to my room. Once inside, I closed and locked the door. I placed my hands on his chest and pushed him backward until his legs bumped the side of my bed. He sat down on its edge, and I backed away slowly a few paces. I reached behind my back and slid down the zipper of my dress.

"Angie… What are you do—?"

"Shhh." I stopped him before he could finish.

I slid the straps down over my shoulders, and the dress fell to the floor at my feet. I stood before Chad in a black, strapless, lace bra and matching thong. I stepped over my dress, slipped off my high heeled sandals, and slowly strolled back to him, while keeping my eyes locked on his. I wrapped my arms around him, and drew him close to me. He began to kiss my neck, and his hands trailed from the back of my thighs up to my nearly bare behind. His hands squeezed and kneaded me. A low moan rumbled in his chest.

"My God, Angie. Your body is a work of art, and you feel so good in my hands." His hands caressed my back and unhooked my bra, releasing my breasts to spill before him. I leaned in and pressed my lips to his as his thumbs rubbed over the aroused buds upon my breasts. I licked over his bottom lip and probed my tongue into the crease of his mouth. Our kiss deepened into a boiling passion. Our tongues were twirling and caressing one another. Heat surged within me and settled in my sex. I gasped and moaned into his mouth.

Chad leaned back onto my bed and pulled me on top of him. Then, he rolled me over, placing me beneath him. His mouth left mine and trailed smoldering kisses down to my chest. His lips latched onto one of my breasts while his fingers rubbed and teased the other one. I unbuttoned his shirt and slid it over his shoulders. He finished taking his shirt off. Then, he leaned down and kissed me from my ribcage down to the front of my panties. There, he placed one single, soft kiss. I ran my hands through his hair and whimpered his name.

"Oh, Chad."

"Yes, baby?"

"Please, don't stop."

He eased the sides of my panties over my hips, down my legs to my feet, and tossed them on the floor with my bra and my dress.

"I never thought I'd be lucky enough to see you this way. You are breathtaking."

"Make love to me, Chad. To hell with the whole chosen mates thing. Bond with me, baby. We can be together forever."

"Angie..." Chad sat up and seemed taken aback.

"What?" I leaned up on my elbows to look at him. "What's wrong?"

"As much as I want to make you mine, I'd rather wait until our connection awakens. Call me selfish, but I want to feel the sensations that chosen mates feel when they bond. I want our connection to spark so that I can feel everything with you. I want to show you the love I have for you and marry you." I bit my bottom lip and turned my face away from him, so he wouldn't see the tears forming in my eyes. I bared myself before him, and he rejected me. That alone hurts me to the core like a knife to my heart.

"Please, Angie. Don't get upset."

"You don't want me to get upset? Are you kidding me?" I asked as tears fell from my eyes. "Here I am, laying here stark naked, offering myself to you. You reject me, and then expect me not to get upset? Are you serious?"

"Angie, please. I'm not rejecting you. All I'm saying is that I'd rather wait until our connection awakens, and we're married to make love to you. There are other ways we can be intimate. We can still show one another how much we love and want one another without actually making love."

"Yes, I know that. I'm just tired of having to wait on our connection to spark. It isn't fair."

"I'm sorry, baby. I know it isn't fair. I'm as frustrated as you are about it. This *urge* to bond is killing me!" He raked his hands through his hair and closed his eyes. "I don't know how long I'll be able to resist, but I have to try."

"We can make love and not bond, Chad. There's more to bonding than just making love, you know. We'd have to hold hands and combine energy as we climax together. We can also use a condom. That'll prevent the bond from forming too."

"We'd just be cheating ourselves, and you know it. That's why *we* wait to be with our chosen mates."

"Then why even bother with the 'other ways' of being intimate? Wouldn't that still be considered cheating ourselves?"

"No, I don't think it would."

"How do you figure that?"

"Because I'm not taking your virginity or giving you mine until our bond awakens. I want to complete our bond the first time we make love. I want it to be something special. Something neither of us will ever forget." He took my hands in his and kissed them both. "Angie, you are more special to me than just a romp in the sheets to stave off the *urge* until our connection sparks. I love you so much more than that."

How can I stay mad at him after that speech? He is right but damn! I still want him to make love to me. I looked down at my naked body, suddenly feeling ashamed of myself. "All right."

"All right, what?"

"I mean all right, we'll wait. I love you, Chad. I'm sorry I threw myself at you and tried to push you into making love to me."

Chad placed his hand on my chin and lifted my face. "Please look at me, Angie. Don't be upset or embarrassed. You've done nothing wrong."

"I love you, Chad. I always have. I'd do anything for you. So, if you want to wait, then that's what we'll do."

"I've always loved you, too."

I pulled back the covers on my bed. We laid there under the blankets and cuddled, watching *Guardians of the Galaxy Vol. 1* on television. The alarm on his phone went off, letting him know he needed to start heading home to be back in time for his curfew. I wish I had powers like Molly, so I could keep him here a few more minutes, and just transport him home at the last minute. I don't, though. So, I put on my bathrobe and walked him down to the front door. We kissed goodnight, and I watched him pull out of our driveway.

I went back upstairs, straightened out my bed covers once again, and went to my en-suite bathroom to shower. My parents will be home in a few hours. I'll be in bed by then. I stood under the warm water and thought back on my date with Chad. He'd taken me to a romantic dinner, just the two of us, and had shown me how much he really loves me. He'd rather wait and make our first time together something special. He'd done all of this to make *me* feel special. He'd done all of this for *me*.

I bathed, washed, and dried my hair. Then, I brushed my teeth, put on my pajamas, and crawled under my covers once again. This bed felt much better when I was all cuddled up to Chad. Maybe someday, we will have our bed, in our own house, and we can sleep cuddled up together every night. I just wish that could be sooner than later.

Chapter 2

Chad

I had a great time with Angie. She looked amazing! She always does, but she looked like a movie star tonight. I felt like I was the luckiest man alive with her on my arm. I hope she knows how special she is to me. I feel like I've known her my entire life. We've grown up together, we know everything about one another, and as far as I know, she is my first love. The only way she isn't my first love is if she isn't my chosen mate, as I'm hoping she is.

Today is the last day of our summer break. It's hard to believe that it's already over. I'm ready, though. Football practice has been fun for the last couple of weeks. We have an outstanding team this year and may have a shot at winning the state championship again.

Toby is probably the best quarterback this school has ever had, but even with his amount of skill, Molly is still our best player. She doesn't know that I know, but I've figured out a few things on my own. I've seen her powers at work. She watches out for us and keeps our players from getting hurt. If we do get hurt, she heals us somehow, so we barely even realize it. I saw Max turn too fast and twist his knee pretty severely during a play. Thank goodness Molly was at the practice. She had him healed before we could even get him up and off of the field. That woman is remarkable! She is going to be an amazing Queen to our people. She doesn't just care about our people, though. She cares about all people. She can't stand seeing others in pain.

I think that the incident with Lilly earlier this summer got to her. She desperately wanted to heal Lilly but couldn't. When her powers kicked in, and she was able to heal her, it made her feel like she had a purpose. She wanted to help as many people as she could.

She'd even healed Paisley O'Riley at the Demolition Derby. A car went through the barrier wall and struck the announcer's stand. Paisley fell, hit her head, and had broken her arm. I'd gotten to her first. I held her hand to comfort her until help arrived, and I shocked her hand with static electricity.

That's when it hit me. My head seemed to spin as realization swept over me. Toby mentioned the spark of a connection between two chosen mates and how it feels like static electricity when they touch. No, that couldn't be what I'd felt. Could it? It had to be static electricity. I'd just ran like hell to get to Paisley to help her. Static electricity on my clothes is a more likely cause. Angie is supposed to be my chosen mate. I don't have any romantic feelings towards Paisley. I hardly even know her. Sure, we've hung out since the Derby on our triple dates, but she was with Max, and I was with Angie. That doesn't mean I know a whole lot about her. Let alone enough to fall in love with her and want to be with her for eternity.

Then, I recalled what Molly asked me right before we returned to our seats, *"You felt something, didn't you?"* At the time, I thought she was asking me if I was okay after seeing Paisley get hurt. Now? I think she was wondering if I'd felt something when I'd held Paisley's hand to comfort her. Molly said she'd felt Lilly's soul calling out for Ryan, her mate, when she'd healed her. Did Molly feel Paisley's soul calling for her mate when she healed her as well? Was she calling out for me? No. She couldn't have been. Could she? I'm in total freak-out mode. Panic and anxiety are coursing through my body. I can't seem to wrap my head around the possibility that Paisley O'Riley could be my chosen mate.

One part of me wants to talk to Molly to see if she'll tell me something, anything about what she'd felt or sensed that night. The other part just wants to forget about it altogether and move on. There's one way to find out without talking to anyone. I'll casually bump into Paisley tomorrow at school. I'll make sure to touch someone else first, so I can rule out static electricity.

If I do feel a spark, how do I tell Angie about it? She'll be heartbroken. Hell, I'll be heartbroken. I love Angie. I don't want to hurt her in any way. What have I done? Angie will think I used her as a place holder if Paisley is my chosen mate and not her. If Paisley is my chosen mate, it wouldn't be fair to string Angie along. I can't do that to her or either of them for that matter. I'll eventually be in love with Paisley instead of her. Ugh, what a mess.

And then there's Max. Oh, boy. How do I tell one of my best friends that his girlfriend is *my* chosen mate and that they have to break up so I can be with her? Man, I feel like a total douchebag. Some friend I am. As though I'm just going to go up to him and say something as stupid as, "Hey Max, I know you were lonely for a while before Paisley came along, but you have to break up with her. She's *my* chosen mate and it's time to move on. Okay. Thanks, man. Good talk." No. No way. That is not going to happen.

Two of the people I genuinely care about would hate me forever. Forever is a long time as immortal beings. Why can't we all be normal teenagers, free to love whoever we want, without having a *chosen mate*? How fair is it to not know all this time and then find out once we've fallen in love with someone else? I have wondered if Angie is my chosen mate all summer. Well, at least since I found out about being a Nymph and the whole ordeal that went along with it.

I think what burns me up the most about all of this is the idea of my Angie not being "my Angie" after all. If she isn't my chosen mate, that means she is someone else's chosen mate. I'll never again get to wipe away her tears, hold her close, make her laugh when she's feeling down, kiss those luscious lips, or feel her curvy body pressed against mine. I'll never get to make love to her through the night and wake up with her in my arms the next morning. No, not I, but someone else will.

Maybe I should just avoid Paisley altogether. That way, perhaps I won't be drawn to her at all. If I'm not around her to help a connection develop, maybe nothing will happen. Wait. Why am I freaking out about this? I don't even know if there's anything to worry about yet. Chill out, Chad. No use in freaking out about something that's not up to me anyway. It all comes back to fate. Fate will decide if and when whatever happens, happens. I just hope that everyone else is ready for any fallout that comes with it because, at this moment, I most certainly am not.

Thank goodness for the Sunday lake goers. Business at the marina is picking up for the day. That is just what I need to keep my mind occupied on. At least, something other than the *chosen mate* thing. Then, a familiar, red, convertible MINI Cooper pulled into the parking lot. Paisley hopped out and walked inside the store. I guess she's grabbing some snacks and heading to Angie's house for the day. I waved but made sure that I looked too busy to make small talk. She browsed around, made her selections, and started walking to the counter. Julie, the cashier, called out to me and asked if I'd mind ringing her up so she could take a quick bathroom break. Great. That's just my luck.

I rang up her snacks, and she handed me her money to pay. Our hands touched very briefly. There it was—the spark. It felt like a sharp electric shock. It was like static electricity, but slightly different. It almost felt like the shock was warm somehow. I don't think she noticed it, but I did. Damn, I'm so screwed.

Angelina

Waking up with sunlight streaming through my window is the best way to wake up, in my opinion. Last night's date with Chad was the most amazing one we've ever had. Our relationship has never been better. I mean, sure, the whole *chosen mate* thing is still a touchy subject, but we've gotten so much closer. Chad said he wanted to marry me and share our virginities on our wedding night when we bond. The thought of marrying Chad makes my heart flutter. He's the only guy I've ever loved. I honestly can't imagine loving or falling in love with anyone else.

My parents must've gotten in pretty late. The house is still quiet. I got up, went to the bathroom, and washed my face. I put my robe on over my pajamas and walked downstairs. There was a note on the counter.

"Gone to breakfast with friends. You looked so peaceful that we didn't want to wake you up before we left. Call or text if you'd like us to bring you anything.
XOXO
Love,
Mom & Dad"

Did they sleep at all? I hope I have their stamina at their age. I texted Mom and asked her if she'd bring me a bacon and egg sandwich on toast. She replied that she would and that they'd be home in a little while. It's such a beautiful, sunny day. Chad has to work at the marina today. I wonder if the girls would want to come swimming and soak up some sun.

Molly and Toby are spending the day together, but Stacy and Paisley will be here in a couple of hours. I'll make us some sweet tea, a fruit salad, and ham and pimento cheese pinwheels for our lunch. I've got the portable radio with fresh batteries, tanning oil, and beach towels in the boathouse, and the rafts are inflated and are ready to go.

Mom and Dad came back from town with my breakfast and told me all about their evening. I told them about my date with Chad, and how we'd enjoyed the restaurant. I told them it would be the perfect place to celebrate an anniversary and nudged Dad's arm. He got the hint and winked at me. Their anniversary is coming up next month. They are so cute together. I hope Chad and I are like that after being married as long as they have been, and hopefully even longer. Eternity sounds good to me.

Paisley called and told me that she was stopping at the marina before coming over and asked if I wanted her to pick anything up. I told her that I'd have lunch ready soon, but she was more than welcome to grab a few things to snack on.

Stacy pulled up a few minutes later. She came in and sat down at the bar while I finished making the fruit salad. Stacy loves my fruit salad. She's crazy about my homemade strawberry kiwi dressing that I make for it, too. It's my secret recipe. As much as I love Stacy as my bestie, I won't even divulge my secret recipe to her.

"So, Angie, when are you ever going to give in and tell me how you make this stuff?" She dipped the tip of her finger into the dressing and smiled as the sweet and tangy flavor hit her tongue.

"Hahaha! I think you know the answer to that question, so stop asking."

"Can't blame me for trying. That is some good stuff, Angie. You could bottle and sell it. It's so good; you'd make a fortune!"

"Yeah, maybe. I wouldn't even know where to start, though."

"Me either, but it might be worth looking into."

"I'm just glad my family and friends enjoy it."

"I know I do. Where's Paisley? Isn't she coming too?"

"She's on her way. She stopped at the marina to get some snacks for later. She should be here in about fifteen minutes or so. Do you want to help me with some pinwheels?"

"Sure! I love those things!"

"Is there anything I make that you don't like?"

"Hmm... nope. Not that I can think of."

"Yep, just as I thought. I didn't think there was. Hahaha!"

"I hail to your culinary genius. How can I help?"

We washed our hands, laid out some burrito-sized tortillas, and layered them with ham, pimento cheese, and baby spinach. Then, we rolled them up, sliced them into pinwheels, and put frilled cocktail picks in them to hold them together. The sweet tea and fruit salad are already chilling in the refrigerator. Everything is ready. All we are missing is

Paisley. Stacy and I put everything away and poured some sweet tea to sip until Paisley arrived. Before we knew it, she was knocking on the door. We enjoyed our lunch and made our way to the boathouse.

The sun felt so good! We laid out for a while to let our lunch settle before we went swimming. The topic of conversation turned to our guys, of course. I told them about my romantic date with Chad. I didn't tell them about what happened afterward, but the rest was still pretty swoon-worthy. I felt kind of bad about sharing my romantic evening with them. Yes, Paisley has Max, but Stacy hasn't had a boyfriend since our sophomore year. She'd dated her last boyfriend, Mark, since the sixth grade. He moved away when his grandmother got sick. His mom wanted to be closer to her to help take care of her. She was so heartbroken that she hasn't even bothered dating anyone else. I hope she can find someone to love her and treat her right. She's a great girl and deserves to be loved by a great guy. I asked Paisley how things were going with Max, and I wish I hadn't.

"So, Paisley, how are things going with Max? Is there a steamy romance blooming, or *sparks* flying?"

"Yes and no. I mean, Max is fun to hang out with, he's a great kisser, and I do mean great, but I'm not sure where it's going, or even if it will go anywhere at all."

"Oh, no! What do you mean? You guys are so adorable together!"

"No, I can't say that there are any *sparks* flying, so to speak. Don't get me wrong. Max is attentive, sweet, funny, passionate, and so *hot*! Wow, is he ever, but I'm just not so sure he's the one for me, you know? I just feel like something is missing. I can't put my finger on it. I don't even know if it's him or if it's just me. As perfect as he is, I'm just not so sure he's perfect for me."

"Oh, Paisley. I'm so sorry to hear that," Stacy said.

"It's okay. I mean, I'm fine. I don't think our relationship is over or anything like that. It's probably just me. I've never had a serious relationship. So, this is all pretty new to me."

"Just give it some more time. It's still a new relationship. I think things will heat up before too long."

"Yeah, you're probably right. I'm still just enjoying things they way they are, I guess. I'm not rushing or pushing for anything at this point. There just hasn't been a *spark* for me."

"Join the crowd," I said. "You aren't the only one."

"Haven't you and Chad been together for years, though? There's gotta be some kind of *spark* between you two. Look at how romantic your date was last night. Y'all have got to be feeling some *serious urges* by now."

"Oh, the *urge* is certainly there, but no *spark*, at least not like I've been waiting for."

"Okay, okay," Stacy said. "Angie, I've seen the chemistry between you and Chad. There are definitely sparks flying there. Max is crazy about you, Paisley. He can't take his eyes off of you. He looks like he's been love-struck with cupid's arrow every time you walk into the room. How is there not a spark?"

How do we explain this? Stacy isn't a Nymph. At least, I don't think she is. We don't advertise the fact that we are Nymphs and are different than humans. We have to protect the secret of our existence at all costs. "It's different for everyone, I suppose. Some sparks are more obvious than others. I'm waiting for that spark of electricity each time we touch. One that leaves hot tingles on your skin and then courses through your entire body."

"That sounds like hormones to me," Stacy laughed, "like cats in heat. That's not love, girls —that's lust." She sighed. "At least you two get to fool around with your hot guys. I still haven't had the heart to move on from Mark."

"Oh, sweetie. You have got to let yourself love again. I know you loved him, but he's not coming back."

"I know. I like the idea of moving on and dating someone new, but when it comes down to it, I get sick to my stomach. It feels like I'm cheating on Mark."

"You shouldn't feel like that, sweetie. I'm sure he's moved on and dated other girls. Don't feel bad for wanting to move on. There's a great guy out there for you somewhere."

"Thanks, Angie. I'll eventually let go, but a part of me keeps holding on, hoping he'll come back."

"Maybe you should try calling him. You might even get the closure you need to move on."

"That's not a bad idea. I'll do that. Thanks for listening to me whining about my lost love."

"Hey, that's what friends are for," Paisley said. "What do you think about taking a dip? It's getting pretty hot out here. Not to mention, we've got to cool off our hormones a bit. Hahaha!"

We all laughed and went down to the dock below to get the rafts and get in the water. It has been a fantastic day so far. I've enjoyed hanging out with Stacy and Paisley. If anyone would've told me a few months ago that I'd be this close to Paisley, I would've shot them a snide comment. Now, I'm so thankful to have her in my life. She has been an excellent addition to our crew. I'm so fortunate to call her my friend.

Chapter 3

Paisley

Sparks—hot, static electricity-like tingles that linger on your skin and course through your body. Chad shocked my hand at the Derby. I'd asked him to hold my hand until help arrived. He did it again today at the marina when I'd handed him the money for the snacks. It could've been static electricity. Chad and Angelina are very much a couple. It won't do me any good to sit and wonder if what I'd felt was anything more than just static. He loves her so much, he hardly even notices any other girl exists—much less me. It doesn't matter. I've moved on. I have a boyfriend of my own now.

Anyway, I should call Max. I know they had a lot to do on the farm before school starts tomorrow. I'd hate to bother him, but a good girlfriend would at least call and see how he's doing.

"Hey, handsome!"

"Hello, gorgeous! I wasn't expecting you to call, but I'm glad you did. I miss you."

"I miss you too. How's your day going?"

"It's been busy, but we got it all done. Toby and Molly have been a huge help this summer. Molly wanted to go to practice in Kilchoman for a while. Toby went with her so they could hang out. I think he trains with her to learn physical fighting techniques, so he can help protect her. It seems like some pretty cool stuff."

"Sounds like it. Molly and Toby have a lot of responsibility coming to them next summer."

"Yes, they do. What have you been up to?"

"Stacy and I went to hang out with Angie today. We ate lunch, laid in the sun, and went swimming. It was a much-needed relaxing day."

"That's awesome, babe. I'm glad you got to hang out with the girls. I'd like to treat you to a romantic supper and hang out with you for a little while if that's okay."

"I'd love that. What time should I be ready?"

"It's still early, but I can pick you up anytime you'd like. I just got out of the shower, so I'll be ready in about ten minutes. I don't want to rush you, though."

"I can be ready in about forty-five minutes. How's that sound?"

"Fantastic! I'll see you then, babe."

"Okay, handsome. I'll be waiting."

Mama and Daddy were doing some last-minute school shopping for Caden. There were a few things on his school supplies list they still hadn't been able to get. I don't need much for this year, just some more pens, pencils, and spiral notebooks.

I went upstairs to shower and get ready for my date with Max. I can tell that I'd gotten some sun today with the girls. The warm water is stinging my skin a little. I turned the heat down and cooled it off a bit. Much better. As fast as we heal, it'll go away in no time. I enjoyed my girl-time today. It felt good to get some things off of my chest and talk about my relationship with Max. It did surprise me to hear that Chad and Angie still hadn't felt a *spark* after all the time they've been together.

Max and I hadn't felt one either. Our relationship is still new, but at the same time, I don't know if we ever will. Something still feels... off. I can feel myself pulling away from him, and I don't know why. He's such a great guy. He's a sexy cowboy, for goodness sake. The way he fills out a pair of jeans should be illegal. Damn! Max is F-I-N-E, *fine*! He's got the whole package going for him, too. I could make a list that went on and on to describe how wonderful he is. We have chemistry when we're together, but there's just something missing that I can't explain. I don't understand. I wish I did. I feel terrible because of it. I have no idea what to do about it, either. I don't want to break up with him because I really do like him, but it would be selfish and string him along if this isn't going anywhere, either. I'm so confused.

I picked out a blue and white plaid sundress to wear and slipped on a pair of white sandals with a kitten heel. Max said he likes to see me in lavender and blue hues. He says they bring out my eyes. I can't disagree. I finished getting ready and headed down the stairs just in time to see Max's truck pull into the driveway. I wrote a quick note on the dry-erase board in the kitchen and headed out the door.

Max hopped out of his truck, picked me up, and twirled me around in his arms. He sat me back down to get a good look at me.

"You are absolutely beautiful, babe. How did I get this lucky?'

"How long do we have? I can list so many ways, but we'd be here a while. Hahaha!."

"I must be a pretty lucky guy then," he said with a huge smile.

"I think we're both pretty lucky. I have a sexy cowboy all to myself for the evening."

"Babe, you can have me all to yourself anytime you want."

"Careful, I may hold you to it."

"Oh, please do!" He pulled me close to him, leaned down, and pressed his lips to mine. His tongue licked over my bottom lip and darted inside my mouth. Damn, his kisses make my head spin. They are so addictive! I could kiss him for hours and still want more. He broke the kiss, and a soft whimper escaped my lips. He chuckled and took my hand. "There's more where that came from, babe, but I don't exactly want to stand here and make out in your driveway." He winked and flashed that sexy smile of his. "I'd prefer a bit more privacy."

I nearly melted. All I could do was nod. I followed Max to his truck. He opened the door and helped me inside. He makes me feel so special. Max treats me like any girl dreams of being treated by a guy. He respects me and treats me like a lady, makes me feel desired and sexy when we kiss, and when we're together, I feel like I'm the only girl in his world.

I'd held out for Chad for so long before I'd finally given up hope of him ever noticing me. I've never had a serious relationship or had a boyfriend at all for that matter. I mean, sure, I've had plenty of offers, but I've never been the type of girl that had to have a boyfriend. I'm pretty independent. I always have been. Plus, I'm picky. If I'm going to have a boyfriend, I don't want just some random guy to have male companionship. He has to be someone special; someone I'd miss when we're apart; someone I'd look forward to talking to and seeing each day; someone like Chad or Max.

Max is unlike any of the guys I've ever known, yet I still feel something pulling me away from him. What is wrong with me? I have a perfect guy right here in front of me. He makes my hormones race with how hot he is and how amazing his kisses are. With all that in mind, it seems like there's still something keeping me just far enough from falling in love with him. I don't understand it. I like the idea of falling in love with him. I care about him—a lot. I can even go as far as saying I love him, but I can't exactly say I'm in love with him just yet. Why? I haven't a clue. It's almost as though my heart and my hormones are at odds with one another and won't come to an agreement.

We talked and held hands while he drove. I gave him a sideways glance when he turned towards the Carolina Forest Clubhouse. He pulled into a parking spot and turned in his seat to look at me. He leaned closer to me and flashed the sexiest smile I've ever seen. Then, he raised my hand to his lips.

"You truly are wonderful, Paisley," he said. "I don't want you to feel like you have to say anything back or feel pressured in any way, but I do want you to know that I'm falling in love with you."

My breath caught in my chest. "Oh, Max," I whispered. A whisper was all I could muster.

He leaned in closer and captured my lips with his. Of all of our kisses, this one is filled with more passion than any of them, and all of them combined. It wasn't a wild and crazy kiss filled with heat and lust. No, this kiss was nothing like that. It was tender, caring, and loving. It was at that moment that I realized I could very possibly fall in love with Max, too. I just had to stop fighting against it and let it happen. That must be what I've been doing. I've been fighting the idea of letting myself fall in love with Max. I decided right then and there that I would give in. I would allow myself to fall in love with Max. Max broke the kiss and whispered, "I love you, Paisley," against my lips.

"I love you too, Max." There, I'd said it. My heart fluttered when I finally realized it was true. I do love Max Brody. He kissed me once again. It felt good to tell him I love him. I can tell by his kiss that he's pretty happy about it, too. This kiss was more eager, hungrier, and yet just as passionate as the one before. A long make-out session with Max could make a girl forget her name.

He broke the kiss and sat back with a huge, satisfied grin. "You love me too, huh? Man, I am one helluva lucky guy."

I smiled back at him and said, "Yes, I do love you, Max. You are absolutely everything a girl could want, all wrapped up in a gorgeous package. I'm the lucky one, baby."

He winked at me and said, "Well, what do you think about having a romantic picnic supper with me?"

"I'd love that."

"C'mon, babe, let's do it."

He got out, walked around to my side, opened my door, and helped me out of his truck. He grabbed a cooler, a small duffle bag, and a bag of charcoal from the bed of his truck. We walked down to the picnic tables between the clubhouse and the water. He set everything down at a table near a grill. He opened the duffle bag and removed everything he'd packed inside. There were utensils to clean the grill, a set of tongs, disposable plates and cutlery, lighter fluid, and a basket for grilling vegetables. He cleaned the grill, prepared the charcoal, and lit it so it could get hot. When it was ready, he opened the cooler. He removed a container with two marinated steaks, one with sliced peppers, onions, and mushrooms, and another container with a beautiful fruit salad inside.

"What would you like to drink? I brought bottled water, Cheerwine, and Mt. Dew."

"I'll have a Cheerwine, please."

He twisted the cap open and handed it to me. "Now, how do you like your steak, babe?"

"Medium rare, please."

"Mmmm. My kind of lady. Coming right up." He placed the steaks on the hot grill and put the vegetables into the grilling basket. I couldn't believe he'd put all of this together.

"You know, if you keep this up, you're going to spoil me."

"Busted. That's the goal, babe. I'm going to spoil you so rotten; no other guy will stand a chance."

"Goal achieved. I've never had anyone do this for me, Max. You continue to amaze me more and more every day."

"I just want to make sure I treat you right. You deserve it, babe."

"Thank you. I hope I can treat you as special as you do me."

"You're welcome, and you do, just by being you."

We both laughed and talked about everything from funny stories of our childhoods to our upcoming class schedules. We have one class together this semester. That means my attention will be divided between Max and the lessons. How am I supposed to pay attention to the teacher with this hottie in the same room? I'll have to make sure he's sitting near me, so I can make it not look so obvious. He's always gotten good grades, just as I have. I have no idea how he does it with all of those football practices and working on the family ranch, too. He truly does amaze me in so many ways.

We enjoyed our supper together. We'd had the picnic area all to ourselves. I helped Max clean up after we ate, and we took everything back to his truck. Then, we walked down to the floating dock and sat on one of the benches together. We gazed out over the water, and he put his arm around me. I scooted closer to him and snuggled into his side.

"This has been the best date night ever. Thank you, Max."

"It's not over yet, babe. I'm far from ready to take you home."

"Good, 'cause I'm not ready to go home yet."

He kissed the top of my head and held me tighter against him. I tilted my head up and kissed his cheek. He reached up to my face, gently tilted my chin up, and captured my lips with his. He placed a series of soft and tender kisses on my lips, followed by a deep and sensual kiss that sent heat radiating through my body.

Max broke the kiss, picked me up, cradled me in his arms, and sat me on his lap. Then, his lips were back on mine. Our lips embraced, our tongues swirled together and danced like they never have before. My fingers are in his hair. His arms are wrapped around me, holding me as close to him as possible. One hand slowly trailed up my leg and rested on my knee. Max's fingers stroked my soft skin, and his thumb circled my kneecap. His touch sent scorching heat surging into my sex. I heard a soft moan and realized it had come from me. Then, a more resounding groan rumbled in Max's chest.

"Paisley," he panted, "if I could kiss you forever, I'd still never get enough of you."

"Who says you have to get just 'enough' of me? I never want to get just enough of you, Max. I want all of you. The good, the bad, and everything in between."

"You've got me, babe. I meant it when I said I'm falling in love with you."

"I'm falling in love with you too, Max." I laid my head on his chest and snuggled closer to him in his arms. "My heart has been guarded for so long. Then, you came along and broke right through its defenses."

"I promise to protect your heart, babe. I never want to do anything to hurt you. I love you, Paisley."

"I love you too, Max. I never want to hurt you either. I've always been so afraid of getting hurt. I've seen so many other girls I know, going through broken hearts with their breakups. I didn't want to put myself out there to go through that if I could prevent it."

"Hell, I had a crush on one girl pretty much my whole life, but she never gave me the time of day. I'd given up on dating anyone. Then, this cute little strawberry blonde Derby Queen fell into my life."

"I know how you feel. I had a huge crush on a guy, and he barely knows I exist. Who was she? Your crush, I mean. That is if you don't mind me asking. I don't mean to pry."

"It doesn't matter. It's in the past. I never told anyone that I liked her in that way or about having a crush on her. Besides, I got a better deal in the long run. Have you seen my girlfriend? She's smoking hot!"

"Hahaha! If you say so."

"Oh, I definitely do!" Max took my hand and brought it to his lips. "Paisley, you are gorgeous inside and out. Whoever your crush was, must be blind. I'm selfishly glad he never paid you any attention, because his loss is my gain. There's nothing I'd ever want to change about you. Well, maybe just one thing later on down the road."

"What would that be?"

"Your last name. If we end up being chosen mates, I'd love to be the one to change your last name to Brody someday. If you'd have me, that is."

"I'll be honored if you are my chosen mate. If not, we can still bond with one another. We just wouldn't have the same connection that chosen mates would have. We wouldn't feel the spark and tingles, sense one another, or speak to one another telepathically."

"I'd never want to deny you of that connection, Paisley. No matter how much I love you and want you to be mine forever. If you were to find your chosen mate, I'd let you go to be with him. It would hurt like hell, but I'd do that for you. I love you that much."

"That's still something I don't get. Why do we have to be with our initial *chosen mate* for any of that to happen? Why can't we have that connection with anyone we fall in love with and choose to be with regardless of whether they are our *chosen mate* or not? Fate sure is taking its sweet time to step in. In the meantime, we fall in love with someone other than our chosen mates, and hearts get broken when fate does step in. It's just not fair."

"I know, babe, but it's a risk I'm willing to take. I know we won't mean to break one another's hearts if or when that day comes. Once two chosen mates are reunited, the connection is established, and we can't fight it. Our souls choose one another. Their connection is on a deeper level than we can ever imagine being possible. We are drawn to them more and more as time passes. If you end up being my chosen mate, I'll consider myself the luckiest guy alive. If not, I'll still consider myself just as lucky because of the time that you were mine."

"Oh, Max. That's the sweetest thing anyone has ever said to me. I feel the same way about you. I'd have no choice but to let you go to her, whoever the lucky girl is. I'd be heartbroken on the inside, but I'd wear a smile and be happy for you."

"I mean every word, Paisley. I love you enough to lose you to someone else if it meant you'd be happy."

"I am happy, Max. I'm happy with you."

"I know, babe. I'm happier with you than I've ever been, but even that won't matter once a connection sparks with our chosen mates. That is, if we aren't one another's chosen mates. We still could be. The timing just might be a bit off."

"I really hope that's it, baby.

"Me too, babe. Me too."

Max held me in his arms, and we watched the sunset over the water before he took me home. Max is right. Our love for one another won't matter if a connection sparks with someone else as our chosen mate. They say "love conquers all," but even love can't conquer the connection between chosen mates.

I slumped down on my bed and said a silent prayer for Max Brody to be my chosen mate. I

had let him into my heart and allowed myself
to fall in love with him. I'm sure that my heart
would shatter if he turned out to be someone
else's chosen mate. I told Max I would be
happy for him, but the truth is that I'd be
broken.

Chapter 4

Chad

Angie and I usually ride to school together since we share the same practice days and times after school. Garrett and Tabby are in the back seat. I'm dropping them off at their school along the way. I pulled up to Angie's house to pick her up. She came bouncing out the door in a knee-length, floral skirt, a white tank top, and a pink cardigan. She is adorable. Her hair shines like strands of gold as the morning sunlight touches it. I'm in complete awe of her beauty. I opened her door for her, as I always do. She stood on her tiptoes and kissed my cheek.

"Good morning, handsome. Are you ready for the first day of our senior year?"

"Good morning, gorgeous. I'm as ready as I'm ever going to be." I got back in on my side, pulled out of her driveway, and headed straight for school.

"Yeah, same here. I'm not quite ready for the summer to be over, but I'm ready to see everyone again."

"I've seen everyone I wanted to see this summer. I got to hang out with my best friends, our families, and my gorgeous girlfriend. What more could a guy want?"

"Hmm. I guess you're right, but it'll still be nice to see everyone again."

"Have you had breakfast, or would you like for me to stop along the way for a biscuit?"

"Oh, I've already had breakfast. You can still stop to get something for yourself, Tabby, and Garrett if you'd like."

"Nah, we are good to go. We all ate before we left. I just wanted to make sure you were all taken care of."

"You're so sweet to think of me. Thank you, baby."

"What kind of boyfriend would I be if I didn't?"

"You wouldn't be a boyfriend of mine, that's for sure."

"Exactly my point, hahaha!"

"I love you, Chad. You're the best."

"I love you too, Angie. You deserve the best."

She smiled at me and then turned her attention to the road ahead of us. Tabby and Garrett both rolled their eyes at me in the rearview mirror. Neither of them is old enough to understand teenage relationships yet, but it won't be long before they have their first boyfriend and girlfriend. We continued making small talk about our class schedules and wondered who would be in our classes with us. Angie hoped the girls were in most of her classes. We have one class together. I highly doubt she'd be the least little bit interested in taking the other courses I've enrolled in this semester.

We pulled up at the high school after dropping Tabby and Garrett off at the middle school. Toby was opening Molly's door for her. I'm still a bit jealous of their connection. From the looks of it, Angie is too. She is watching them with a sad smile on her face. I hopped out, opened her door, and took her hand so that I could help her out of my truck. I saw Max's truck and Paisley's MINI Cooper parked a few spaces over.

Angie and I held hands as we walked to our old spot in the quad. All of our friends met us there. We always got to school early enough to hang out for a while before the bell rang for homeroom. The only one of our friends without a significant other is Stacy. She seems to be okay with it, though. She is happily talking to Molly and Paisley.

The moment I saw Paisley, I immediately thought back to Saturday, when I'd once again felt the static shock the brief moment our hands touched. I still wonder if she'd noticed it or felt what I'd felt. Now isn't the right time to ask her, though. She and Max are sitting side-by-side at our usual table with Toby and Molly. They still look like a happy couple—for now.

I wonder what'll happen if what I felt is proof of a connection between Paisley and me. Will Max and Angie understand that we can't fight the connection as it gets stronger? Will they hate us until they find their chosen mates? Only time will tell. I'm not going to be the one to stir the pot. As much as I'd like to pull Paisley aside and talk to her alone, I dread doing so because of having to face the possibility of hurting Angie and Max.

Molly and Toby are telling everyone about their eventful weekend in Kilchoman. Arren, the High Priestess, had broken out of prison. She'd planned to kill Molly and Toby after taking Molly's powers for herself. Arren's mate saved Molly and Toby, and ended up having to kill his mate to keep her from continuing her evil schemes.

Everyone is comparing their class schedules. Paisley and I have Biology II and Chemistry II together. None of our other friends are in them with us. If that *spark* is legitimate, we will end up having a lot more to discuss than just those classes together.

"Hey, Paisley, I think we have Biology II and Chemistry II together. Do you want to be lab partners?"

"Sure, why not?"

"Cool. I hope you're better at those subjects than I am. I suck. Hahaha!"

"I'm pretty good with both. I can help you study if you need me to."

"I appreciate it, Paisley. My dad would be furious if I get benched for bad grades."

"That's what friends do for one another. We help each other when we can. I'm sure you'd help me with my speech class if you could. You've always been a great public speaker. Toby is too. Me? Not so much."

"I thought you did a great job announcing the drivers as the Derby Queen, babe," Max said.

"That's because you couldn't see how nervous I was from where y'all were sitting. I was shaking like a leaf on a tree."

"I'd be happy to help you with your speech class for helping me with the science ones. I don't have that class this semester. If you tell me what the topics are, I can help you write them, give you tips on giving the speech, and on calming your nerves."

"That'd be awesome. Thanks."

"No problem at all."

That was easier than I thought it'd be. I'll have study time with Paisley, and I'll be able to talk to her in private about the *spark*. There's no way she didn't feel it like I did. It's happened twice now, and it may even happen more often with us studying together. Either way, I'll be able to test my theory. I'll sit with her at the lab tables in the classroom. Then, I'll casually bump her arm or tap her shoulder to get her attention, and ask her a question about the lesson. If there's a *spark* every time I touch her, I'll know. Well, that, and as we spend more time together, the connection will grow stronger, if there is one.

The bell for homeroom rang, and I walked Angie to her class before going to mine down the hall. I made sure no teachers were watching. I gave Angie a quick kiss on the cheek and turned to walk away. I didn't see Paisley walking in my direction, and I bumped right into her as I'd turned to leave.

The *spark*. It was stronger this time because our bodies bumped and not just our fingers. Only, it wasn't just a *spark* this time. It felt like a jolt followed by hot tingles that rushed through my whole body. Paisley looked up at me and gasped. Her eyes were as wide as saucers. That's when I knew. She'd felt it too. Paisley and I are chosen mates. Damn, I'm so screwed.

Paisley

"Chad—"

"Paisley, I'm so sorry. I didn't mean to bump into you. Are you all right?"

"Yeah, I-I'm fine. I think."

"We need to talk." We'd said it at the same time. What in the hell is happening? The *spark*... and... *hot tingles*. Oh, no! *Chad* can't be my chosen mate. *Max* is supposed to be my chosen mate. I love *him*. I'm falling in love with *him*, not with *Chad*. My heart is racing and breaking at the same time. My breath is ragged, and I feel light-headed. All I can manage to do is dumbfoundedly nod at him.

"Chemistry class," he said. "We'll get a lab table in the back if we can. You don't look so good, Paisley. You may want to sit down before you fall out."

"Good idea. I'll see you in a few minutes."

It's a good thing homeroom only lasts long enough to take roll call. I need to talk to Chad. I'm glad that Max and Angie aren't in our science classes. It'll give us a chance to talk about what just happened and what is going on between us. This can't be happening, not between us. If it is, why couldn't it have happened before we'd fallen in love with other people? I'm sure Chad and Angie are in love, especially as long as they have been together. This is so not fair.

I know that Max and I have only been dating a short time, but we are falling in love. I can feel it deep inside me. I've guarded my heart and fought against falling in love for so long. Just when I finally let myself fall in love, this happens. Oh, no! What am I going to tell Max? I know he said he'd let me go if I found my chosen mate, but how is he going to feel about my chosen mate being one of his best friends? This is bad. This is really, really bad! I'm not far from being in full-on panic mode.

The bell for the first period finally rang. I grabbed my backpack and darted out the door. Chad and I have to talk—now. I hurried through the hallway and was the first one in the chemistry classroom. Max's homeroom and first-period class are in another wing of the school. I'll see him at lunch and in my third-period class afterward. Hopefully, I'll know what to say to him by then. Right now, it's all I can do to keep from throwing up. I headed for the lab table in the very back of the classroom and waited for Chad. He came in and sat down beside me. He doesn't look as shaken up as I feel at the moment. Maybe he is just better at hiding it than I am.

"So... what do you suppose we do now?" Chad asked.

"How are you so calm? I'm freaking out here." He placed his hand on my shoulder. The *spark* sent hot tingles through me once again. The tingles felt soothing, yet so wrong. I don't want to feel them. At least, I don't want to feel them with *Chad*. I want to feel them with *Max*. It feels like my soul is betraying my heart.

"Paisley, everything is going to be okay."

"Is it? How is any of this going to be okay? I'm falling in love with *Max*. You're in love with *Angie*." I lowered my voice so our classmates wouldn't overhear our conversation. "*You* and *I* aren't supposed to be *chosen mates*, Chad."

"We are, though, Paisley. You do know we can't fight this, right?"

"I can't do this, Chad. I can't hurt Max. I feel like my heart is shattering."

"Paisley, Max will understand. Our connection will get stronger, whether we want it to right now or not."

"What about Angie? Will *she* be as understanding as you say Max will be? Somehow, I highly doubt it."

Everyone had found their seats, and Mr. Duncan started talking about class expectations and lab safety. Chad and I opened our textbooks to lab safety practices and pretended to follow along. Meanwhile, we continued to whisper amongst ourselves.

"Paisley, we will get through this together."

"What choice do we have, Chad? I'm about to break the heart of the only guy I've ever loved. Our relationship has been so wonderful. Now?" Oh, God, I'm going to be sick. "It's over."

"Angie thought you had a crush on me earlier this summer. I guess she was wrong."

"No, she wasn't, at least, not exactly. I did have a crush on you. I had a crush on you for years. I finally gave up on the idea of you ever giving me a chance on the day of the Derby. Mama and I saw you guys eating together at that burger place in Troy. You and Angie looked very much in love. So, I gave up and moved on.”

“Do you think you could ever reignite that crush?”

“I don’t know, Chad. Right now, all I can think about is how much this is going to hurt Max. Angie will be heartbroken, too. What are we going to do?”

“We should tell them sooner than later. This connection is going to be hard to ignore for too much longer. I’m sure you remember how fast it hit Toby and Molly. I’d rather tell them and end things now, so neither of us has to feel guilty about falling in love with one another.”

“You’re probably right, but I still dread going through with it. The thought of it makes me physically ill.”

All I want to do is curl up on my bed and cry. I never wanted to hurt Max. We just had this discussion yesterday. We’d just confessed our love for one another. Then, he’d told me that he loved me so much that if I found my chosen mate, he’d let me go to be with him if it meant I’d be happy. I’m not happy about this at all. I’m devastated, crushed, shattered, and even angry. They say, “All’s fair in love and war.” How is this fair?

“Should we tell them both at the same time, or separately?” Chad asked.

“Probably separately. Breakups are still intimate moments. I don’t think it’d be appropriate to tell them together. I wouldn’t want Max to bring his chosen mate to break up with me. It'd seem like a slap to the face, followed by a punch in the gut."

"Yeah, I'd be pretty furious if Angie did that to me, too."

"It's probably best to wait until after school to tell them. They'll have time to process everything before school starts tomorrow. I still can't process it myself. My relationship with Max will be over today, and our relationship will be just getting started. Ugh. Chad, this is so freaking awkward."

"Yeah, it is."

"I have a feeling our circle of friends will never be the same again. Y'all were just fine before I came along and ruined everything."

"Don't say that. You have made Max happier than I've ever seen him. Angie has been nicer to everyone, and they've finally accepted her as a friend and not just the girl I'm dating. So, you see? You've had a great impact on our group of friends, Paisley."

"Yeah, and I'm about to screw all of that up when this bomb drops." My eyes are burning, and I can feel tears welling up in them. Two more people are about to be devastated by this news. I don't know how Chad is so calm. He doesn't seem to be phased by this new development at all.

"It won't be that bad. You'll see."

"Again, how are you so calm?"

"Paisley, I've wanted to feel the connection with my chosen mate since the day my parents explained everything. All they would tell me was that I had chosen my mate and that fate would decide when we'd find one another again. To be honest, yes, I did want it to be with Angie because I do love her. She's all I've ever known, but something inside me told me she wasn't the one. I know she will find her chosen mate and be happy again someday, too. Max will find his chosen mate someday as well. Fate will show them who their mates are when the time is right for them. The time is right for us, or it wouldn't have happened."

"I suppose you're right."

We stayed silent for the remainder of the class. Chad kept looking at me periodically and smiling. I honestly think he's relieved to finally know who his chosen mate is, even if it isn't who he'd wanted it to be. Could he and I fall in love like he'd said we would? I know I was attracted to him for a long time. Am I still? The only guy on my mind right now is Max.

I remember my parents telling me that the connection is awakened by a spark when our palms touch. When had our palms touched? We bumped into one another in the hallway. Then, I remembered asking him to hold my hand at the Derby when I'd gotten hurt. He'd shocked me with what felt like static electricity. That was it—the *spark*. That was about a month or so ago, though. We hadn't touched one another after that, other than when he shocked my hand again at the marina on Saturday. Our fingers touched when I'd paid for the snacks. That's why we'd never paid attention to the tingles before today. We'd never really touched one another long enough and had barely touched then. Even still, the connection has been awakened for a while now. Why haven't we been drawn to one another?

The bell finally rang to end the class. I shoved my book and my notebook into my backpack and started to stand. Chad placed his hand on my shoulder. The spark zapped me again with more tingles.

"Wait a minute, will you?"

"Why, what's up?"

"I want to try something, but let's wait for everyone to clear out first."

I nodded and tried to look as though I was busy getting my things together. Once everyone was gone, Chad tilted my face towards his and placed a soft kiss on my lips. The spark and tingles spread from our lips and heat surged through me to my core. My heart started pounding. It was the most intense rush I've ever felt. The kiss ended just as fast as it happened, but his lips left mine sizzling with tingles that lingered on them. Yep. Chad Greene is my chosen mate. No doubt about it. I'd never felt that sensation, even with as many times as Max and I had kissed. Not even once.

Chad looked into my eyes, and it felt as though he was looking into my soul. I felt bare before him. His hazel eyes seemed to glow with specs of amber and gold—the color of honey. Something, an odd feeling, stirred inside me. I felt our connection. It was almost as though I'd felt my soul calling out to Chad's as his soul was calling out to mine. The look on his face told me he'd felt the same thing. His lips parted slightly, and he drew in a small gasp of air.

"Paisley, you felt that too, didn't you?"

"Yeah, I did." I broke our eye contact and looked away from him. "Um, we should probably get to Biology II before we're late." I grabbed my backpack and started walking towards the front of the classroom. Chad reached for my hand and brought it to his lips. Sparks and tingles ran up my arm and into my chest.

"I'm looking forward to getting to know you better, Paisley."

All I could do was look at him in stunned silence. We walked next door to class together and sat down at an empty lab table at the back of the room. Other students were still coming in. Despite feeling the connection we share, I felt guilty. It felt wrong. I felt as though everyone was watching us because they all knew he was dating Angie. Not everyone knew I was dating Max. Our relationship wasn't exactly common knowledge. I've managed to stay lucky enough to avoid drama and dodge being in the rumor mill my whole life. Something tells me that my luck is running out where that's concerned. The rumors will surely fly tomorrow. Everyone will think that I've broken up their happy little romance and stolen Chad away from Angie.

Little do they know, that neither one of us are to blame. We won't be able to fight the *urge* to complete the bond as our connection grows stronger. I suppose I'd better get ready for this rollercoaster because it is going to be one helluva ride.

Chapter 5

Chad

Paisley is so selfless. She's more concerned about hurting Max and Angie than anything else at the moment. I've never met anyone like her. I feel the need to reassure her that everything is going to be okay in the long run. It'll be rough at first, but we will get through it together. I reached over and placed my hand on top of hers on the lab table. She retracted her hand, looked at me like I'd lost my mind, and then looked around the room to see if anyone had seen it. I guess we shouldn't be seen holding hands right now. Well, probably not for a while to let the rumor mill settle down from the breakups that'll hit everyone's ears pretty soon.

If I want to spend time with Paisley, it'll have to be in private for now, which I fully intend to do as often as I can. I've wanted to feel this connection for so long now. I'm going to do everything in my power to make sure it grows into something incredible. I'm ready to claim Paisley as my chosen mate and love her for eternity.

Chemistry II and Biology II classes are the only ones I have with Paisley this semester. So, I have to try to take advantage of this time to learn what I can about both subjects and her. I'd never gotten the chance to know her beyond her just being Max's girlfriend. Angie's jealousy has pretty much kept me from getting to know any other girls. I'd gotten to know Molly because she lives across the water from me. Angie is no longer jealous of her because she is Toby's chosen mate and is not interested in me in the least little bit.

I can't stop looking at Paisley. I want to memorize every detail of her beauty. She is stunning. I'd never really noticed before, but I can now. I can, because she's mine. Paisley O'Riley is mine. Her strawberry blonde curls fall perfectly down her back and over her shoulders. Her lavender-blue eyes sparkle like polished tanzanite. The perfectly formed pout of her lips makes me want to feel them pressed against mine again.

I already can't stand the thought of Max's, or any other guy's hands or lips on her. How am I going to get through our lunch period, knowing he'll hold her hand, walk her to class, and maybe even kiss her? They have History class together after lunch, and I have English Literature with Angie. How am I supposed to act normal with Angie until after school and football practice, when the only girl I want to touch and kiss for all eternity is Paisley?

Then, there's my friendship with Max. He's one of my best friends. How am I going to face him, knowing I'm taking his girlfriend from him? The answer is, I'll do what I have to do and act normal. Will he still want to be my friend after this? I wouldn't blame him if he didn't. I'll do my best not to rub my relationship with Paisley in Max's and Angie's faces. I'll have to wait to be affectionate with her until we are alone, or at least until I know Angie and Max are okay.

I know Paisley will probably want some time to get over Max or at least time to get over hurting him. She'd said she felt like her heart was shattering. I wish I could do something to heal her pain. I'd hold her in my arms and just let her cry if it'd help. I want to comfort her and tell her everything will be okay. I want to be here for her now and for eternity.

I watched her all through Biology II class, while Mrs. Isleson explained the class expectations and the syllabus. Once a review of last year's Biology I class was underway, I nudged Paisley's elbow.

"Are you okay, baby?" I whispered.

"Please, don't call me that, Chad."

"Paisley, please. You are *my* chosen mate. Please, talk to me. How can I make you feel better about us?"

Paisley drew in a ragged breath. If I didn't know any better, I'd say she was on the verge of tears. "Please, Chad. I need some time, okay? This... this thing between us... it feels... I don't know... wrong. You shouldn't have kissed me. I feel guilty for enjoying it when I still love Max."

"We belong to one another now, Paisley, not to Max and Angie."

"I know that, but it still doesn't help ease the pain I feel inside at the moment. I just need time to process it all. I'm still telling Max about everything tonight. I owe him that. I need some time before we work on starting an 'us,' okay?"

"Okay. Take all the time you need. Just know that I'm here when you're ready. I'm not going anywhere, Paisley."

She nodded and wiped a tear from one of her eyes. Damn, I hate this. I was so looking forward to finding my chosen mate, feeling the spark and tingles with her, relishing in our connection, and falling deeply and completely in love. Now that our connection has awakened, my chosen mate is in too much pain to enjoy it with me, because she will have to break the heart of her first love and her own just to be with me. I'll give her time to mend her heart and be here for her, whether she needs or wants me to be or not.

I do understand how she's feeling, though. I dread telling Angie about my connection with

Paisley. It'll be one of the hardest things I've ever had to do. Paisley will have me to comfort her through her heartbreak and getting over Max. Who will soothe Angie to help her get through hers? I'm sure she'll turn to Stacy and maybe even Molly, but she will more than likely alienate Paisley from her circle of friends. She may also alienate herself from our group all together. I still love her and care about her. I want her to be okay, but most of all, I want her to find her chosen mate and find true love with him.

The ninety-minute Biology II class went faster than I thought it would. The bell rang, and Paisley stood up to leave. I had to stop her. I reached for her hand. The spark and tingles rushed through me once again.

"Paisley, wait. Please?"

"Yes, Chad?"

"When you tell Max about our connection, when are you going to say it began, today, or at the Derby?"

"I'm going to tell him the truth. I'm going to tell him I'd felt something at the Derby, but thought it was just static electricity at the time."

"Okay, good. That's what I'm telling Angie too. I'll have to wait until after football practice to tell her. Max will be at football practice too."

"Yes, I know. I still want to tell Max in person. Breaking up with someone isn't something to do over the phone."

"Yeah, I agree. I just wish it didn't hurt so much. I hate that people I care about are getting hurt at all. I know we just figured everything out, and we aren't an 'us' yet, but it still hurts me to see you in pain, Paisley. I remember how scared I was when you fell off the platform at the Derby. I ran faster to get to you than I'd ever run in my life. I was terrified and couldn't explain why I'd felt so strongly towards you then. It hit me when I felt our souls calling out to one another back in the Chemistry II classroom. I think we were calling out to one another even back then."

She shrugged her shoulders and bit her bottom lip. "I guess it's possible. I remember asking you not to leave me. I wonder if that accident was fate's way of bringing us together?"

"I think it was. As much as I've loved Angie, my soul will always choose *you*, Paisley. *I* choose you."

I couldn't resist touching her another minute longer. I reached up, cradled her face with one hand, and stroked her cheek with my thumb. The spark and tingles flowed from my hand, up to my arm, and into my chest. My heart started beating faster and faster. Before I even realized what I was doing, I leaned down and pressed my lips to hers.

"Chad? Paisley? What's going on here?" Max asked.

"I'd like to know the same thing!" Angie said.

Damn, I'm so screwed. I didn't consider the fact that Max and Angie, or anyone else for that matter, would walk in and see me kissing Paisley. I didn't even realize what I was doing until it was too late. Resisting her is going to be more challenging than I thought. So much for waiting to tell Max and Angie after school.

"I owe you both an explanation," I said.

"Damn right, you do! I didn't see Paisley in the quad or the lunchroom, so I came looking for her at her last class. Just what do I find? My so-called 'friend' has his lips on my girlfriend! How do you explain that?"

"Max, Angie, please listen. There's something I need to tell you. It isn't easy for me to say, because neither of us expected this to happen. Paisley and I just found out that she and I are chosen mates. We'd planned on telling you separately this evening in private. I guess I screwed that up. I am so sorry."

"No! When did this happen?" Angie asked, with tears streaming down her cheeks.

Max slumped down in a nearby empty chair and just looked down at the floor. His initial anger has now turned to heartbreak. Angie sat in a chair at another table and buried her face in her hands. The first girl I ever loved and one of my best friends are hurt, and it's all my fault. I cautiously walked to the table where Angie was and sat down on its edge beside her. Paisley sat down beside Max and tried to console him. Tears are now streaming down her cheeks too. This is not how I'd imagined telling Angie and Max about Paisley and me.

Paisley took a deep breath and started trying to explain through her tears. "We think our connection started at the Derby when I fell, and Chad came to help me. His hand shocked mine, but we'd both blown it off as static electricity and didn't think anything more about it. We accidentally bumped into one another in the hallway this morning. The *spark* hit us again, followed by the tell-tale tingling sensation. That's when we knew. I told him I needed time because I'm still in love with you, Max."

"I told her I'd wait for her and would be here when she's ready. I didn't mean to kiss her just then. Something just came over me, and I couldn't fight it."

Max turned to Paisley and took both of her hands into his and kissed them. A pang of jealousy hit me like a freight train. I had to tamp it down, though. Max is my friend, and until now, has loved Paisley as his girlfriend. This can't be easy for him either.

"Paisley, I told you that I love you enough to let you go to be with your chosen mate, if or when that day came. When I said that, I had no idea that day would be today, and that your chosen mate would be Chad. Regardless of all that, I meant what I said. I still love you, Paisley. My heart is breaking, but I'm a man of my word. I want you to go to Chad, and be happy with him as your chosen mate. I'll be happy for you both in time, but for right now, I need time to make peace with letting you go."

He kissed her hands once more. Then, he stood, kissed her cheek, and walked out of the classroom. Paisley looked over at me and then at Angie.

"Angie, I am so sorry. Chad and I never meant for any of this to happen. I love Max so much. My heart is breaking, Max is hurting, and there's nothing I can do to fix it. I prayed so hard for Max to be my chosen mate. I'm sure you prayed just as hard, if not harder, for Chad to be yours."

"What do you know about love? You've only been dating Max for what, a few weeks?! Chad and I have been together for almost six years!"

"Angie, this is not her fault. It's not even my fault. I am so, so sorry that our connection is causing so much pain and sadness. I don't want you to be sad. I want you to find your chosen mate and be happy."

"Right, because this is all about what you want, and it's so easy for me to just find *my* chosen mate. Well, apparently, it's not who I want to be with, so what does it matter? Just leave me alone. Don't talk to me, don't look at me, and please don't call or text to check on me later. Stay out of my life. You've done enough harm already. The same goes for you too, Paisley. I thought you were my friend."

"Angie, please, try to understand. I am still your friend."

"No, Paisley. Not anymore."

Angie stormed out of the classroom. I hopped off the table and walked over to where Paisley is sitting. I squatted down beside her and took one of her hands into mine. "Paisley, I am so sorry. I know we'd had plans to tell them in another way. I never meant for it to happen like this."

"I know, Chad, but the damage is done. I've got to go. Lunch is almost over, and my next class is on the other side of the school."

"Mine is too. Do you want me to walk with you?"

"I don't think that's such a good idea. Max will be in that class with me. He's probably already there if he didn't leave school for the rest of the day. I wouldn't blame him if he did. Besides, I need to go freshen up in the ladies' room anyway. I'm sure I look like a huge mess."

"You're probably right about Max. You are still so beautiful, Paisley. You're even pretty when you cry, not that I want you to cry, or be the reason you cry ever again."

"That's sweet of you to say, Chad. Thank you. I still need time to get over Max. I hope you understand."

"You're welcome, and yes, I understand. I told you I'd give you all the time you need. I'll be here when you're ready." I stood, kissed her hand, and helped her up from her chair. She wrapped her arms around me and placed her head on my chest. The spark and tingles I felt surging through me were comforting and reassuring.

"Thank you, Chad."

I wrapped my arms around her, placed a kiss on the top of her head, and held her as close to me as I could. "You're welcome, sweetheart. I'll be waiting patiently. Here, I'll put my number in your phone. I want you to call or text me anytime, okay?" She simply nodded and handed me her phone. I put in my number and gave it back to her. I walked with her to the closest ladies' room, and we said our goodbyes.

The rest of the school day, including football practice, was a hazy blur. All I could think about was how much all of this mess hurt everyone. I left practice and drove home. Alone. Angie caught a ride home from one of the other cheerleaders on her squad. They all kept giving me dirty looks the entire time we were on the field for practice. So, it begins. The word around the school will be that I dumped Angie for Paisley, I'm sure. As though I have a choice in the matter. Paisley and I are meant to be together. Our souls are connected. We will eventually be inseparable, but not right now. Right now, Paisley is trying to process it all with a broken heart. We all are.

Dad was in the living room, and Mom was cooking supper when I got home. Dad took one look at me and saw how my day had gone. It was displayed all over my face.

"Hey, son. What's wrong, did you have a bad first day of school?"

"Yeah, you could say that."

"What happened?"

"I figured out who my chosen mate is, that's what."

"Don't you like her?"

"That's not the issue, Dad. Paisley is gorgeous, smart, has a heart of gold, and a great sense of humor. The problem is, she was dating one of my best friends."

"Oh. I see."

"Yeah. That's not all. We have two classes together. We'd decided to tell Max and Angie after school. That didn't get to happen, though. I'd held Paisley back after class to talk to her. Something came over me, and before I knew it, I was kissing her. Max and Angie walked in and saw everything. Max is taking it better than Angie is. He's heartbroken because he's in love with Paisley, but agreed to let her go. Angie, on the other hand, is completely crushed. She hates us both and doesn't want to speak to Paisley or me ever again."

"Wow. I'm sorry, son. Fate can sometimes have impeccable timing, huh?"

"Yeah, that's the understatement of the century. Angie had just practically thrown herself at me over the weekend. She begged me to bond with her, regardless of who our chosen mates were. I rejected her, though, because I wanted to be with my chosen mate, whoever that turned out to be."

"Aren't you glad you did? I thought you'd be happy when you found out about Paisley. I've known her dad, Taggart, for years. We served on Queen Isabella's Royal Guard together. We were pretty ecstatic when you and Paisley chose one another.”

“Really? I had no idea.”

“We were close back then. We still talk now and then, but we had to separate you two to let fate step in when the time was right.”

“I really like Paisley, and I am happy with my choice, but Angie and I have been together for almost six years, Dad. I still care about her, and feel like crap for hurting her.”

“I know you do, son, but we can’t avoid the connection between chosen mates forever. You’ll always be drawn to Paisley. Now that your connection has awakened, it will continue to grow stronger. Your feelings for Angie will fade, Chad. Before you know it, it will seem as though you and Angie never dated at all.”

“I don’t want to forget, though, Dad. I’ve cherished my memories with Angie all these years. How do I just let all of that go?”

“Well, you don’t have to if you don’t want to.”

“What do you mean, Dad?”

“You still have a choice. You can stay with Angie and bond with her, after your wedding, of course, and try to ignore the connection with Paisley. I don’t personally recommend it, though. You’ll never feel the same for Angie as you once did. The love you feel for her will just be a shadow of the much deeper love you could experience with Paisley.”

“So, I could fight the connection if I wanted to?”

"It wouldn't be easy, but yes, if that's what you want. You'd still be drawn to Paisley and would be for eternity, even though you'd be bonded to Angie. It'd be a hard road to travel, but the choice is yours to make."

"I don't know what to do, Dad. Max and Paisley were a happy couple. All of that has changed now. I think I've known for a while that Angie wasn't my chosen mate. I can already feel the pull of my connection to Paisley. I think it was awakened at the Derby. It's taken a few weeks for us to figure out that the spark we'd felt wasn't just static electricity. We felt the tingles when we accidentally ran into one another at school today. That's how we knew. Then, something else happened. I'd kissed her very briefly after our first class. I looked into her eyes, and we felt our souls calling out to one another."

"It seems to me like your choice has already been made."

"Yeah. I suppose so."

"Go ahead and wash up for supper. It should be ready by the time you've had a shower."

"Thanks for talking with me, Dad."

"No problem, Son. I just want you to be happy with whatever choices you make in life."

I smiled at him and headed upstairs. My cell phone dinged with a text message as I walked into my room. I didn't recognize the number, but I opened it up anyway out of curiosity.

"Hey, Chad. It's Paisley. Can we talk?"

"Sure, are you okay?"

"Yeah, I think so. Mind if I call you?"

"I don't mind at all." My phone rang a few seconds later. "Hello?"

"Hey, Chad, it's Paisley again."

"Hey, sweetheart. What's up?"

"Not much. Am I calling at a bad time?"

"No, not at all. I was just about to jump in the shower. My phone case is waterproof. I can take you with me."

"Um... o-okay."

"Does that make you uncomfortable?"

"No, it's fine. "

"Okay. So, what's on your mind?"

"I'm just not used to being the topic of conversation in the rumor mill, that's all."

"I'm sorry about that. It was bound to happen no matter how we broke the news, though. Angie has always been a bit of a drama queen."

"I'm sure it'll pass before too long. I've just had people, who I thought were my friends, calling me a home wrecker, a trollop, a slut, and a whore in texts and other various social media messages all day."

"I'm so sorry, sweetheart. That's all my fault. I shouldn't have kissed you again so soon. I don't know what came over me. I didn't realize I was even doing it until it happened."

"It is what it is, I suppose. Molly called me and made sure I was okay. She said Toby talked to Max. He's still pretty hurt."

"Yeah, he seemed out of it at practice. I can't say I blame him. I probably would've been upset too if I'd lost you to someone else."

"What about Angie? Would you have been upset if she'd found her mate first?"

"I think I would've been hurt for a little while, but I would've been happy for her in the long run."

"I'm sure you wish she could've been your chosen mate instead of me, huh?"

"I don't know; I think I did pretty well by choosing you. It's hard to say, but I think I've known for a while that Angie and I weren't meant to be together."

"If that's the case, why didn't you let her go sooner? If you don't mind me asking, that is."

"I don't know. I guess I was still hopeful. I've loved her for so long that I just assumed she was my chosen mate. We both thought that our connection would awaken any day now. When it didn't, I began to wonder if it ever would."

"I can imagine how frustrating that must've been for you both."

"It definitely put a strain on our relationship. It made her super jealous of any girl that got within touching range of me. She was afraid a spark would happen with someone else."

"Then, I came along, and it happened anyway."

"Paisley, I'm thrilled you came along and joined our group of friends. I'm even more thrilled that you turned out to be mine."

"I am too, really, I am." She took a deep breath and sighed. "I just hate that people we care about are hurting."

"They will be okay in time, sweetheart."

"Yeah, I know. I hope so. It still doesn't make it suck any less at the moment."

"Paisley, sweetheart, are you sure you're okay?"

"Yeah, I'm okay. Well, I will be." Her voice cracked a little as if she's about to cry. "I do want to apologize for snapping at you earlier today. I really am very sorry. It just struck a nerve when you called me baby so soon. Max used to call me babe. Calling me baby was just too close to that, I suppose. Hearing you call me that seemed so wrong at the time, and i shouldn't have said, 'the damage is done.' I'm sorry for that too."

"It's okay. I know today wasn't easy for you. It wasn't easy for me, either. If you don't want me to call you baby, what would you like for me to call you?"

"Did you ever call Angie sweetheart?"

"No. I always called her Angie or baby. You're the only girl I've ever called sweetheart, Paisley. You're so sclfless. You were more worried about Max's and Angie's feelings than your own. You truly are a sweetheart."

"Thanks. I guess I could get used to you calling me sweetheart, then since you put it that way. What would you want me to call you?"

"Whatever you'd like. Maybe one day, I'll earn your heart and your love. I'd really like for you to call me yours."

"You're already mine, Chad, and I'm yours. I've never felt anything as intense as I did with you today. When you kissed me, even though it was just a simple kiss on the lips, the tingles that flowed through me were beyond anything I'd ever felt when Max and I had kissed. I admit that I doubted the connection before, but I don't anymore."

"I know what you mean. I could get used to kissing you, Paisley, among other things, in due time, of course."

She giggled. "You think so, huh?"

"Yeah, I do, but I'm willing to wait for you. You're worth waiting for, Paisley. I mean that."

"Thanks, Chad. I appreciate you saying that. What if we just start by getting to know each other better as friends and see how it goes?"

"I'd like that. I think that's a great idea, sweetheart."

"Thanks for talking to me tonight. I already feel a lot better."

"Good. I'm glad. I don't ever want to be the cause of your pain or sadness, Paisley. I want to be the one to dry your tears, soothe your pain, calm your nerves, and chase away your fears. I want to make you smile and laugh every day."

"That's very sweet of you to say. I hope I can do all of those things for you, too. Eternity is an awfully long time to be with someone. It means a lot just knowing that we can love and appreciate one another for more than just the physical bond we will share one day.”

“We will. I know we will. In time, we will share a love so deep and so pure that nothing or no one will be able to come between us.”

“I’m looking forward to sharing that with you, Chad.”

“Me too. Our love story will be a great one. You’ll see.”

“I’m sure it will. Well, Mama just sent me a text, saying supper is ready. Would you want to chat later?”

“Sure. Call or text me anytime, sweetheart.”

“Thanks, honey. I really appreciate it.”

“Honey, huh? I like that.”

“Really? Good, I’m glad you do. That’s what I’ll call you, then.”

“I’m curious. Why honey, though?”

“Your eyes are the color of honey when they glow. I’ll never forget the way they looked when you gazed into my eyes today. You really got to me.”

“You got to me too. I think that’s pretty obvious, though. I couldn’t stop myself from kissing you.”

“To be honest, I didn’t want you to stop. My heart was racing.”

“Mine was too. I’d like to kiss you again sometime if you’ll let me.”

“I’d like that. Well, I’ve got to go.”

“Okay. No worries. Bye, sweetheart.”

“Bye, honey.”

Chapter 6

Paisley

I went downstairs, fixed my plate, and poured something to drink. Then, I sat down at the table to have supper with the rest of my family.

"Everything looks great, Mama."

"Thank you, Paisley. I found the recipes in a new cookbook that I bought last weekend. Anyway, enough about that. Tell me about your first day of your senior year."

"I don't exactly want to talk about it. It wasn't all that great."

"Oh, Paisley. It couldn't have been that bad."

"Oh, but it was."

"What happened?"

"Well, I figured out that Chad Greene is my chosen mate, for starters."

"That's wonderful! We were hoping your connection would awaken soon. Aren't you happy with him?"

"Oh, Mama." I looked down at my plate and slowly shook my head. "I think I would've been happier if both of us weren't dating other people at the time."

"I'm sure Max will find his chosen mate before to long."

"He's hurt right now, Mama. Angelina is even more upset than Max is about it. We'd planned on breaking the news to them separately in private, but that's far from what actually happened. Chad kissed me after our second class together. Max and Angelina walked in and saw us. Everything went downhill from there."

"What does Chad think about your connection?"

"He's sorry that things went the way they did with Angelina and Max, but he's happy about our connection. He's wanted to find his chosen mate since his parents told him about his heritage."

"And you?"

"Mama, you know I've had a crush on Chad for years. I just never thought that I had a chance because Angelina had her claws in him. I'd given up on him and had fallen in love with Max. I feel horrible for hurting him. Max and I just had the *chosen mate* discussion yesterday. He told me he was falling in love with me. Then, he said he loved me enough that he'd let me go to be with my chosen mate if it wasn't him because he wanted me to be happy. When he found out about Chad and me, he said he was a man of his word and that he'd be happy for us in time. Oh, Mama. I hate that he's hurting. I want to go to him and make sure he's okay, but I don't know if he'd even talk to me right now."

"Well, you could try calling him and see if he answers. If he does, just tell him you were worried about him and wanted to make sure he's okay. If not, text him that same message. He may not want to talk to you, but then again, he may appreciate you checking on him as a friend."

"Angelina told Chad and me to never speak to her again and that our friendship was over."

"I think she'll come around once she discovers her chosen mate."

"Yeah, but who knows when that'll be."

"She's a beautiful girl. Even if she doesn't find her chosen mate right away, she'll have another boyfriend before you know it."

"I don't know, Mama. She and Chad were a couple for a long time. She is pretty upset."

"I'm sure she is, but she will be okay. Just give her time for her broken heart to mend."

I just nodded and continued to eat my supper. Mama had done a fantastic job. She made roasted Cornish hens with carrots, potatoes, onions, and steamed broccoli. Once everyone finished eating, I cleaned up the kitchen and headed upstairs to call Max. It rang three times, but he answered.

"Hey, Paisley. Are you okay?"

"Hey, Max. I'm just calling to check on you. I'm worried about you and feel horrible about the way things ended between us. My heart still aches for you, Max. This isn't fair." Tears filled my eyes and threatened to spill down my cheeks.

"I know, babe—sorry. It's a habit. I probably shouldn't call you that anymore, huh?"

"Max, this isn't easy for me either. Why couldn't it have been you, Max? You're the one I love. You're the one I'm in love with—not Chad."

"Give it time, Paisley. Your heart will catch up as the connection grows stronger. You'll eventually get over your love for me and fall in love with Chad. It may or may not happen overnight, but it will happen. That's why I told you I'd let you go if you found your chosen mate. Your connection with him is on a level I can't compete with."

"I know." I took a deep breath to try to fight back my tears. "I wish there was a way to change it. I'd choose you if I could."

"I'd choose you too, Paisley, but we can't change who our souls are meant to bond with. I'm still trying to process everything. Yes, it still hurts, but I'll be okay. I don't blame you or Chad. Neither one of you planned for this to happen. I'd still like to have both of you as my friends if that's okay. I've known Chad my whole life. I'd hate to lose him as a friend. I'd hate to lose you, too. I'd rather have you in my life as a friend than not at all. At least then, I'd know you're happy."

"Thank you, Max. I'd really like that."

"Well, I'm going to get off of here. I still have homework to do before going to bed."

"Yeah, I still have a little bit to do as well. I started it after I got home from school, but I didn't quite get to finish. Let me know if you need any help. I'd be glad to help you get it all done at a decent time. You work too hard not to get a decent night's sleep."

"Thanks, I'll keep that in mind. I don't have much to do, so it shouldn't take too long."

"Okay. Good night, Max. Thanks again for talking to me."

"Good night, Paisley. You can still call or text me anytime. That's what friends are for, right?"

"The same goes for you, too. I mean it. Bye, Max."

"Bye, Paisley."

I'm glad I talked to Max. I feel a little bit better now that I was able to get some closure with him. At least he doesn't hate Chad or me for what happened. I wish I could say the same about Angelina. I hate that she's hurting so much and wish she understood as Max does. She'd told everyone at school that I'd stolen Chad from her.

My "good-girl" reputation was gone in the blink of an eye. All of the cheerleaders, Stacy included, gave me dirty looks in the hallways and uttered derogatory names under their breath as they passed me. As though I wasn't hurt enough by the situation. They just added insult to injury, and kicked me when I was down. They didn't realize or care that my heart shattered, too. They didn't care that I was in love with Max and had broken both of our hearts.

They are also human and don't understand the connection that Nymphs form with their chosen mates. Angelina knows, though. She is just so crushed that she doesn't care who she takes down with her. Chad told me that Angelina knew I'd had a crush on him earlier this summer. I'm sure she thinks I did this on purpose to steal him from her. I hope that her parents can explain to her that neither one of us are to blame and that we can't fight it. We will always feel the gravitational pull of one another. Our souls have been calling out to one another. I didn't know that was possible and wouldn't have believed it if I hadn't experienced it first hand.

I hope Angelina finds her chosen mate soon. She may not want to be my friend right now, but I still care about her. I even forgive her for smearing my name through the mud at school. As much as I hate that she did it, I know that it was her pain talking. Everyone could see how distraught she was. She was very clear in telling everyone exactly what she'd seen that had her so upset. Oh well, I'm sure something else will happen that'll take the spotlight off of Chad and me soon enough. This is high school, after all.

I grabbed my pajamas and headed to the bathroom to take a shower, so my hair will be dry before I go to bed. I stood under the warm water, and my mind drifted to Chad. I wondered if he'd tried to talk to Angelina and console her, as I'd done with Max. I'm glad I did. It gave me a sense of closure. I feel like I can start to move on. I'm still not ready to have public make-out sessions with Chad just yet. I stepped out of the shower and put my pajamas on. My phone was ringing when I walked back into my room. It was Chad calling me. "Hey, honey."

"Hey, sweetheart. How are you?"

"I'm feeling a little better. I just got out of the shower."

"Oh, okay. Well, I just spoke to Max. He called me and told me he's not mad and still wants to be friends with both of us."

"Yeah, I was worried about him and called him earlier. I think he and I were able to get the closure we needed to start moving on."

"Good. I'm glad to hear that, sweetheart. I wish it were that easy with Angie. She still won't talk to me. She's taking this pretty hard."

"Well, she's heartbroken, Chad. I can imagine how she feels. She's had you all these years, and then all of a sudden, she doesn't. There was no downward slope, no relationship issues, and no warning signs of a breakup. Then, boom! It's over. It's a lot to process."

"Things were a bit strained with us, though. We just didn't make it a topic of discussion with everyone. I'm not sure she'll get over it as easily as Max has."

"They say, 'time heals all wounds.' I hope Angie can find closure and doesn't make herself suffer. I still want her as a friend, even if she doesn't consider me as one. I also forgive her for smearing my name all over school."

"You truly are a sweetheart, Paisley. I can see why my soul chose yours."

"I'm glad we chose one another, too, Chad. I think I've always known somehow. Maybe that's why I'd had such a strong crush on you all that time, and why I never dated anyone until Max. I had plenty of offers but just wasn't interested. Guys finally gave up trying to date me after I'd gotten the reputation of being undatable. A few of them even called me 'the touch-me-not,' like the flower."

"Some people can be very mean when they don't get their way. So, you gave up on me and dated Max?"

"Yeah, I did," I sighed. "I don't regret dating Max, though. He's a great guy. His chosen mate is a lucky girl, whoever she turns out to be."

"I agree. I'm glad Max doesn't hate me after taking his girl."

"I'm glad this didn't ruin your friendship. Y'all have been friends for so long. It'd be a shame if it fell apart over me."

"Sweetheart, he doesn't blame you."

"I know he doesn't. I just wish Angie didn't either."

"I think she'll come around once she finds her chosen mate and realizes how strong the connection can be."

"I hope so. That's what Mama said too."

"She will. Just wait and see. I know you said you wanted time to get over Max, but could I interest you in going on a friendly date with me this weekend? We can either go out after the scrimmage football game Friday night, or Saturday after I get off work at the marina, or maybe even both if you'd like."

"I'd like that. Let's plan on both. What did you have in mind?"

"Well, we could go for a drive Friday night and just talk. I want to learn everything I can about you, Paisley. Then, maybe Saturday, I can take you on a real date somewhere."

"That sounds great. I'd like to learn everything about you too, Chad. We are going to be together for quite a while."

"That, we are, sweetheart. I'm personally looking forward to it."

"Me too. Oh, I almost forgot. How's your homework coming for Chemistry and Biology? Did you need any help?"

"Nah, it's not too bad so far. I think I understood it once I reread the chapters. I'm sure it'll get harder as the class goes on. I'm just glad I have a super-smart girlfriend to help me."

There it was. Chad called me his girlfriend. I'd waited so long to hear him call me that. It was music to my ears and made my heart flutter. At the same time, it felt as if it was a bit too soon. I know I won't be able to fight the connection we have for too much longer. So, I might as well accept it and let my heart catch up to my soul. I have to let go of Max and move on. "Girlfriend, huh?"

"Yeah. Paisley, sweetheart, I know we're chosen mates, but is it okay if I call you my girlfriend now?"

"Sure, I suppose that's okay. We'll be much more before too long. Once the *urge* kicks in, we won't be able to keep our hands off of one another."

"Paisley, I assure you. I'm already going to have a hard time keeping my hands off of you. I promise I won't do anything you don't want me to, though. I'll give you all the time you need. We will go at whatever pace you're comfortable with."

"Thank you, honey. I appreciate that. Let's just see how things go, okay? I don't want to put a timeframe on anything. If things progress slowly, so be it. If things heat up fast, and our relationship becomes hot and steamy, that's okay too."

"I can respect that. I don't think you realize how happy I am about us, Paisley. I've wanted to find my chosen mate all summer long. I'm so excited about everything to come and having you by my side through it all."

"I am too, Chad." I felt my heart flutter once again. It felt like it was covered in butterflies, fanning their wings. Our connection is already intensifying. I can feel it. Chad's voice is so soothing. I am already beginning to imagine how his touch will feel on my skin, and how his kisses will feel on my lips, among other places on my body. Wow! It's getting hot in here!

"Well, sweetheart, I should probably let you go so you can dream about me, huh?"

"Hahaha! I guess so. I'll see you in the morning."

"Okay. I'll see you then. Goodnight, sweetheart."

"Goodnight, honey." Wow! Chad Greene is my boyfriend and my chosen mate! I didn't want to accept it at first, but I feel better about it now that I have closure with Max. Chad is so handsome! He did get to me when his eyes burned into mine and, our souls called out to each other. That feeling was so intense it nearly took my breath away. All I can think about is my connection with him. It's hard to believe that it has been there all along, but we've only just realized it today. I wonder why we didn't feel the magnetism sooner? The first spark happened at the Derby. Could it be because we were focused on other people, or simply because we hadn't been around one another enough for it to develop?

I pulled back the covers and crawled into bed. I closed my eyes and saw Chad's glowing, honey-colored eyes in the darkness behind my eyelids. Those eyes. The eyes are the doorway to the soul. Even now, I can feel him calling out to me. How is this possible? Something tells me that our relationship is about to get a whole lot more intimate. I won't be able to hold back for too much longer. I drifted off to sleep, thinking of nothing but Chad.

I began to dream about him. He had just picked me up for our date. We were in his truck, and he was holding my hand. The spark and tingles felt so real. They flowed through my body in soothing waves. Being with him felt so natural. It seemed as though I had always been with him. I didn't even feel guilty over Max and Angie, nor did I feel awkward with him. I didn't feel nervous around him, either. I felt good, really good. I felt like being anywhere with Chad is where I belong—where I am meant to be.

Chapter 7

Chad

My first thought as I opened my eyes was of Paisley. I wondered if she'd slept well, if she'd dreamt of me as I had of her, and if she longed to touch me as much as I longed to touch her. I want to hold her hand and walk her to her classes. Although, I'd love to wrap my arms around her and kiss her senselessly. I can't wait to just feel her near me. I'd even settle for that at this point.

I hurried through my morning routine and had to wait on my siblings to get ready. Tabby has started to primp in the mornings. I'm not so sure how I feel about that. I think she has a crush on a boy at school. Garrett was ready in no time and was eating cereal while Tabby finished getting ready. She came prancing down the stairs and put two pastries in the toaster.

"What's gotten into you, Tabby?"

"Nothing, why?"

"Uh-huh. Nothing, huh? What's up with the hair and makeup?"

"Oh, leave her alone, Chad. She's growing up, that's all," Mom said. "I think she looks beautiful. She didn't go overboard with the makeup, so I'm okay with it."

"I was just teasing, Mom. I think she looks beautiful, too. I'm just not used to seeing my little sister all dolled up."

"Thanks, Chad," Tabby said. "Do you really think I look beautiful?"

"I sure do. It won't be too long before I have to beat the boys away with a baseball bat."

"You wouldn't do that, would you?"

"Hahaha! It's what big brothers are for."

"There's just one boy, and you don't have to beat him away with a baseball bat. I like him, too."

"Uh-huh. That's what I thought. So, who is he?"

"Good luck getting that out of her. She won't even tell us who he is."

"Well, I won't have to hurt him as long as he respects you and is a good guy."

"Chad!" Tabby scolded me.

"What? I mean it. He'd better be good, or he'll have Dad, Garrett, and me to deal with. Isn't that right, Garrett?"

"Yep," Garrett said between bites of his cereal.

"Are y'all about ready to go?"

"Just about. I'll be ready as soon as I eat and brush my teeth," Tabby said.

"Me too," Garrett said.

"All right. I'll go ahead and start my truck, so it'll be cooled off and ready to go when y'all are." I went outside, started my truck, and called Paisley.

"Good morning, sweetheart. Did you sleep well?"

"Good morning, honey. Yes, I did. I dreamed about you."

"Oh? All good, I hope. I dreamed about you too."

"Yes, it was a good dream. I dreamed about going on our first real date."

"I dreamed about holding you in my arms and kissing you like you should be kissed."

"Oh?"

"Oh, yeah. I'll have to show you sometime."

"Hmm. I may hold you to that."

"I miss you already. If our connection keeps getting stronger, being away from you is going to drive me nuts."

"I miss you too, Chad. I'm looking forward to seeing you."

"I'll be seeing you soon. Be careful on the way to school."

"I will. I promise. I have to take Caden to school first, and I'll be on my way after that."

"Same. I have to drop off Tabby and Garrett on my way there."

"I'll see you then, honey."

"I can't wait, sweetheart."

Tabby and Garrett came out and hopped in the truck with their backpacks. We all put on our seatbelts and were off to school. They talked about their new friends and how they couldn't wait to see them. We also talked about sports practices and how they were going. Tabby is in cheerleading, and Garrett is the quarterback on the middle school team. He's a fast runner like I am and has an arm on him like a cannon for his age.

I'm very proud of him and Tabby, too. Tabby always idolized Angie when she cheered at the games. She was sad to hear that Angie and I had broken up but was happy for me. She told me she likes Paisley and thinks I did pretty good at picking her. For the record, I think so, too.

The commute to school went pretty fast. Traffic wasn't too bad. I dropped Tabby and Garrett off at the Uwharrie Mountain Middle School and headed off to the high school. I got there just as Paisley was pulling into the parking lot. I parked beside her little red MINI Cooper and hopped out of my truck. I walked up to her and took her backpack from her. To my surprise, she reached for my hand and laced her fingers with mine. The spark and tingles felt terrific.

"Mmmm. That feels nice," she purred.

"I can't agree more."

I pulled her beside my truck and sat our backpacks on the ground. My heart began pounding inside my ribcage. I wrapped my arms around her and pulled her close to me. The spark and tingles surged through me everywhere we touched. Her lavender-blue eyes sparkled in the morning sunlight. Her plump lips slightly parted as she drew in a short gasp. I leaned down and captured her lips with mine. I felt her arms wrap around my neck and her fingers ran through the hair at my nape. Her lips opened further, and the kiss deepened. Our tongues twirled and danced together in a hungry kiss as though we'd been apart for too long. She tasted of ripe strawberries, sweet and tangy. I want more. I want all of her. The sparks and tingles surged through me so intensely that I'd forgotten where we were for a moment. I broke the kiss and looked into her gorgeous tanzanite eyes.

"I-I don't know what came over me, Paisley, but I couldn't resist kissing you."

"Wow!" She panted. "That was—just wow! You are an incredible kisser, Chad."

"Likewise, sweetheart. Mind if I kiss you again?"

"Please, Chad. Please, kiss me again."

I'm so glad she wasn't mad that I'd kissed her and wanted me to kiss her again. This kiss was even better than the one before. I savored the flavor of her kiss and the feel of her body pressed against mine. She feels amazing. We fit together like puzzle pieces. I can't get enough of her. Thank God she's mine. I slowed the kiss and reluctantly broke away from her once again. A tiny whimper escaped her lips.

"There will be many, many more of those, sweetheart. I promise," I said as I stared into her eyes once again and grazed her bottom lip with my thumb.

"Good. There'd better be. I can hardly wait to have your lips on mine again."

"Don't tease me, woman, or we'll be late for class."

We both laughed and enjoyed one last kiss. I picked up our backpacks and slung them over my shoulder. We walked to the quad, hand-in-hand. I didn't even care about the sneers and dirty looks we got on the way to our usual table. Let them talk. They are going to anyway. Why not give them something to talk about? We are still earlier than the rest of our crew. I sat our backpacks down and sat at the table beside Paisley. Her hand feels so good in mine. I can only imagine how the rest of her skin will feel against my fingertips.

Toby and Molly walked up to the table next. Molly took one look at Paisley and smiled. Paisley's lips are a little swollen from our kisses. I'm sure Molly knows what we'd been doing this morning. Toby playfully slugged my shoulder and told me congratulations. Max walked up to the table last. He looked directly at Paisley, then at me, and took a deep breath.

"Chad, may I have a word with you?"

"Sure."

I leaned over and whispered in Paisley's ear. "I'll be right back, sweetheart." She nodded, and I stood and walked around the corner with Max.

"Hey, man. I just wanted to say that I am happy for you and Paisley. It's hard for me to see her with you, but if her chosen mate had to be anyone but me, I'm glad it's you. I know you'll do right by her."

"Thanks, man. I appreciate that. I promise you I will treat Paisley like she deserves to be treated. I'll love her, honor her, respect her, and be here for her."

"I know you will." He stuck out his hand. "Friends? No hard feelings."

"Of course, we're friends, Max." I shook his hand. "We always will be, no matter what."

We walked back to the table with the rest of our friends. I sat back down beside Paisley, and he sat beside Toby. We all talked about the elephant in the room, and the mood suddenly lightened. Everyone congratulated Paisley and me on our connection awakening and the beginning of our relationship. Well, everyone but Angie. She is still nowhere to be seen. If she is here, she is likely hanging out with the other cheerleaders for emotional support.

The first bell rang for homeroom roll call, and I walked Paisley to her class. I handed her backpack to her and kissed her cheek before heading to my homeroom class. I felt a void as soon as I left her side. Damn, I'm so screwed. I already can't stand to be away from her. I'm going to go nuts if the magnetism of our connection gets any stronger. I'm going to have to talk to Toby and see how he and Molly overcome it.

The bell for the first period finally rang, and I practically ran to meet up with Paisley. I darted into the Chemistry II classroom and claimed the table in the very back of the room. Another girl in our class attempted to sit down next to me, and I shook my head at her. She scoffed and walked away. Paisley walked in, and we locked eyes. I smiled at her and patted her seat beside me. She smiled and sat down. I reached for her hand and held it up to my lips. I pressed a kiss to each of her knuckles. The spark and tingles of each one made her giggle. I love her laugh. I want to hear it as much as possible.

The teacher came in, and we opened our textbooks. We passed our homework to the front of the class, and today's lesson began. I laid my hand on Paisley's thigh. I can only guess where the tingles traveled because she jumped, and her cheeks displayed a lovely shade of pink.

She glanced over at me and whispered, "Honey!"

I grinned slyly and winked at her. I lightly caressed her thigh with my thumb. She placed her hand on top of mine and laced our fingers together. She smiled sweetly at me and bit her bottom lip. Oh, how I'd love to bite that lip, too.

She squeezed my hand, and we looked back down at our textbooks to follow along with Mr. Duncan. I'm going to enjoy having Paisley as my lab partner in these science courses, but what I'm looking forward to the most is having her as my partner for eternity.

Mr. Duncan read from the book and explained stoichiometry while I tried to pay attention and soak it all in. It's so hard to pay attention and stay focused. All I can think about is kissing Paisley. I can't wait for class to be over so I can try to sneak in another kiss between classes. Her lips are so tempting. I glanced at the clock above the dry-erase board. Only fifteen minutes had passed. This could legitimately be considered torture in some countries. Focus, Chad. You have to pass all of your classes or no sports for you. Knowing my parents, that could also mean no extracurricular activities, period, which could very well mean no dates with Paisley. I can't let that happen. I need to be able to spend as much time with her as I can.

So, I followed along. I started understanding it. Mr. Duncan wrote out a chemical equation for a volunteer to complete. I raised my hand and went up to the board. I finished the equation and got it right. I'm quite impressed with myself. I'm beginning to understand at least a portion of the Chemistry II class. Maybe I just hadn't had the right motivation to pay attention in the past.

I don't know how I'm going to wait until after the game Friday night to have some alone time with Paisley. I may still try to squeeze in a study date or two between now and then. We have a quiz on Friday morning. I want to make sure I pass for a few reasons now. Before Paisley, I focused on my schoolwork so that I could play sports. Now, I can add spending time with Paisley to that list.

Mr. Duncan gave us a few equations to complete for practice. Paisley and I finished rather quickly and compared our answers for accuracy. I had gotten the same solutions that she had. Everyone in the class was talking to their lab partners, so I took the opportunity to speak to mine.

"I think I'm starting to get the hang of this stuff."

"I think so, too. You did great up at the board and on the practice ones."

"I think I still need a few study dates to make sure."

"Well, I know just the girl to tutor you," she said with a wink.

"When would you like for me to come over?"

"I'm free every evening after your practice if you'd like."

"Your parents won't mind?"

"I doubt it. Mom and Dad are pretty ecstatic about our connection. I'm sure they'd love to have you over unless you'd like to meet somewhere else more private. I'll meet you anywhere you like."

"Hey, now there's an idea. Would you like me to pick you up at around 6:00 tonight? We can go eat supper, study there for a while, and then go for a private drive."

"I'm in. I'll ask my parents and make sure it's okay with them. I'm sure they won't mind if it's a study date."

"Great. I'm looking forward to having you all to myself."

"It'll give us a chance to get to know one another better and see where things go from there."

"Exactly. I want to know everything about you, Paisley."

"Same here. I'm looking forward to getting to know you, too."

Mr. Duncan grabbed everyone's attention again, and we went over the practice equations. Paisley and I had gotten them all correct. The bell rang right as we'd finished going over the last one. Mr. Duncan assigned us a few more equations to do in our book for homework. The classroom cleared out, except for Paisley and me. Our Biology II class was right next door to this one, so we didn't have to hurry out.

I took advantage of the newly found alone time. I picked Paisley up and sat her on the lab table. Then, I tilted her face upward and captured her lips with mine. Sparks and tingles surged through me as our lips embraced. Her lips parted, and our tongues caressed one another. The taste of ripe strawberries hit my tastebuds once again. I could kiss her for eternity, and it still wouldn't be long enough. I reluctantly broke the kiss and caressed her bottom lip with my thumb.

"Every time I see you bite this lip, it makes me want to bite it, too."

"Oh? Well, if anyone can bite my lip, it's you, Chad Greene."

I smiled slyly at her. "Good, 'cause I fully intend to do just that and so much more later on." Her cheeks blushed that lovely shade of pink again. Her eyes went wide, and she sucked in a quick gasp. I love her little reactions to things I say and do. She is adorable. "Come on, sweetheart." I helped her down from the lab table. "Let's get to our next class, shall we?"

"Yes, honey. Let's go. The sooner this school day gets over and done with, the sooner we get to go on our study date."

"Mmmm. I can't wait."

I packed up our backpacks and headed next door for Biology II. We claimed the table in the back of the room and opened our textbooks to the page number that Mrs. Isleson had written on the board. She was still wrangling students inside when the bell rang. Paisley and I kept glancing at one another and smiling throughout the entire class. Mrs. Isleson didn't give us any written homework. We just have to read the next chapter and be ready for a pop quiz tomorrow morning. Paisley and I will be studying together this evening, so that should be easy enough.

Paisley and I walked together, hand-in-hand, to the lunchroom to grab some food. Then, we went to the quad to meet up with our friends. Molly and Paisley caught up on current events and were whispering to themselves. I took the opportunity to talk about football with Max and Toby. Everything seemed like it was back to normal again. I don't know what I would've done if there were hard feelings between Max and me. I'm glad I don't have to find out. Our group of friends has been there for one another, basically our whole lives. We will be friends for the rest of our lives, too, if either of us has any say in it.

The third-period bell rang, and I walked Paisley to her class. I stole a quick kiss while none of the teachers in the hallway were looking. How can her lips be so addictive? The more I kiss her, the more I want to kiss her and hold her, among other things. I simply can't get enough of her.

Angie sat in the front row of our English Literature class after lunch so she wouldn't have to look at me. She's still pretty upset. I can tell she's been crying. Her eyes are puffy and have a trace of a shadow under them. I hate that she's still hurting like this. I wish I knew who her chosen mate was, so I could help fate along the way to bring them together. I think that would help her feel better because she would put me in her past and move on with him.

The rest of my classes were painful. I missed Paisley. I needed her with me. Just having her near me made me feel complete in a way I'd never felt before. It feels like there is a void when we are apart. I wonder, does she feel the same way? Does she miss me, too? I sent her a quick text message, hoping she doesn't get in trouble for checking it.

"I miss you, sweetheart."

"I miss you too, honey. How's your day going?"

"Painful without you."

"I know how you feel. I wish we had all of our classes together."

"Me too."

"Just a few more hours until our study date."

"Tell me about it. Time can't go by soon enough."

"I messaged Mama. Study date is on."

"Fantastic! Wait for me in your last class. I'll walk you to your car. I want my goodbye kiss before football practice."

"Okay, will do. I'll see you soon, honey."

"Okay, sweetheart."

Chapter 8

Chad

School is finally over for the day. I hurried to Paisley's Speech class. She was standing there, waiting for me. I took her backpack and slung it over my shoulder. I reached for her hand, and she laced her fingers with mine. The sparks and tingles surged through me and settled in my core. I felt very protective over her all of a sudden. I looked around and saw Angie and some of the other cheerleaders heading straight for us. I held onto Paisley's hand and kept walking towards the exit to the seniors' parking lot.

"Yeah, there she is. There's the little whore that took my man. Oh, look. They're holding hands, and he's carrying her backpack. How sweet."

"Angie, leave her alone."

"She certainly isn't leaving you alone, is she? We were happy before that little trollop came along. This is all her fault, Chad!"

"This is not her fault or mine, Angie, and you know it! I'm not going to argue with you or explain everything here in front of all these people. You know good and well why. If you want to chat, we can. We'll chat, but you will not have your posse with you when we do."

Angie crossed her arms over her chest and rolled her eyes. "Fine. Then you can't have your little whore with you either. We can chat alone."

"Angie! One more derogatory name or insult toward Paisley, and we won't have anything to talk about—ever again. Do you understand?"

"Fine!"

"I'm going to walk Paisley to her car. I'll see you at the field." I turned towards the exit and opened the door for Paisley. I walked her to her car, opened her door, and placed her backpack on the back seat. Then, I wrapped my arms around her. She stood on her tiptoes and wrapped her arms around my neck.

"I've been waiting for this moment for a while now."

"Me too. Kiss me, Chad. Give me something to look forward to for later."

I didn't dare make her ask twice. I captured her lips, and our kiss deepened. Sparks and tingles surged through me and settled in my groin. I felt my hardness press against her soft tummy, and a deep groan rumbled in my chest. Damn, I want her. I need to possess her and make her mine. I want her naked and writhing beneath me as I plunge deep inside her. I want to hear her moaning my name as I bring her over the edge over and over again. I want to feel her energy mixing with mine as we bond for eternity.

Damn. The *urge*. I don't know how much longer I can fight it. It almost feels like there's something inside of me trying to take over—a "beast." A ravenous monster that is clawing at my insides. All this "beast" wants is to possess Paisley. To make her mine once and for all, and ravish her again and again.

"Paisley, sweetheart, the *urge*. It's growing stronger. I can feel it. I want you so much, Paisley."

"Oh, Chad. I feel it too," she panted. "Wow... just... wow. I've never wanted anyone as badly as I want you."

"How is this happening so fast? All I can think about is making love to you, completing our bond, and making you mine."

She reached up and touched my face with her delicate hand. "I know, honey. I want that, too. I want to be yours, Chad, and I want you to be mine."

"We will be, sweetheart. I can promise you that. I also promised you I'd give you time. I don't know how long I'll be able to resist you, though."

"You don't need to give me any more time, Chad. I'm ready to move on. I'm ready to be yours for eternity."

I crushed my lips to hers and, she moaned into my mouth. That sweet sound, combined with her flavor of ripe strawberries, the spark, and the tingles, nearly unraveled my self-control. She ran her fingers through my hair. The tingles ran down my spine as I held her tighter. Close wasn't nearly close enough.

"Paisley, sweetheart, if I don't let you go, I'm afraid I won't be able to stop myself. I'll skip practice, take you for a drive, and make love to you right now."

"Oh?"

"Don't tease me, woman."

She giggled and pressed one last kiss to my lips. "Okay. I'll go, but I'll be looking forward to our study date."

"Most definitely."

"I'll see you then, honey."

Paisley got into her car, and I closed her door. She waved and blew me a kiss as she drove away. The void returned. I miss her already. I can't wait to get through this chat with Angie and football practice, so I can get a shower and pick Paisley up for our date.

Angie was waiting for me on the top row of the bleachers. Everyone else was already either on the field or in the locker room inside the field house, changing for practice. I walked up to her and sat down beside her.

"Hello, Angie. Let's get this over with, shall we? I have to change for practice. What do you want?"

"What do I want? Isn't it obvious?"

"If you want me to ignore my connection with Paisley and be with you, the answer is no. I can't."

"Can't, or won't?"

"Both. I can't and won't ignore the connection I share with Paisley. I feel our souls calling out to one another. Our connection is growing stronger, and it will continue to grow even stronger every day, Angie. You'll understand when you find your own chosen mate."

She is sobbing uncontrollably now. "I don't want to find my chosen mate. I want *you*, Chad!"

"You can't have me, Angie. It's over between us."

"Maybe for you, but not for me. I'm still in love with you. Please, don't do this to me—to *us*."

"I'm sorry, Angie, but there is no *us*. I'm going to be with Paisley. She's my chosen mate. We chose one another before we were born, just as you chose your mate. Trust me. When your connection awakens, you'll be thankful that we aren't together. You won't have to choose between him and me."

"I'd always choose you, Chad. I'd choose you over any man in the world!"

"No, Angie, you won't. The connection and the love you'll share with him will be so much deeper and more powerful than the love we ever had for one another or ever would, for that matter. You'll see. I just hope fate steps in for the both of you sooner than later. I do still care about you, Angie. It hurts me to see you in pain. Please, don't do this to yourself. You have to let me go."

"I can't. I've loved you for so long. How can I just let go after all these years? After all that we've been through, the intimacy and love we've shared?"

"You have to, Angie. This obsession isn't healthy. Don't let this bring you down or make you bitter. You have made so much progress in being a nicer person over the summer. You're so much better than this, and you know it."

"I don't want to move on and let you go, Chad. I'm miserable without you. Please, come back to me. I need you."

"No, Angie. That's not going to happen. I'm sorry you're taking this so hard, but I choose Paisley. My choice is made, Angie. I'm not going to change my mind. She and I will be getting married. The date hasn't been set, but it will happen. I plan on asking her to marry me very soon."

"I'm not going to stop, Chad. I'm not giving up on you or us until that day comes. I will do everything in my power to get you to come back to me. You will come back to me."

"No, Angie. I won't. You need to move on. You'll be much better off when you do. I'm going to go change for practice. I suggest you do the same, so you don't upset your coach."

I stood and left her there, sobbing on the bleachers. It hurt to see her so upset and so broken, but I can't go back to her. I won't. I'm meant to be with Paisley. She's who I want more than anyone or anything in this world. She will be mine. We will complete our bond and be together for all eternity. No one will stop me from being with her, not even Angie. No one.

Angelina

How am I supposed to face anyone right now, much less go to practice today? My eyes are red and swollen, my makeup is ruined, and my nose is so stopped up from crying that I can hardly breathe. I grabbed my backpack and my gym bag and headed to my car. I can't believe he chose her over me, after everything we've been through together. This can't be happening to me. He's supposed to be mine. I would always choose him over anyone, no matter what. He told me he loved me, wanted to marry me, and bond with me on our wedding night. How can he just flip a switch and throw our love away like that?

I cried the whole way home. It's a wonder I made it safely, or even at all, for that matter. I could hardly see the road through my tears. Six years together, and he turns around and tosses me aside like an empty wrapper. That pretty much sums up how I feel. I feel like an empty wrapper, used and tossed aside. My heart hurts so badly. Chad ripped it out of my chest and shattered it at my feet. He was my everything. Apparently, all I was to him was a placeholder; someone to keep him occupied until his *chosen mate* came along. I have never felt this hurt, this betrayed, or this cheap.

My nerves are shot. I passed my parents' liquor cabinet on the way to my room. I opened the door and grabbed a bottle of whiskey. I honestly don't care what kind of liquor it is at this point. I just need something to calm my nerves and drown my sorrow. I unscrewed the lid and took a swig. The liquid tasted horrible and burned my throat going down. It could've tasted like goat piss, not that I know how goat piss tastes, and I still would've downed another swig if I knew it would make me feel better, even for a little while. I sucked down a few more large gulps and put it back in the cabinet.

I went up to my room to lay down before the liquor kicked in. I didn't want to fall into a drunken stupor and get hurt if I could help it. It'd just add insult to injury. I laid there on my bed, thinking about Chad and all of the things we'd been through together. All I can do is cry. Am I not good enough for him? If I were, he would've chosen me over anyone else no matter what.

I tried to close my eyes and rest, but I can still see his face. I can still hear him saying, *"No, Angie. That's not going to happen. I'm sorry you're taking this so hard, but I choose Paisley. My choice is made, Angie. I'm not going to change my mind. She and I will be getting married. The date hasn't been set, but it will happen. I plan on asking her to marry me very soon."*

I feel like my world is crashing down around me. Every plan I've ever made has involved Chad in some way, shape, or form. We were going to get married after high school graduation, go to the same college, and start a family together. He can't marry Paisley and bond with her. He just can't. He's going to come back to me. I just know he will. He has to. I can't live without him. Not like this. It can't end like this. He's supposed to be mine.

My head is starting to feel fuzzy. I think the liquor is finally kicking in. Good. I'm tired of feeling anything for today. I just want to forget this whole thing and wake up tomorrow with Chad as mine once again. I tried to close my eyes again, but I saw his glowing amber eyes in the darkness. More tears came flowing down my cheeks. I didn't drink enough to not think about him. I got up from my bed, went downstairs to the liquor cabinet, and chugged a few more gulps of whiskey. Then, I went back to my room and laid down once again.

Chad

Football practice went very well. Our team's cohesion is unbreakable. We executed each play with acute precision. The opposing teams won't stand a chance against us this season. Toby's arm has gotten so much stronger, and his aim is almost surgical. He can land a pass like no other quarterback I've ever seen, aside from the pros, that is. This football season is going to be epic!

I didn't see Angie practicing with her squad. She must've gone home after our chat instead of going to practice. I admit I am worried about her, but I will not go to her. I tried to give her closure, but she wouldn't accept it. She is not willing to move on. I can only hope and pray that fate steps in soon and awakens the connection with her and her chosen mate sooner than later. I'm afraid if it doesn't, she will continue into a downward spiral of self-destruction. I hate seeing her like this, but I will not go back on my decision to be with Paisley.

As strong as the *urge* to bond with her is now, I don't know that I'll be able to wait until marriage. I'll do my best to resist, but I can already tell it's not going to be an easy feat. Our connection has developed so intensely over the last few days. I have a feeling that we won't be able to wait too much longer, especially when I can't think of anything but her.

I showered and changed after practice and headed to pick her up for our study date. Her dad, Taggart, answered the door and called her downstairs. She came down in a short, floral printed romper with spaghetti straps that tied on each shoulder. She may be short, but her shapely legs go on for days in that outfit. Damn, I'm so screwed. How am I supposed to resist the *urge* to bond with her when she wears something as tantalizing as that?

She flashed me the sweetest smile I've ever seen. "Hey, honey. Shall we go?"

"Hey there, sweetheart. Yeah, I'm starving after football practice. Where's your backpack? I'll carry it out to my tuck."

"Oh, why thank you. It's right there by the door."

"I want you home by 10:00 p.m, Paisley," Taggart said.

"I will be, Dad. No worries."

"I'll be sure to have her home by then, Mr. O'Riley. I promise."

"Okay. You kids behave and good luck with homework. I don't miss having to do that one bit."

"Thanks, Daddy. I love you! Bye!"

I walked her to my truck, opened her door, and helped her up inside. Then, I put her backpack on the back seat, closed the door, and hopped in on my side. I finally had her to myself. Damn, she smells good. The scent of ripe strawberries and freshly picked flowers filled my truck. I could get used to this.

"Damn, sweetheart. You smell good enough to eat."

"You're just hungry, honey. That'll pass once we get some food in you."

"No, I mean it, Paisley. You smell amazing."

Her cheeks flushed into that same lovely shade of pink that I love so much. "Thanks, honey. I'm glad you like it."

"Like it? I love it! I could get used to having your scent all around me forever."

"You smell pretty good yourself."

"Thank you, sweetheart."

I flipped up the center partition and patted the seat for her to scoot closer to me. She undid her seatbelt, slid over, and fastened the middle seat belt over her lap. I backed out of her parents' driveway, and we headed off on our study date.

Paisley reached over and placed her hand on my thigh. The spark and tingles shot up my leg and settled in my groin. It was so intense that it nearly made me jump.

"Uh-huh. Now you know what it did to me when you touched my thigh in class."

"A taste of my own medicine, huh?"

"Hahaha! Yes, indeed!"

"That's okay. I'll take it. You can touch me anywhere you want, sweetheart. I'm all yours, after all."

"The same goes for you too, honey. I'm all yours. I want to feel your touch everywhere."

"Everywhere, huh?"

"Yes, everywhere."

I rested my hand on her knee. "Here?"

She gasped when the spark and tingles hit her. "Yes."

I slid my hand higher up her thigh. "How about here?"

She gulped and bit her bottom lip. "Yes, there too."

I slid my hand even higher and rested it on the spot just below the apex of her thighs. "And here?"

She squeezed my thigh, tilted her head back, and began to pant in short, ragged breaths. "Yes, definitely there too."

Damn, I'm so screwed. There's no way I'm going to make it until we get married. Not if she doesn't stop me from making love to her. I can feel her heat through her satin romper. I pulled my truck onto a side road and put it into park. I slid the seat back, unbuckled my seatbelt, and then unbuckled hers.

I picked her up and sat her on my lap, so that she was straddling me. She wrapped her arms around my neck and crushed her lips to mine. I wrapped my arms around her, caressed her back, slid my hands down, and cupped her perfectly-shaped butt. I squeezed it firmly, and a low groan rumbled in my chest. I pulled her closer to me, so she was now sitting on top of the bulge in my jeans. The sparks and tingles between our bodies are so intense that I can't think straight. The *urge* is taking over. Its pull is overwhelming.

I trailed more kisses down her neck to her shoulder. I untied one strap and then the other one. Then, I unbuttoned the front of her romper. It fell to her waist, exposing her white, strapless, lace bra. I kissed a trail from her neck, down to the lacy fabric. She arched her back, grinding onto me. I reached around her, unhooked her bra, and tossed it onto the back seat. Her beautiful breasts fell free. I gathered them in my hands and wrapped my lips around one of her perfect buds. The most beautiful moan escaped her lips, and I nearly lost control.

"Oh, Chad! Please, don't stop!"

I picked her up and laid her on the seat. Then, I crawled over her, being careful not to crush her beneath me. I continued to kiss, lick, and suck on her gorgeous, aroused buds. I gently slid her romper down further and over her hips, leaving a searing trail of kisses down her magnificent body. I placed a gentle kiss on the front of her white lace thong. Her back arched, and she moaned my name once again.

"Oh, God, Chad!"

"Yes, sweetheart?"

"I want you so much! Please, Chad!"

"I want you too, Paisley. I want you so badly it hurts."

"Then, take me. Make love to me, Chad. Bond with me and be mine."

Without another word, I slid off her romper and her thong and buried my face in her heat. I licked over her sensitive flesh, and her whole body shuddered. I darted my tongue into her tight channel, and she writhed against me. The flavor of ripe strawberries mixed with her peppery arousal and was like heaven on my tongue. More. I want more. I reached up and found her bundle of nerves and began to circle it with my thumb. Her soft moans and whimpers are all the encouragement I need. I continued to tease her with my tongue as I rubbed her sensitive spot.

I love watching her. She is so beautiful. Her back arched once again, and colors began to swirl around us. Her body shuddered, and she moaned my name as her pleasure surged.

"You are so beautiful, Paisley."

"That was… oh, my goodness… wow! Did you see the swirling colors too, or was I hallucinating?" Paisley asked, still panting.

"You weren't hallucinating, sweetheart. I saw it too."

"Is that what happens when we… um… orgasm?"

"I think it only happens like that between chosen mates. Other couples don't experience the same sensations that chosen mates do together."

"I've heard that, too. I've never felt anything that intense before."

"I'm not nearly done with you yet, sweetheart. I can't get enough of you."

"Oh, Chad! Please, make love to me. Don't make me wait any longer."

"I'm afraid I'll hurt you, Paisley. I'm… not small."

"I'll be okay, Chad. We can go slow. I need you. I need to feel you and your energy inside me."

"Are you sure, sweetheart?"

"Yes, I'm sure. I've never been so sure of anything. I love you, Chad. I always have."

"I love you, too, Paisley. What about protection? We can't use a condom when we bond. There's a chance I could get you pregnant."

"No, honey. I'm on the pill. I have been for years. Supposedly, our kind has a hard time regulating our cycles. We need the hormones in the pills to keep everything on a more normal schedule."

"Oh, Paisley. You're sure this is what you want? We can't go back once we complete our bond."

"We'll be married and bonded after graduation anyway, right? We're of bonding age. Why wait in pain as the *urge* gets stronger?"

"You make a very valid point, love. I promise I'll be as gentle as I can. I never want to hurt you, Paisley. I love you on a level I've never thought was possible."

"I love you too, Chad. I love you so very much."

I sat up on my knees, took off my shirt, shoes, then my pants, and boxer briefs. Paisley's eyes were as wide as saucers when my hardness sprang free.

"You weren't kidding about not being… small."

"I told you, sweetheart. It's probably going to hurt. I'll stop anytime you tell me to, or if you change your mind, okay?"

"Okay. I'm ready to bond with you, Chad. I've wanted you for so very long. I can't believe you're finally going to be mine."

"Believe it, my love. I'm going to make love to you and make you mine. No one will ever be able to come between us."

"Please, Chad. I need you."

"Your wish is my command, my love."

I lowered myself on top of her. My hardness nudged the entrance of her warm center, and I eased inside of her, little-by-little. The spark and tingles at our joining were the most intense feeling I've ever felt. A low groan rumbled in my chest. She drew in a gasp and began panting.

"Ow, ow, ow!"

"Are you okay, sweetheart? Do you want me to stop?"

"I'm fine. Please, don't stop. It hurts a little, but I'm okay."

I seated myself deep inside of her and stayed there for a few seconds to let her get used to my size. I hate the thought of hurting her. Yet, I can feel "the beast" and its need to possess her, to claim her as mine.

"How about now, sweetheart? Are you okay?"

"Yes, I'm okay."

"Okay. Good. Let me know if I hurt you, and I'll stop."

She nodded, and I began to move in and out of her very slowly. She wrapped her legs around me and lifted her hips, grinding onto me and matching my rhythm.

I increased my tempo a little, and she egged me on by lightly scratching down my back and pulling me into her harder and faster. Colors began to swirl around us as our pleasure began to build. I wasn't far from going over the edge. She released my back and grabbed my hands. We laced our fingers together, pressing our hands, palm-to-palm. I felt my energy pouring into her as hers poured into me. Sparks of light, like lightning strikes, joined the swirling colors as she spasmed around me. I couldn't hold off any longer. We began to soar into our climax and over the edge together. My whole body spasmed as I spilled deep inside her.

It is done. Paisley and I are now bonded mates for all eternity. She's mine, and I'm hers. I stared into her glowing tanzanite eyes. I can feel her and sense her like never before. I feel her pleasure. She's happy and in love—with me. I've never felt anything so pure and so true. Then, I heard her voice in my head.

"I love you, Chad. I love you more than anything in this world."

"I love you too, Paisley, with my heart and my soul. I'm yours for all eternity."

"Yes, Chad, as I'm yours for all eternity."

"It's a good thing because I can't get enough of you, woman. You are out of this world amazing." I was still inside her and was already getting aroused again. *"As a matter of fact, if it's okay with you, I'd love to make love to you again."*

"Yes, my love. Please do. I can't get enough of you either. I want more. I need more."

We made love again. Sparks and tingles surged through us as we relished in our joining. We held hands and soared once again as the colors began to swirl around us. Flashing lights mixed with the swirling colors as our energy flowed between us and mixed once again. Paisley is mine, and I am hers. No one can change that now.

Chapter 9

Paisley

Chad Greene is finally mine. I'd loved him from a distance for so many years. He is mine now, and I'm his. Making love and bonding with him was the most wonderful and beautiful experience I've ever felt. I can still feel his energy swirling inside me, mixing with mine. I feel his love for me, too. I've never felt so loved. He is honestly, truly, and deeply in love with me and me alone.

"Are you sure I didn't hurt you, sweetheart?"

"I'm a little sore, but I'll be fine. I'm already starting to heal."

"I hope it's not painful for you next time and after that. I don't want to hurt you, Paisley. Ever."

"I'm sure my body will get used to you in time." I flashed him a seductive smile and bit my lip. *"I suppose we'll just have to keep making love as much as we can to make sure that happens sooner than later."*

"Don't tease me, woman, or we'll never make it to the restaurant. I'll take you again and again until time to take you home."

"Oh, honey. Don't threaten me with a good time. I might just take you up on it."

"Damn, I'm so screwed. You're going to drive me insane."

"Hahaha! Good! I want you just as crazy about me as I am about you."

"Done. I'm already there, sweetheart. If I weren't starving, I'd ravish your body over and over again."

"Well, I guess we'd better get you some food. I can't have you starving, now can I?"

We got dressed and headed to the Golf Club Grille for some food and to get our homework done. The restaurant was pretty packed, but there was an open booth near the bar. We sat down and placed our orders with the waitress and nibbled on some chips and salsa.

"You are the most beautiful woman I've ever seen."

"Thank you, my love. You are, by far, the most handsome man I've ever seen. I've loved you for so long, Chad. I was afraid you'd never notice me or know I existed. I'm so glad you're finally mine."

"Same here, Paisley. I couldn't be happier that you're mine. So, tell me everything about you. We probably should have had this conversation before completing our bond, but you know what they say, 'Better late than never.'"

"Well, I was born on July 28th, my birth name is Paisley Rose O'Riley, my favorite colors are rose gold and amber, I love animals, I love to sing, I like my steak medium-rare, and I love sweet tea, but I like a nice cold Cheerwine now and then. Mama's name is Fiona, Daddy's name is Taggart, and I have a little brother named Caden. What about you?"

"I was born on July 9th. My birth name is Chadwick Owen Greene. My favorite color is blue, my favorite fruit is strawberries, which is how you smell and taste, by the way. I love playing sports; I also like my steak rare to medium-rare. I love sweet tea and Cheerwine too. My mom's name is Shannon, and my dad's name is Trevor. I have a sister named Tabby and a brother named Garrett."

"Well, it's nice to finally get more acquainted, seing how we are bonded for eternity. So, you really think I taste like strawberries, huh?"

"Yeah, you do, ripe strawberries that are sweet and still a little bit tangy. I taste strawberries on your lips when we kiss, and everywhere else I kiss you. I do mean everywhere." He waggled his eyebrows and shot me a wickedly handsome smile.

I felt my skin flush across my chest and spread into my cheeks. "You taste like honey and salted almonds. I can't get enough. I'm addicted to you, Chad."

"I'm pretty addicted to you too, Paisley. Thank goodness you're mine." He reached for my hand, and I laced my fingers with his. The spark and tingles flowed up my arm and into my core. "I don't know what I'd do if I couldn't get my fix."

"Well, you can have your fix anytime you want."

"Good, because I already can't wait for dessert."

The waitress brought our food. We ate and laughed about stories from our childhoods. We confessed all kinds of embarrassing stories and ways we'd gotten into trouble over the years. I love being with him. He's athletic, perfectly sculpted, and has the most gorgeous eyes and tanned complexion I've ever seen. He's sweet, naughty, and has a great sense of humor. I know deep within my soul that he loves me more than I've ever felt or thought was possible to be loved by anyone. He's the definition of perfection, in my opinion. I still can't believe he's all mine.

The waitress took our plates and cleared the table once we'd finished eating, and we hit the books. We finished our homework in what seemed like no time at all. We still had almost two hours until I had to be home. Chad placed our backpacks on the back seat, and we hopped in his truck. We drove into the country towards Love Joy and pulled onto a dirt road that led to an abandoned hunting cabin.

Chad turned off the engine and locked the doors. Then, he moved the seat back as far as it would go. We unbuckled, and I sat on the seat on my knees. I wrapped my arms around his neck, and he pulled me onto his lap. I crushed my lips onto his, and our kiss went wild with hunger, need, and passion. The sparks and tingles flowed through me and settled in my sex. We made love nice and slow at first. He grabbed my hips and pulled me down on him harder, yet keeping the same pace. My soft whimpers turned into moans. A low groan rumbled in his chest, and he brought his mouth to one of my breasts. His tongue circled the sensitive bud, and his teeth lightly nipped it. I felt my climax began to build. Chad grabbed my hands, and we laced our fingers together. My whole body shuddered as I soared into a mind-blowing climax. Lights flashed, colors swirled, and our energy mixed within our bodies. Our rhythm increased, harder, and faster. I took all of him and ground him deep inside me when I circled my hips.

"Damn it, woman! Ah!" He groaned and sucked in a gasp. *"Oh, that feels so good! Please, don't stop!"*

"Like that, my love?"

"God, yes, Paisley! Ah!"

I felt another round of pleasure building. Flashing lights and colors started swirling around us. We soared higher and higher into bliss. Both of our bodies spasmed, and I slowed down the pace as we came down together. The sparks and tingles continued to flow through us and seemed to pulse at our joining.

"I love you so much, Chad. Thank you."

"I love you too, sweetheart, but thank you for what?"

"For choosing me to be your mate."

"It wasn't just me who chose you. We chose each other, sweetheart."

"Yes, we did, initially, but you could've chosen to bond with Angie instead."

"That's not what I wanted, though. Yes, I loved Angie for a long time before our connection awakened. You're the only woman I want, the only woman my heart and soul long for, and the only woman my body aches for. I only wanted to bond with the woman I initially chose as my mate eighteen years ago. Something inside told me it wasn't Angie. I couldn't explain it, but I began to have doubts about my relationship with her the night of the Derby."

"The night our connection awakened."

"Yes, that's right."

I took a deep breath and shook my head. "I still can't believe you're finally mine after all these years."

"I've always been yours, and you've always been mine. We just didn't know until now."

"True. I feel so empty when we aren't together. It feels like there's a part of myself missing."

"Like a void."

"Yes, exactly like a void."

"I feel it too, sweetheart." He reached up and caressed my cheek. I pressed a kiss into his palm.

"At least now, we can sense each other and communicate mind-to-mind from anywhere in the world. We'll never feel entirely lonely again."

"Sweetheart, I'll still feel lonely unless I have you in my arms."

I crushed my lips to his, and our kiss deepened. I felt his love pouring into me. He sucked and nibbled on my lips, and our tongues twirled and danced. I felt him harden inside me once again.

"Again, my love?"

"I told you, Paisley. I can't get enough of you."

"You can have me anytime you want, as many times as you want, my love. I can't get enough of you either. You are my only addiction, Chad. I wish I could make love to you every day, several times a day."

"Marry me, Paisley."

"We are already married as far as the Ancient Nymphean tradition goes."

"Yes, I know, but just think. We can have a fall or winter wedding with all of our *friends and family members there. Then, you'll be my wife in modern traditions, too."*

"Yes! Of course, I'll marry you, Chad! I can't wait to be your wife and have you as my husband."

"Oh, Paisley, my beautiful Paisley. I'm the luckiest man in the world, all because you're mine."

"That makes me the luckiest woman in the world because I have you."

We made love again before he took me home. I felt like I was walking on cloud nine. My head was fuzzy, and my body was coursing with Chad's energy from our lovemaking. I have never felt this good in my entire life. As many times as we'd made love, I still wanted more. I am addicted to him. We pulled into my driveway at 9:55 p.m. Chad carried my backpack and walked me to my door. We said our goodbyes and shared an amazing good night kiss. The void returned as he got into his truck and drove away. I tossed my backpack on the floor by the door and headed upstairs to shower and go to bed. My parents were in their room. I knocked on their door and told them I was home, good night, and that I loved them.

I grabbed my pajamas and my bath towel and headed into the bathroom. I wished I could shower with Chad and fall asleep in his arms. I turned the shower on and let the water warm up. As I took off my clothes, my thoughts went back to Chad and our evening together. I closed my eyes and replayed our lovemaking in my mind. I reached down and touched the tender flesh between my legs. I was still a little sore, but it was a good sore. I had bonded with my chosen mate, my Chad. I am his, and he is mine.

I stepped into the shower and stood under the warm water. I washed and conditioned my hair. Then, I grabbed my shower poof and lathered it up with body wash. I gently washed the sensitive flesh between my legs. Then, I heard Chad's voice in my head.

"I miss you already."

"I miss you too, my love. I missed you the second you walked away."

"I love hearing you call me 'my love' and 'honey.' I also love hearing you moan my name as it caresses your gorgeous lips."

"You are the man I love, Chad."

"I love you too, sweetheart."

"I have no doubts in my mind about that. I felt your love when we completed our bond."

"As did I, my love. I still feel your love inside of me."

"Yes! It's amazing. I wish you were in this shower with me and that we could fall asleep together."

"Soon, sweetheart. Soon. We'll figure out a way to be together each day. If we have to slip away for daily 'study dates,' we will."

"Good, because I don't know if I could be away from you for too long without going stir crazy."

"Trust me, sweetheart, I know."

"It's going to be hard to sit in class, knowing you're right there, and I can't have you.

"Tell me about it. It'll be harder for me to hide my intentions than it will be for you."

"Oh, my! Hahaha! That is so true! I'll try not to tease you or turn you on, then. I'd hate to have to fight off all the girls at school if they get a look at your massive package."

"You have no competition, Paisley. No woman in this world could ever come close to holding a candle to you."

"I feel the same way about you, Chad. I'm so in love with you. I can't even think about anyone but you."

"It may be wise to keep our completed bond to ourselves for a while."

"Yes, I agree, my love. I'm sure my parents' heads would spin if they found out."

"No kidding! I'd hate for your dad and mine to be after me for deflowering you before marriage."

"Luckily, we aren't royalty, like Molly and Toby. They do have to wait until marriage. The council's medical examiner has to verify her virginity before their wedding."

"We aren't royalty, but we were born of noble blood. We will have certain expectations, but thankfully that isn't one of them."

"I wish you were here. This bed feels so empty. I'd love to have your arms around me."

"I know, sweetheart. It sucks to be this far away from you. I will have you back in my arms as soon as I can."

"All right, my love. I can accept that... for now. I am looking forward to the day that we will be married and have our own place, though."

"You and me too, sweetheart. Well, I'm out of the shower and getting ready to hop into bed. We should both try to get some sleep."

"All right, my love. Good night. I'll see you in my dreams."

"Good night, sweetheart. I'll see you in mine."

I drifted off to sleep with Chad on my mind. My Chad, my bonded mate, and my future husband.

Chapter 10

Chad

Paisley is the first thought that crossed my mind as my eyes opened. I can sense her; even though she isn't here with me, I still feel her energy inside me. I closed my eyes and reached out for her with my soul. She's just waking up too.

"Good morning, sweetheart. Did you sleep well?"

"Good morning, my love. I slept better than I ever have. I had the most wonderful dreams about you. How about you? Did you sleep well?"

"I sure did. I fell asleep with you on my mind. I had some pretty amazing dreams about you too. Damn, I wish you were here right now."

"I do too, honey. I miss you so much."

"I miss you too. I can't wait to get my hands on you."

"Hands, lips, your arms wrapped around me; I'll take what I can get!"

"Don't tease me, woman. I'll drive over there, sweep you up, and carry you away."

"Hahaha! That does sound nice right about now."

"What do you think about another study date tonight?"

"That sounds amazing."

"I'll pick you up at 6:00 p.m."

"I can't wait. What am I saying? I can't wait to see you at school. I'll see you in the parking lot."

"I'll meet you there, sweetheart. I'm so addicted to you, Paisley. I'm afraid I might lose control with you."

"You won't hear me complain if you do. I can't get enough of you, Chad."

"Damn it, Paisley. I want you so badly right now. I can't think of anything else."

"I want you, too, honey. I need you. Our study date can't come soon enough."

"I love you, Paisley. I love you so much it hurts to be this far from you."

"I love you too, Chad, so very much. I know how you feel."

"Well, I'm going to finish getting ready, sweetheart. I'll see you in a little while. Please drive safely and watch out for all of the idiots out there on the roads."

"Same to you, my love. I'll see you soon."

I can't stop smiling. I'm happier with Paisley than I ever have been. It could also have something to do with the *urge* to bond being nonexistent now, too. I finished getting ready and headed downstairs. Mom was making breakfast. She turned to me and smiled as I sat down at the table with Tabby and Garrett.

"You look pleased this morning, Son. I'm guessing your study date went well."

"Yeah, it did. Chemistry and Biology are finally sinking in. Paisley is a great tutor."

"Uh-huh, sure she is," Tabby said with a giggle.

"She is. She's so much smarter than I am with math and science stuff. I'm helping her with her speech class. She's still shy when it comes to public speaking."

"Oh, that's nice of you to help one another out then," Mom said.

"Yeah, it also lets us get to know one another better."

"Good, Son. I'm glad you two are getting along then."

"Yeah, me too."

"How's Angie taking it?"

"Not well. Angie's still convinced that we'll be together, regardless of my and Paisley's connection. I told her that she and I were over and that I'd chosen Paisley, but she's not willing to accept it."

"Oh, dear, the poor thing. I hope she finds her chosen mate soon. That'll probably be the only way she'll move on."

"Yeah, that's what I'm thinking, too. I could tell that Angie has cried a lot. Her eyes were puffy and had dark circles under them. She didn't even go to cheerleading practice yesterday after our talk."

"Oh?"

"She was insulting Paisley and calling her all kinds of names, saying she stole me from her, among other mean and nasty things. I made her stop, though. I won't put up with anyone disrespecting my chosen mate."

"I'm glad you're protective over her. You should be. She's going to be a big part of your life."

"Very true. I want to buy Paisley an engagement ring and propose to her. The sooner, the better. I know we're chosen mates, but I'd like to make everything official."

"Oh, how exciting! Let me know if you want my company when you go ring shopping. I happen to have great taste in jewelry," Mom said with a wink.

"Thanks, Mom. I'll keep that in mind, and I will probably take you up on that."

"You know, that may not be a bad idea. If Angie sees an engagement ring on Paisley's finger, she may let you go and move on. Then again, rumors may go around that you and Paisley are getting married because she's knocked up. We don't want that going around if Angie is already stirring up trouble."

"That wouldn't be good at all. Paisley's good-girl reputation is already at stake. Angie's slinging mud at school about her pretty badly."

"I do hate to hear that. You may want to wait on the ring then, at least for a little while longer. You two just started dating as far as the kids at your school are concerned. They won't understand how fast we fall in love with our chosen mates."

"I honestly don't care what people will say or think about us. I want to marry her as soon as possible, maybe even over Christmas break. Then, we can get our own place after the wedding. We are both of bonding age, after all."

"What about college?"

"I guess it will depend on where we get accepted. Maybe we could rent a house or an apartment until graduation. Then, we could buy a place of our own around here afterward."

"Okay, that sounds fair. We will help you both out in any way we can."

"Thanks, Mom."

"So, when do we get to spend some time with the new addition to the family? She might as well be considered family. After all, she's going to be married and bonded to my eldest son before too long."

"I could ask her over for supper sometime if you'd like."

"Oh, please do. Maybe Paisley could come and hang out with us at the lake on Saturday too."

"I've got to work on Saturday."

"And? What's that got to do with us? She can come and hang out with the rest of us without any distraction from you, hahaha! It'll give us a chance to get to know her on our own."

"Okay. I'll ask her."

"Thanks. I'd appreciate that. Y'all should probably get going. It's almost time to leave for school."

Tabby, Garrett, and I climbed in my truck, and we headed off to school. I dropped them off at their school and headed to mine. I couldn't wait to get to Paisley. Her car was already in the parking lot when I pulled in. I parked in the empty spot beside her MINI Cooper. She hopped out when she saw me pull in. I got out of my truck and wrapped my arms around her. The sparks and tingles surged through us, and a wave of calm came over me. Damn, I've missed her.

I leaned down and captured her lips with mine. A sweet little whimper resonated in her mouth. It was all I needed to hear. I picked her up, sat her inside my truck, and climbed back in with her. The skirt she was wearing made it hard for me not to take her right then and there. It wouldn't have taken much to slide her panties off and have her straddle me in the backseat. The windows are tinted so dark that no one would've seen a thing. I resisted, though, because I know I won't have enough time to make love to her as long as I want. We sat in my truck and kissed and held one another until time to go to homeroom. I hate letting her go, but I know I'll have her with me again shortly. I walked her to her homeroom and placed a kiss on her temple.

"I'll see you in a few minutes, sweetheart."

"Okay, honey. See you soon."

I saw Angie walking into her homeroom class. She looked at me very briefly with tears glistening in her eyes and then looked down. She doesn't look any better than she did yesterday. I'd be very surprised if she's even wearing makeup. She's always worn makeup everywhere she went. Today, her face is pale, and she looks exhausted. I hate that her heart is broken, but I can't go back to her. I wouldn't, even if I could. I'm meant to be with Paisley. She and I are bonded mates now. There's no going back from that, no mulligans, and no do-overs. I wish fate would just show Angie who her mate is, so she won't make herself miserable over me anymore. She deserves to be happy with him, whoever he may be.

I headed into my homeroom and waited for the bell to sound for our first-period class. I couldn't wait to see Paisley and have her near me once again. I shot up like a rocket when it finally sounded. I hurried to Paisley's homeroom and walked with her, hand-in-hand, to the science hall. We went to our claimed table in the back of the class and sat down. I reached under the table and placed my hand on her thigh. She closed her eyes and bit her bottom lip when the tingles hit her. Then, she put her hand over mine. We held hands the entire class. We relished in the sparks and tingles surging through us, enjoying the guilty pleasure that our connection provides us.

We spent the second period very much the same way. By the time the lunch bell rang, Paisley was so turned on; she practically dragged me to my truck. We got into the back seat, and I locked the doors. She pulled off her thong, and I undid my jeans and slid them down to my knees. She straddled my lap and took all of me inside her. Sparks and tingles surged through us and seemed to pulse and intensify at our joining. I feasted on her lips as much as possible, so our moans wouldn't be heard outside the truck in case anyone did walk by. Bright colors swirled around us as our pleasure began to build.

"Hold my hands, sweetheart," I said to her mind-to-mind.

"Yes, my love. Oh, Chad! Yes!"

Flashing lights joined in with the swirling colors, our energy mixed within our bodies, and we both shuddered as our climax washed over us. Paisley leaned forward against me, and I wrapped my arms around her while we caught our breath.

"Damn, sweetheart! I'd say how incredible that was, but it'd be the understatement of the century."

"You said I could have you anytime I wanted you."

"That, I did."

"You knew exactly what you were doing in class. I could hardly focus on what the teachers were saying. It was all I could do to

keep from moaning in front of everyone. I wanted you so badly."

"So, that's all I have to do, huh, just rub your inner thigh and send those little sparks and tingles right where I want to be?"

"Oh, Chad! Yes, I loved it! Wow!"

"You are incredible, Paisley. I love you so much."

"I love you too, Chad, so very much."

There was still enough time left of our lunch period to grab a quick bite to eat and head to the quad. Molly and Toby were the only ones at the table. Max had already left to go to his class on the other side of the school.

"Where have you two been?" Molly asked.

"We needed some... um... private time," I said, "I can't keep my lips off of her."

"Yeah, good luck with that," Toby said. "Trust us. We know the feeling. That damned *urge* to bond is a painful thing."

"Tell me about it," I said. "I've never wanted anything more in my whole life than to bond with her and make her mine."

Toby slapped me on the back a couple of times and said, "Not too much longer, though. We all have, what, nine months or so until graduation? You and Paisley are already eighteen and don't have the obligations that Molly and I do. You two could technically get married over Christmas break."

"Oooh! A winter wonderland themed wedding would be beautiful." Molly said. "I'd love to help you plan it and decorate the venue."

"Well, I did propose last night. I haven't gotten her a ring yet, but that's coming." I pulled Paisley closer to me and stole a quick kiss. "I couldn't have been happier when she said, 'yes.' I can't wait for her to be my wife and make her mine for eternity. Don't go spreading it all around, though. Mom thinks it'd be a bad idea to be engaged so soon. I told her I wanted to get Paisley a ring and propose to her sooner than later. She said humans wouldn't understand how fast things go with us, verses in their culture. She's afraid people would spread rumors of us only getting married because of a baby coming."

"Congratulations to you both! That's very true. Rumors spread like wildfires. The only thing that kept that rumor from going around about us is because no one's ever seen me with a girlfriend. They bought the whole long-distance relationship story," Toby said.

"That's why I was going to hold off on getting her a ring for a few months, but if we plan on getting married over Christmas break, I'd better get a move on it. A lot goes into wedding planning, or so I've heard. I want our wedding to be her dream come true, not just something thrown together at the last moment."

"I can't say I blame you there."

"I don't need anything fancy, honey," Paisley said. "I just want to marry you. That's all that matters at the end of the day."

"I know, sweetheart, but where would we live? I don't exactly want to spend our wedding night in either of our parents' houses if you know what I mean."

"Oooooh," she cringed. "No, I don't want to either. Maybe we'd better just hold off until after graduation. I'll see if I can get hired at the diner or at the cafe to make some extra money. Every little bit counts and will help us get our own place. I could work weekends while you're working at the marina."

"Speaking of the weekend, Mom wants you to hang out with her, Dad, Tabby, and Garrett on Saturday while I'm working. She wants to 'get to know the new addition to the family without any distraction from me.'"

"That doesn't sound awkward at all," Molly said and snickered behind her hand. "I'm just kidding, of course. I'm sure you'll have a blast. Chad's family is great. You'll love them, and I just know they'll love you too. In fact, I'm sure of it."

"I'm in. It sounds like fun. I met your family over the summer, but I wouldn't mind getting to know my new soon-to-be-in-laws a lot better. I'll have to ask your mom what time she'd like for me to come over."

"You are amazing, sweetheart. Mom is going to be thrilled! She was already making plans this morning while we were getting ready for school."

"Well, I'm looking forward to it."

"Molly's right, you know. They're going to love you."

"I hope so."

"They will. Our dads were pretty ecstatic that we'd chosen one another. They'd served together on Queen Isabella's Royal Guard before we were born. They're as close as Toby, Max, and I are."

"Wow, I had no idea."

"Neither did I until Dad told me."

The bell rang for us to head to our third class of the day. I walked Paisley to her class, told her I love her, kissed her temple, and walked to mine. I walked in just before the tardy bell rang and headed to my usual seat at the back of the room. Angie was already sitting in her chair at the front. She still looks rough. She looked up at me as I walked by. Her eyes are bloodshot and are glistening with tears. She's been crying, likely over our breakup. I glanced away and kept walking. I don't want to make her think that I still care about her in that way and string her along. If she believes I am still in love with her, she'll hold on to that notion and not move on. I'm a bonded man. I am no longer on the market for anyone but Paisley. My thoughts were interrupted by my phone buzzing in my pocket. I checked it to see eho had texted me. It was from Angie.

"I miss you."

"I'm sorry, Angie. You need to move on."

"I can't. I need you."

"No, you don't. You need to pull yourself out of this."

"Come back to me, Chad. Please, I'm begging you."

"No, Angie. I'm not coming back to you. Not now. Not ever."

"I feel so broken and empty without you."

"There's nothing you can say or do to make me come back to you, Angie. I told you. It's over."

"I can't accept that, Chad. I won't. I love you too much to let you go."

"I don't love you anymore, Angie. I love Paisley. I'm in love with her. I'm dedicated and devoted to her now."

She stood up, grabbed her backpack, and left the classroom, sobbing. Other people in the class turned in their seats to look at me and gave me dirty looks. Great. Now, I look like a jerk. Well, so be it. I'll do whatever it takes for her to move on. I'll be the jerk, the bad guy, the heart breaker. It doesn't matter what anyone thinks about me. I could honestly care less.

"What are you looking at? Mind your own business, will you?"

Everyone turned back around as Mrs. Anderson came in and started today's lesson. Angie didn't come back to class. I don't know if she went home or if she just went to hide for a while. She was very distraught by what I'd said to her. I may try to call her parents later and see if they have been attempting to talk to her.

I'm sure they have if they've taken one look at her at all this week.

"Are you okay, honey? You seem... off."

"Yes, sweetheart. I'm okay. Angie still isn't, though. She texted me, begging me to come back to her. I told her there was nothing she could say or do to make me go back to her. She left class, crying before it even began."

"I hate that she's in such pain. She would be so much happier if she could just let you go. Holding onto you could be keeping her from finding her chosen mate."

"It's possible. That could be why it took so long for our connection to grow stronger. It took a while for us to realize it was there, but once we did, it hit us pretty hard."

"Wow, did it ever! I love you so much, Chad. I'm so glad you're mine."

"I love you too, Paisley, so very much. I'm glad you're mine. I hope you know that I wouldn't have gone back to Angie even if we hadn't completed our bond yet."

"I know, my love. I wouldn't have gone back to Max either. My love for you is stronger than I ever imagined it could be."

"I didn't know what love was until our connection awakened and got stronger."

"I'm looking forward to our study date later. I miss you."

"Me too. I miss you too."

My last two classes were nearly painful to sit through. The school day was finally over for the day, including football practice. Angie wasn't at her cheerleading practice yet again. I'm going to call her mom to make sure she's all right. I can talk to her on my way to Paisley's house for our study date.

"Hello?"

"Hello, Mrs. Simpson. It's Chad. I'm worried about Angelina. She's been skipping classes and cheerleading practices. She's also been crying a lot and tried to start a fight with Paisley in front of a lot of other students. Have you or Mr. Simpson had a chance to talk to her?"

"Yes, we both have. It doesn't seem to do any good, though. Angelina is very headstrong and spoiled. She's used to getting her way. That's our fault, and I'm sorry about that. Right now, you are what she wants more than anything in the world."

"I'm not up for grabs, though, Mrs. Simpson. I'm devoted to my chosen mate now. She and I are in love and will eventually be getting married."

"I know all too well how chosen mates work. I just hate that Angelina got so attached to you before her connection could spark with her chosen mate."

"I'm sorry that it hasn't happened for her yet. I hope that fate steps in soon for them."

"That's very nice for you to say. I'm just not so certain that Angelina will be satisfied with him because *he* isn't *you*. She's made it very clear that she doesn't want to be with her chosen mate and that she is determined to bond with you anyway."

"I'm afraid that won't be possible, Mrs. Simpson. I'm not going back to Angelina. I want the deep connection and bond that can only be shared with my chosen mate."

"As will she when her connection awakens. She's just heartbroken right now and isn't thinking clearly. She will be just fine in due time."

"Thank you for talking to me, Mrs. Simpson. Angelina and I were together for a long time. I may not be in love with her or love her in that way anymore, but I do still care about her wellbeing."

"I can respect that, Chad. Thank you for checking in on her."

"No problem, Mrs. Simpson. I suppose I'll talk to you later."

"Anytime, Chad."

I'm glad her parents are aware of everything. I just wish there was more that I could do to help her move on. Besides lining up eligible bachelors and having them touch their palms together, I'm not sure what else to do. Now, there's an idea. We could make a sign that says, "Free High Fives From Our Varsity Cheerleading Captain, Angelina Simpson!" It may get everyone excited about the upcoming game and possibly find her mate if he's here at our school. She'd never go for it, though, especially if she doesn't want to be with him because he isn't me.

∞

I spent the evening at Paisley's house, having dinner with her and her family, and then studied there in her room afterward. They want to get to know me like my family wants to get to know her. Everyone is pretty excited about us being together. I like her family. Her little brother, Caden, is a pretty cool kid. He showed me some of his favorite action figures and told me about his school crush, who just happens to be Max's little sister Alyssia. I told him I knew her and that I'd put in a good word for him.

We went up to Paisley's room and turned on some music to listen to while we studied. It is so hard to resist making love to Paisley. We are alone in her room, with the door closed and locked, so we can study in private, without her little brother barging in. I should try to behave and wait to have her again another time, but I'm not sure I can. She is so cute when she's trying to focus, especially when I'm doing my best to distract her. I started talking dirty to her, mind-to-mind, without looking at her, pretending to read over my homework.

"I want you, Paisley. I want you naked, squirming, and begging me to take you."

"You're terrible; you know that?" She giggled.

"What?" I laughed. "I don't know what you're talking about."

"I want to hear you screaming my name."

"Uh-huh, sure, and you're not doing anything but innocently reading your book, right?"

"Then, when you're good and ready, I want to make love to you until neither of us can move."

"Yep, that's right," I said with a wink.

"You want me too, Paisley. I can feel it. I can sense how aroused you are. You're throbbing right now, aren't you?"

She bit her bottom lip. I leaned in and took her bottom lip between my teeth and gently tugged on it. Then, I captured her lips with mine. She opened for me, and our tongues danced and twirled, licked, and tasted. She let out the cutest little whimper that unraveled my self-control. I had to taste her. I couldn't wait any longer. I laid her back on her bed, dove under her skirt, pulled off her thong, and tossed it on the floor. I swirled my tongue through her wet folds and circled her throbbing bundle of nerves. I inserted two fingers into her tight channel, probing and massaging inside her. I teased and flicked her sensitive flesh with my tongue. She began to writhe against me, and colors began to swirl around us.

"That's it. Let go for me, sweetheart."
"Oh, God! Chad! Ah, yes! Oh, my God!"
Her legs started shaking as her pleasure spiked. I licked along her slit and savored her sweetness on my tongue. She is and always will be my favorite flavor. I can't get enough of her.

Even eternity may not be long enough for me to fully enjoy her. The tantric way she moves, the glow of her lavender-blue eyes, and her musical voice are enough to make me weak in the knees.

"Do you think you can be quiet, Sweetheart?"

"Do you?"

"Is that a challenge?"

"Maybe."

"Challenge accepted. Although, I do want to hear you moan my name, Paisley. I love hearing my name on your beautiful lips."

"What if someone hears us? We don't need to get caught, Chad."

"Well, I guess you'll have to be as quiet as possible. I'll settle for hearing your voice mind-to-mind. I'm still going to do my best to drive you up the wall."

I climbed over her, and Paisley frantically loosened my belt and undid my jeans. I slid them down, and she wrapped her legs around my waist. I eased inside of her slowly, inch-by-inch, and captured her mouth with mine. Soft whimpers began to escape her throat as I plunged deeper inside her. I began thrusting slowly at first, allowing her to adjust to my massive size, and then gradually increased my tempo.

"Oh, Chad!"

"Yes, my love. I told you I'd have you moaning my name and begging for more. You're mine now, Paisley."

"Yes, Chad! Yes!"

Paisley was writhing and grinding against me. Hearing her sweet voice in my mind, calling out my name, and feeling her reaction to my movements made it hard to remain in control of "the beast" inside me. It wants to possess her and ravish her completely. That part of me wants to give in to "the beast." I need to feel Paisley's submission as I conquer her. It's a need I'd never experienced with Angie. I have to keep it in check. I'm afraid of what will happen if I don't.

"Yes, Chad! Harder! Faster! Don't hold back. I'm yours, Chad. All yours."

I felt a low growl rumble in my chest, and "the beast" took over. I'd lost the battle with "the beast" inside me. I began pounding into her harder and faster as she'd begged me to do. Colors began to swirl around us. I held her hands above her head, pressing our hands together, palm-to-palm. Our energy began to flow, and flashing lights combined with the swirling cyclone of colors.

"Damn, you feel so good! I can't hold off much longer, Paisley. Soar with me."

"Yes, my love! I'm ready. Oh, God! Yes, Chad! Yes!

Both of our bodies shuddered as we soared into climax. We came down together slowly and caught our breath.

"You are amazing, Paisley. I can't resist you. I told myself that I should behave and wait until we were completely alone to have you again, but it was no use. I had to have you. I couldn't even hold back. I tried to fight

losing control with you. I was so afraid I was going to hurt you.”

“Shh. It’s all right, Chad. You are incredible. You have done nothing wrong. I enjoy absolutely every second we spend making love. Soft and gentle or fast and hard. I can’t get enough.”

“Are you sure I didn’t hurt you?”

“Yes, I’m sure, my love. I’m perfectly fine. I asked you not to hold back, remember?”

“Yes, but I never want to hurt you, Paisley. I worry about that when my inner ‘beast’ takes over. When it does, I want to possess you and ravish you. ‘The beast’ needs your submission.”

“Chad, my love, I am yours. You can possess me and ravish me whenever you want. No holding back, no fighting the urge to lose control. I submit to you, Chad, to you and ‘the beast’ inside you.”

“Sweetheart, I love you more than life itself. I will always ask before I lose control with you unless you ask me to first. I will always fear hurting you and will fight as hard as I can not to.”

“I love you too, Chad. You are my world. Don’t worry about hurting me. I think you forget how fast we heal. I know we haven’t known about the whole Nymphean thing very long, but we do heal very fast. Even if we do get a bit rough in our lovemaking, I’ll heal so fast; it won’t matter.”

I looked away from her, feeling ashamed of myself for being rough with her. I know she’d asked me to, and we do heal very fast. I still feel bad about the possibility of hurting her, whether it was in the past, or whether I'll lose control again and hurt her in the future. I can't let that happen, even with her permission.

"Honey, please look at me. I trust you, Chad. I know you won't hurt me. My body is getting more used to you faster than you think. I crave you. I need to feel you inside me, and your energy mixed with mine."

"I still can't risk hurting you, sweetheart. I would never forgive myself if I did."

"It's okay, my love. You haven't hurt me, not once. Please, don't feel bad about anything. I have no regrets with you."

"All right, sweetheart. Only if you're sure."

"I am very sure, my love."

"I don't deserve you, Paisley. You are way too good for me, but I am so glad you're mine."

"You do deserve me. We deserve each other. Our love for one another is on a level so deep, pure, and so true that no one else could ever come close to competing with. I didn't want to believe it when Max told me that's the way it would be, but it's true. I need you, Chad. I can't wait to be your wife and call you my husband."

"I can't wait either, sweetheart. I'd marry you right now if I could." I captured her lips with mine in a tender kiss, full of passion and love. Paisley responded to my kiss as our lips embraced, and our tongues caressed one another in their own private slow dance. I made love to her once again, but this time, I was gentle and tender with her. I poured my

passion and energy into her to show her just how much I love her, how much I need her, and just what she means to me. She is my world, my everything.

We bared our souls to one another, and I can honestly say that it was the most beautiful thing I'd ever experienced. She is the most beautiful woman I've ever met on the inside and the outside. Her beauty radiates from within her; from her soul. I don't know how I'd never noticed before. Now, it seems so obvious that I think I must've been blind.

Paisley and I are made for one another. Our souls crave one another's closeness. I've never needed anyone as I need her. Our bond is growing even stronger by the day. I already can't stand to be away from her for any length of time. I never imagined that the connection between us would develop and bloom as quickly as it has. That wedding over Christmas break sounds pretty good right about now. I know it isn't convenient, though. We will have to make do with the time we have with one another. Knowing I can sense her and speak to her mind-to-mind at all times does help a little bit. I still crave her closeness, the feel of her tender caress, the softness of her skin, her scent lingering in the air when she's near me, and the taste of her sweetness on my tongue.

The ride home was excruciating. The void returned as soon as I got into my truck. I always hate leaving her side. It feels like a part of me is being ripped away, almost as though a limb is being ripped from my body. I keep telling myself that it won't always be this way. We will be together soon, and won't have to live apart ever again. That day can't come quickly enough.

Chapter 11

Angelina

I can't do this anymore. I can't sit back and watch *my* Chad gallivanting around with *her*. It should be *me* on his arm, not *her*. Tonight's varsity game is only a scrimmage one. I'm not required to wear my cheerleading uniform to school today. So, I'm going to show Chad what he's missing. It's time to bring out the big guns. I'm going to wear the red dress that I had on for our last date. That should spark his memory and make him see what he could have. Paisley can't compare to how I look in that dress, even on her best day. Chad Greene will be mine once again. He won't be able to resist me. I'll seduce him and bond with him in the parking lot at school if I have to.

I put on my rejuvenating mask, my bathrobe, and my cozy slippers. It's time to pamper myself and come back more beautiful and better than ever. Chad Greene won't know what hit him. I showered, curled my hair, perfected my makeup, and slipped on the red dress. The school's dress code requires my shoulders to be covered, so I put on a short cardigan shrug that wouldn't take anything away from the dress. I grabbed a quick breakfast and headed to school.

Chad's truck was already in the parking lot. Good. He'll see me make my appearance in the quad. I'm going to make his mouth water and make him want me again. He'll regret the day he ever chose that skanky Paisley over me. I think I'll walk right up to him, sit on his lap, and kiss him right in front of Paisley and everyone. Hmph. That'll show her. I refuse to give him up. I'll do anything to have him back.

I walked into the quad and immediately spotted Chad and his friends. Paisley was sitting on the table in front of him. Her feet were on his lap, and he was caressing her legs. I think I'm going to be sick. No. Pull yourself together, Angelina. Like Chad said, *"You're so much better than this, and you know it."* Yes, I am better. I'm so much better than that skank, and yes, I do know it.

I tossed my hair, walked right up to him, and sat down beside him. I didn't even acknowledge Paisley sitting there. I reached over and tried to stroke his thigh from his knee to his groin. He grabbed my hand and shoved it away!

"What the hell are you doing, Angie?"

"I'm not giving up, Chad. You're supposed to be mine, and mine alone."

"No, Angie. I belong with Paisley now, and I always will. I told you it's over between us, and I meant it."

I ignored his outburst as though he'd not even said anything. "How rude. You didn't even tell me how beautiful I look today. Don't you recognize this dress, Chad? Or would you prefer to see it pooled around my ankles like it ended up the last time I wore it for you?"

Paisley furrowed her brow and looked at Chad with tears in her eyes. His eyes widened as big as saucers. He scowled at me and then looked at Paisley. Oh, goodie! Operation break up Chad and Paisley is underway. He'll be mine once again before the day is over, and everything will be back to normal.

"Chad? What is she talking about?"

"Angie and I… it's not what you think. I swear. I didn't take her virginity or give her mine. She came on to me really strong, but I rejected her. You have to believe me."

"I do believe you, my love."

They stared into each other's eyes for a moment. Then, Paisley reached down, caressed his cheek, and smiled at him. What… the… hell… is going on here? This can't be happening! I stood up, looked from him to her, and back at him. His gaze never left hers. He's not leaving her, and she's not leaving him either! It's so apparent and is written all over both of their faces. Their connection is growing stronger than even I can compete with. A connection like that could only mean one thing. They have already completed their bond. NOOO! I felt all of the color leave my face, and the world went black.

"Angie! Angie, wake up!"

Molly's voice. She was yelling at me to wake up. Why? What happened? Did I faint?

"I'm okay… I think. Oh, my head. Am I bleeding?"

"No, you're all right," Molly said. "You had a nasty gash on the back of your head, but I healed you before it started bleeding. The pain should subside in no time. Just take it easy standing up. We don't need you falling again."

"Thanks, Molly. I appreciate it. I don't deserve your kindness, but thank you."

"I understand what you're going through, and I know it can't be easy. Please don't shut us out. Let us help you through this. We are all still your friends here."

"Not all of you are. Those two can stay the hell away from me and never speak to me again as far as I'm concerned."

"Angie, please don't be that way." Molly's voice dropped to a whisper. "Chad and Paisley are chosen mates. They can't fight their connection even if they wanted to. You know that."

"Do I? No, I wouldn't know anything about fighting connections because I don't have one... with anyone!"

"Neither do I, Angie," Max said. "I could have turned against them too when their connection took Paisley from me, but I didn't. I couldn't. Chad has been a great friend of mine for too long to let their connection ruin our friendship. Not to mention, I'd rather have Paisley in my life as a friend than not at all. At least I know she's happy, even if she isn't mine anymore."

"You have no idea how painful it is for me to see him with her. He should be with me."

"Listen, Angie," Molly said. "I know you're hurting right now, but you have to look at this a different way. Your heart is now open for your chosen mate to step in and show you how true love feels. I know you love Chad, but even that love can't compare to the love you'll feel when your chosen mate comes along. Believe me when I say that it'll stop you in your tracks, knock you off your feet, and take you higher than you'd ever imagine."

"How do I forget him? He's the only guy I've ever loved." I can feel my eyes stinging with tears. I'm so tired of crying, but it seems like that's all I do these days. Well, that and drink enough whiskey to numb the pain so I can get some sleep.

"Who says you have to forget? Cherish the memories you made with him, but let your heart mend and move on." Molly wrapped her arms around me, and I began to cry on her shoulder. I couldn't fight back the waterworks any longer. "It's okay to cry, Angie, but just don't let this consume you. We've all got things going on in our lives that haven't been extremely easy to get through. We get through them together, though, and then it's not so bad. We are here for you, too, you know."

"I'm sorry I've been such a brat. I know I don't deserve it, but could you please give me another chance and forgive me?"

"Of course. That's what true friends do, Angie. We may fight, go a while without speaking, and say things we don't mean, but we will always be here for you. We are all more than just friends, you know. We are more like a family than anything. There aren't that many of us out there when you think about the grand scheme of things. We have to stick together."

"Thank you. I promise I'll try to get over Chad, but it's not going to be easy. I may keep my distance for a while, but please just know that I'm trying. I'm sorry, Paisley. I've said and done some pretty awful things. Will you ever forgive me?"

"I already have. I did as soon as it happened. I knew that it was your pain talking and didn't hold it against you. I wish you would've let me help you and be there for you, but I understand why you didn't. I'll still be here for you, though, whenever you're ready."

"Thanks, Paisley. I suppose I owe you an apology too, Chad. I shouldn't have tried to come between you and Paisley like that. It just hurts so much to see you two together. I need time to get over you in my own way and in my own time.”

“That’s completely understandable, and yes, of course, I forgive you. I’m with Max on this one. You and I have known one another for a long time, Angie. I’d rather have you in my life as a friend than not at all. I’ll even be happy for you when your chosen mate comes along. You deserve to be happy with him, whoever he may be.”

“Thanks, guys. It means a lot to me that y’all forgive me for my behavior. I have been difficult, huh?”

“You could say that again,” Chad said, “but we don’t blame you.”

“I’m thankful for that. Well, the bell should be ringing anytime now. I’m going to go ahead and make my way to homeroom.”

“I’ll walk with you,” Max said. “You did just faint after all, and I’d hate to know you fell out again on the way there.”

“Thanks, Max. I appreciate it.”

The bell rang as soon as Max and I started heading out of the quad and away from the rest of our friends. They are still my friends after all that I’ve said and done. Now, if only I could just move on from Chad and find my chosen mate. Maybe finding him will help me to forget the love I still feel for him.

Max walked me to my seat, which probably wasn’t necessary, but I wasn’t going to complain. I did still feel a little woozy. "Thanks for walking with me, Max. I appreciate it."

"No problem at all. Here's my number. Text me if you still feel woozy, and I'll come to walk you to your next class too." He wrote his number on the inside cover of my notebook and smiled. He has a very charming smile. How had I never noticed before?

I smiled back and nodded. "Thanks again, Max. I'll let you know either way. Here's my number, so you'll know it's me." I tore off a piece of paper and wrote my number down for him.

He smiled again and said, "Feel better, Angel. I'll see you soon." Then, he turned and walked out of my class and headed to his. He called me "Angel." I wonder why? No one's ever called me that. I've always been Angie or Angelina. Hmm... I'm no angel; not even close. I don't deserve the kindness everyone has shown me today. Not after the way I've acted lately, anyway. I haven't been the most likable person over the last few years, either. I'd been working on being a better friend to everyone before everything fell apart for Chad and me. Maybe I should get back to being a better person. That may even help me get over Chad in the long run.

Molly was right. My head stopped hurting before the end of my first class, and I no longer felt woozy. I sent Max a quick text to let him know I was feeling better. "Hey, Max. This is

Angie. I just wanted to let you know that I'm feeling much better now."

"Hey, Angel. Good. I'm glad. I'm still walking you to your next class, just in case. I'm not taking no for an answer, either."

"Okay. Fine. I suppose there's no way to win this one, is there?"

"Nope. Not a chance. I'll see you in a few minutes."

Max was right on time. He came into my class and walked up to my desk as I was picking up my backpack. He took it from me and threw it over his shoulder. He offered me his arm to help me stand up. I gladly took it and stood up slowly. Wow! His arm is solid muscle! I suppose it'd have to be with all the work he does on his family's ranch.

"Thanks again, Max. I know I keep thanking you, but I do appreciate you looking after me since I fainted."

"It's my pleasure. I don't mind at all."

"You called me 'Angel' earlier. Was that just a Freudian slip, or did you mean to call me that?"

"You noticed, huh?" His cheeks flushed, and he looked away, but I had already noticed. I stopped walking and turned to face him.

"Listen, Max..."

"Say no more. You don't like it. I won't call you that anymore. Don't worry about it. It's fine. I get it."

"No, I mean yes, I mean... ugh. Let me start over. Please?"

"Um... okay."

"I do like it. I think it's adorable. What I don't get is, why? I'm no angel; not even close."

"Really? You don't mind?"

"No, I-I don't mind. I just don't understand why you did, that's all."

"Well, to be honest, I've had a huge crush on you for years. I never said anything because you fell in love with Chad and never gave me the time of day. I've always thought you were the most beautiful girl I've ever seen. In my eyes, you were an angel that fell from heaven. That's why I called you 'Angel.' I never called you that before because I didn't want Chad getting jealous of me calling his girlfriend a nickname or term of endearment."

"Oh. I see." Now, it's my turn to blush. "Just call me, Captain Oblivious, because I did not see that one coming."

"I won't bother you anymore if you don't want me to. I'll leave you alone, and we can just continue being friends if you want to."

"You aren't bothering me, Max. Why on earth would you think you are?"

"Well, because before today, you acted like I barely existed at all. I know we come from two totally different worlds. I mean, think about it. What would a girl like you ever want with a guy like me? I hate the thought of you thinking I took advantage of the situation to get close to you because that's not why I wanted to look after you. When I saw you faint, I panicked.

Something inside me just sort of snapped. I had to make sure you were all right."

"I guess you were my hero, and I was your damsel in distress, huh?"

"Something like that, but there's more to it than just that. As I said, I've had a crush on you for a long time. I don't expect you to go out with me because I said anything, but I don't want to be used as a rebound either."

"Max, I wouldn't do that."

"Wouldn't what, go out with me, or use me as a rebound?"

"I wouldn't use you as a rebound or use you in any way. Despite my piss-poor, spoiled-little-rich-girl reputation, I'm not the kind of girl to use people."

"Oh, all right. Well, I'm sorry I said anything. I didn't mean to offend you."

I turned and started walking toward my class once again, and Max did the same. "No, please. Don't be sorry. It's okay. I know I've not been the nicest person to anyone for a long time. I'm going to change that, though. I'm not my biggest fan either right now, just so you know."

"I never would've thought that."

"Well, it's true. I hate how mean and rotten I've been to everyone who genuinely cares about me. So, I've decided to make some changes in my life. I'm going to be nicer to people and help others whenever I can, even if it's an inconvenience for me. I think it'll help me be a better person in the long run. Maybe I'll even like who I become."

"I can respect that. That's pretty awesome. It takes a lot of courage to admit something like that."

"Thanks."

We finally arrived at my next class, and Max followed me inside to my desk. He sat my backpack down beside me and said, "Well, I'm going to head to class. Let me know if you'd like me to walk you to your next class and to lunch from there. I'll come and get you if you do. If not, I'll just see you at lunch."

"Thanks again, Max, for looking after me and for listening."

"Anytime, Angel. I'll see you later."

"Bye, Max."

He turned and walked towards the front of my class to leave. I couldn't help but notice how well he filled out those jeans. Nice butt! He just so happened to turn to look at me as he was walking out and caught me checking him out. I'm so busted! My face flushed a bright red. Damn! He flashed me that sexy grin of his and walked out. As hot as Max is, I do need to give myself time to get over Chad before I go after the first guy that pays me any attention. It's the right thing to do. If I do decide to date Max or anyone for that matter, it should be for the right reasons, and not because I'm on the rebound like Max said. I'm well overdue for some much needed "me" time.

Chapter 12

Chad

Well, I suppose that could've gone much worse. I'm glad Paisley believed me about not making love to Angie. I only wanted to share my virginity with my chosen mate. Something had to have spooked Angie to make her faint like that. Maybe seeing me with Paisley does bother her that badly. I'm just glad that she's trying to move on and isn't going to stir up any more trouble for us.

I walked Paisley to her homeroom class and gave her a quick kiss while no one was looking. Something seemed a bit off with her, though. I had to talk to her and find out what's on her mind.

"Are you all right, sweetheart?"
"Yeah, I'm all right. It just upset me to hear Angie talking about you seeing her

naked. I know I shouldn't be upset about it because it happened before we found out about our connection, but it still rattled my cage a bit."

"I kind of figured that's what was bothering you. Are you sure you're all right?"

"Yeah, I'm sure. I never went that far with Max, but I'm sure you wouldn't want to hear about all of our make-out sessions, either."

"No, that most certainly would not be my favorite topic of discussion."

"So, you see my point then. I had to assume you two had experimented and done things since you'd been together so long. I just didn't want to hear about it, especially not with Angie rubbing it in my face."

"I agree. That was not pleasant for me either. To be honest, I regretted it as soon as I found out about our connection. I wished I'd known sooner. I would've broken things off with Angie before it even came to that."

"I don't blame either of you, Chad. Honestly, I don't. I just don't like thinking about you being intimate with anyone that isn't me."

"I can imagine why. I'll admit that it infuriated me to think about Max's hands and lips on you after we found out about us. What do you say we just put all of that in the past and leave it there?"

"I'm great with that. From now on, it's all about us, our present, and our future together."

"It's a deal, sweetheart. I love you so very much. The bell for the first period needs to ring already. I need to feel you near me."

"Same here, my love. I love you so very much and can't wait to see you in Chemistry II class."

The bell finally rang, and I nearly jumped up out of my seat to get to Paisley's homeroom so that I could walk with her to the science hall for our Chemistry II class. Her smile is so contagious. She was smiling at me at the other end of the hallway, but every guy she passed smiled and looked back at her, as though she was smiling at them instead. Poor fellas don't stand a snowball's chance in hell. I can't blame them, though. She is gorgeous.

"Hey, handsome! I missed you!"

"Hello, gorgeous! I missed you too!"

"You don't know how badly I want to escape with you and play hooky for the rest of the day."

"Don't tempt me, woman! I'll scoop you up and run like a bat out of hell. Hahaha!"

"That would be wonderful, but we have to play nice and stay here if you're going to play football."

"Very true, sweetheart. Tonight's game is only a scrimmage one, but I still want to play. Are you going to come and cheer for me?"

"I wouldn't miss it! I've already made plans to sit with Molly."

"I'll be looking for you in the stands."

"I'll be there. Then, I'll be waiting for you outside of the field house afterward for our date."

"I can hardly wait, sweetheart. I'm ready for some more alone time with my woman."

"Mmmm, that sounds amazing!"

"It will be if I have anything to do with it."

"You're pretty confident about that, huh?"

"I have a pretty good reason to be. I have it on good authority that I'm a sure thing."

"Hahaha! Is that so?"

"Only for you, Paisley."

"I wouldn't have it any other way."

"Me, either."

We sat down at our usual seat at the lab table at the back of the room and opened our books to the page Mr. Duncan had written on the board. I can hardly focus on anything he's saying. All I want to do is wrap my arms around Paisley and kiss her senselessly. Her scent is driving me crazy. I want to taste her on my tongue so badly that my mouth is watering.

She must be thinking the same thing I am because I sense her arousal. Our date cannot come soon enough. I may not be able to keep my hands to myself until then. As a matter of fact, I know I can't. I reached over, placed my hand on her upper thigh, and slid my fingers inward and between her legs. Then, I tucked my fingers under her thigh and squeezed it. She closed her eyes for a second when the spark and tingles hit her right where I wanted to be.

"I want you so badly right now, Paisley."

"I want you too, my love. Our date is going to be a hot one for sure!"

"I may have to have you before then. I foresee a lunchtime quickie in our future."

"Is that so?"

"Oh, most definitely! I'll be surprised if I don't throw you over my shoulder and sprint to my truck as soon as Biology II is over."

"Hahaha! That'd look a bit conspicuous, don't you think?"

"You're right. We'll have to be careful not to get caught."

"Right. Neither of us wants to explain to our parents why a teacher followed us and ended up seeing us going at it in your truck."

"Oh, no. Absolutely not! Maybe we should just tease one another here and there until our date to build up some heat."

"Honey, if you get me any hotter, I'm going to spontaneously combust!"

"We can't have that, now can we?"

"Not if you want to live for eternity, hahaha!"

"Good point, sweetheart. This life wouldn't be worth living without you in it."

"Awe, you're so sweet!"

"Only to you, sweetheart. A lot of people think I'm a jerk because I dumped Angie and made her cry."

"They're only human, honey. They don't understand. They're not meant to."

"I know. It doesn't bother me. Most athletes are called jocks and are known to be jerks anyway. I guess I fit the bill now."

"Everything will settle down soon, and something else will take the spotlight off of us before you know it. We just have to grin and bear it until then."

"Very true. I'm glad that everything is going to be all right in our circle of friends. It may take a while for Angie to come back around us, but I'm glad she's going to be all right."

"Me too. I miss hanging out with Angie. She is fun to be around. We were making progress in our friendship. I hope we can get back to that someday. I miss my friend."

"Just give her some time. I'm sure she'll be back to normal before too long."

Paisley smiled at me and raised her hand to answer Mr. Duncan's question. I honestly don't know how she divides her attention between our conversation and the lesson so efficiently. She is brilliant. She answered correctly and winked at me. All I can do is smile back and shake my head. She is truly amazing. I'm so lucky that she's all mine.

Mr. Duncan was gracious enough not to give us any strenuous homework over the weekend. All we have to do is study the last few chapters and read ahead for Monday's lesson. There will be a quiz on Monday on everything we've covered so far. Paisley and I packed up our books, and I carried our backpacks to Biology II.

Paisley and I got settled into our seats and opened our books. Mrs. Isleson came in a few minutes late, but she had written our reading assignment on the board for us to get started on in her absence. Of course, I took the opportunity to talk to Paisley.

"What do you think caused Angie to faint like that?"

"Maybe she just stood up too fast. It's not uncommon to get dizzy that way. It's happened to me before."

"Hmm... maybe so."

Biology II class seemed to fly by quickly. We walked to the quad together and joined the rest of our friends at our usual spot. Everyone was chatting happily and enjoying their lunch. Angie still hadn't rejoined the crew, but she had explained that she needed time to deal with everything her way on her time. Paisley and I sat down as Max was telling Molly and Toby about his time with Angie.

"She seems like she's starting to feel better. I walked her to all of her classes so far, but she decided to walk by herself to lunch."

"She should be just fine now as far as her head and a possible concussion are concerned," Molly said. "I can't say about the emotional aspect of everything, though. Unfortunately, I haven't had much luck healing that sort of thing."

"Thank you for healing her, Molly. You're amazing," Max said.

"If I didn't know any better, I'd say you care about her."

"I do. I mean, Angelina's been a part of our group for a long time now."

"Are sure that's the only reason?" Max blushed and looked away. "I'm sorry, Max. I didn't mean to pry. It's just... oh, never mind. Forget I even said anything."

"What is it, Molly?" Max asked.

"It just seems like there may be something there, for you at least, that is beyond friendship with Angie. You don't have to tell us if you don't want to."

"It's okay. I don't mind, but I honestly didn't want to admit it in front of anyone just yet, or at all for that matter. I've had a huge crush on Angelina for a long time. Well, since I met her in Kindergarten. I never said anything because I thought I wasn't good enough for her. I gave up when she fell in love with Chad. I figured I would never have a chance to tell her how I felt."

"She's all yours now, my friend," I said as I patted him on the shoulder.

"Gee, thanks," he said. "I'm not going to pursue anything with her, though. I don't want to be a rebound that she goes for because she's trying to get over you. I may not feel like I'm good enough for her, but I know I'm better than being a rebound."

"Max, you are good enough for me." Angelina was standing right behind him. None of us even noticed her walk up and had no idea how long she'd been standing there because we were all focused on Max. "You're good enough for any girl you decide to date. Truth be told, you're probably too good for them, and even too good for me. I told you I'd never use you as a rebound. You're better than that. Anyway, I've decided to take some time to myself for a while. I'm not going to date anyone until I'm fully ready to move on. I owe that to myself and whoever I do decide to pursue a relationship with later on. Maybe then, if you're still single, Max, and still have a crush on me, maybe we could go out sometime. Well, I just thought I'd let y'all know about my decision. So, I'm just going to go now."

She turned on her heel and left without another word. We were all stunned into silence until Molly finally spoke up.

"Well, that was awkward. I'm sorry I put you on the spot like that, Max. Are you okay?"

"Yeah, I'm okay. You didn't do anything wrong. I told Angelina about my crush on her while I was walking her to one of her classes. I also told her I didn't want to be just a rebound. I guess that's why she came to tell us about her decision."

"Well, at least she knows now, and it sounded to me like she may be interested in you too," Molly said.

"We'll see. I'm not counting on anything. I'm sure she'll have other offers by the time she's ready to move on."

"I've noticed a pattern when I've healed other Nymphs. I can sense their souls calling out to their mates for comfort. Although, I can't always see who their mate is as I did with Lilly. I think Angie may have been calling out to her mate as well. Just be careful, Max. I don't want to see you get attached to Angie and get hurt in case she finds her chosen mate, and he isn't you."

Max sighed and said, "That's the risk we all take when we fall in love with someone before we are reunited with our chosen mates."

"Oh, Max," Paisley said. "You deserve to be loved by someone who will appreciate how wonderful you truly are. I know it isn't up to me or any of us to say, but I'm not sure that Angelina is that girl."

"The crush I had on her wasn't just because of her beauty. That was only a small part of it. Maybe she'll come around; maybe she won't. I'm not getting my hopes up either way. I'm not going to sit around moping either. I've got better things to do. Speaking of better things to do, I'm going to head to class. I'll see y'all later."

"Later, Max."

The bell rang for the third period. I walked Paisley to her class and then hurried to English Literature. I walked in and saw Angie sitting in the seat next to mine. I tried to act like I didn't care that she was even there. I sat down, got my book out of my backpack, and waited for the teacher to start our lesson.

"Can we talk?" Angie asked.

"Sure. What's on your mind?"

"I know, Chad."

"You know what, Angie?"

"I know that you and Paisley already completed your bond."

"What?!"

"Come on, Chad. Don't play dumb. It was never one of your strong suits. I saw how your connection with her had gotten stronger, especially when I tried to start a fight between you two. A connection on that level has to mean you've already bonded. I think that's what made me faint like that. It was such a shock. I guess it was too much for me to handle at the time because I felt like I was too late. I honestly thought I could get you to come back to me."

"I know you did, but I told you that was never going to happen. I'm in love with her, Angie. She's my everything. Please, I'm begging you. Don't tell anyone that you know."

"Don't worry, your secret is safe with me. I'm not going to say anything to anyone else about it. Your completed bond is the reason I've decided to move on. There's nothing left for us. "

"Thank you, Angie. You don't know how much I appreciate it, but you will someday. Your chosen mate is out there. You'll know what I'm talking about when you find one another."

"That's another reason I'm taking time to myself. I want to make sure I'm ready to fully move on with whoever he is and put us in the past. It wouldn't be fair to him or me if I continue to hold onto something that isn't there anymore. I'm letting go, Chad. I want you and Paisley to be happy together. You deserve to be happy. I promise not to stand in the way of that."

"Thank you, Angie."

"You're welcome."

"Paisley, sweetheart?"

"Yes, my love?"

"Angie knows about us completing our bond."

"What? How?"

"She figured it out in the quad. She saw how strong our connection has gotten and figured it out for herself. She said our secret is safe. She's not going to say anything to anyone."

"Are you sure?"

"Yeah. I'm sure. We can trust Angie. She's letting me go, Paisley. She told me that she wants us to be happy and won't stand in the way."

"Oh, Chad! That's wonderful! I think she's doing the right thing by taking time to herself to let her heart mend. You never know. Her chosen mate may pop up at any moment."

"This is true. Fate does have its own agenda."

"Yeah, no kidding."

Paisley

The scrimmage football game is about to start. I found Molly in the crowd, and we snagged some excellent seats in the bleachers. The guys were still in the field house, waiting to be announced. Angie was readying her squad and going over the list of cheers for the evening. She looked up into the stands, waved at us, and flashed us her brilliant smile.

It's been a few days since we have seen her smile. We were all pretty worried about her. She's going to be okay now. I'm glad she's finally letting Chad go. I do consider her as my friend. I hated seeing her in so much pain. We noticed she'd been crying a lot and looked as though she wasn't sleeping much either. We knew she was having a rough time when we'd seen her at school without makeup on. I'd never even seen her with a single hair out of place, much less without makeup on. She always looked the part of absolute perfection. There wasn't a single girl in our school that wasn't secretly jealous of her. It's good to see her getting back to normal.

The announcer came over the loudspeakers and introduced our football team and then the opposing team. The chorus teacher performed the National Anthem. Then, the team captains went out to the fifty-yard line for the coin toss. Our team won the toss and opted to defer to the second half.

Molly has a way of manipulating the elements. I've seen her use the wind to blow a breeze on the players to keep them cool during their practices on hot days. I've also seen her use her powers to help our team in other ways. I've seen her keep the players from getting hurt, and she's healed them when they did get injured during practices. Toby, her chosen mate, is our star quarterback. She protects him most of all, but she also looks after Max and Chad.

Our team took possession of the ball. A massive player on the opposing team was heading straight for Toby. Molly used the wind to slow the player down to give Toby a chance to get out of his way and pass the ball.

I nudged her, giggled, and whispered to her, "I saw what you did there."

"Shhh. You saw nothing. Besides, if I can't sack that quarterback, no one else gets to either. Hahaha!"

"Oh, my gosh! That's hilarious! Hahaha!"

Then another massive player went for Max near the end zone after he'd caught Toby's pass. Molly slowed him down, so Max could make it out of his way and score a touchdown.

"Uh-huh. I saw that too," I said.

"What? I couldn't just let him plow into Max! That guy is huge!"

"That's what she said!" We said it simultaneously and just started laughing hysterically.

I love hanging out with Molly. We always have so much fun. We laughed together and enjoyed the rest of the game. She swore me to secrecy not to tell anyone what she'd done to manipulate the game in our favor. Our team won thirty-four to six. We all went out after the game for some fancy milkshakes.

Chad and I had plans afterward. Our weekend curfew was later than on school nights so that we could catch a late showing at the theater in the Randolph Mall. We'd taken my MINI Cooper back to my house and hopped in Chad's truck to meet up with everyone else. We finished our milkshakes, said our goodbyes to everyone, and headed to the mall.

I had no idea what movies were playing, but I didn't care either. I just wanted to spend time with Chad. We hadn't seen a movie together yet, so I figured tonight was an excellent opportunity for a movie night. We decided to see the new *Fast and Furious* movie. Chad bought our tickets, and I secured a place in the line at the concession stand. We got our buttered popcorn and a Cherry Coke Icee and made our way into the theater.

The theater was nearly empty. We chose two seats in the center of the very top row. Perfect. Those were always my favorite seats. We climbed the steps and sat down as the previews were starting. Chad draped his arm around my shoulders and pulled me closer to him. The spark and tingles coursed through my body and lingered within me. We snuggled together and got comfortable, nibbled on our movie snacks, and watched the previews.

Chad nuzzled my hair away from my ear and nibbled it. Then, he trailed kisses down the curve of my jaw to my lips. I turned towards him and yielded to his kiss. Our lips embraced, and our tongues swirled. I felt Chad's hands begin to roam. I felt him caressing one of my breasts over my clothes. My bud constricted, and I longed to feel his lips on it.

"Chad, my love?"

"Yes, sweetheart?"

"I want you so much."

"I want you too, Paisley, so much it hurts."

"Do you want to skip out on the movie and go somewhere more private?"

"No. Not just yet. I want to tease you a little longer."

"The tingles are working in your favor."

"Good. 'Cause those tingles are about to get a bit more intense."

"Is that so?"

I felt Chad's other hand slide up my thigh and cup my sex. The spark and tingles were more intense, indeed. They surged straight to my already throbbing bundle of nerves. I had to hold my breath to keep from moaning. The sensations were almost too much to bear quietly. His mouth was still on mine; our kiss was full of longing and need.

"Ah! Chad! Oh, my God, yes!"

A low growl rumbled in Chad's chest. *"Mine. All mine."*

"Yes, my love. I'm all yours."

Chad removed his hand from my sex and eased his hand upward. With just one finger, he left a trail of tingles and sizzling heat up to my breast. His thumb circled my aroused bud through the fabric of my shirt and my bra. He gently pinched it, and I whimpered into his mouth. The spark and tingles continued to surge and course through my body. It was time to give him a dose of his own medicine and see how long he could hold out. I slid my hand along his thigh, cupped the massive bulge in the front of his jeans, and gave him a light squeeze. I felt the spark and tingles as they traveled from my hand through his jeans and into his throbbing erection. Chad nearly jumped when the spark and tingles hit him.

"Two can play this game, my love."

Another low growl rumbled in his chest. *"You're playing a very dangerous game, sweetheart. Are you sure you want to play?"*

"Yes, my love. I'm sure."

"Don't tease me, woman. You know there's a chance I'll lose control. I don't want to hurt you."

"You won't, honey. I trust you."

"Paisley, I don't know what it is about you. I've never felt like this with anyone. When we are together, some kind of 'beast' awakens inside me. It's like 'the beast' takes over, and I lose all control."

"Yeah, I've noticed. It's okay. I like that 'beast' of yours. As crazy as it seems, I feel like I'm different when I'm with you too. Outside of

our relationship, I'm headstrong, independent, spunky, and a bit of a smart ass. When I'm with you, all I want to do is submit to your every whim and satisfy your needs and desires."

"I never wanted to change a single thing about you, except for your last name. I love everything about you, Paisley."

"I love everything about you too, Chad. I need you more and more each day. I crave you. You are so addicting. I feel like an addict in need of another fix."

"That's exactly the way I feel about you too, Paisley. I crave your touch, your scent, your flavor on my tongue, and the way you feel when I'm inside you."

"Oh, Chad, how are we supposed to survive living apart from one another until after graduation? If our connection gets much stronger, it's going to get harder and harder to be apart."

"Toby moved into one of Molly's parent's spare bedrooms so they could be near one another. All of our rooms are taken at my place, but maybe we could convince your folks to allow me to move into the spare room there."

"I highly doubt that'll go over well. We may have to look into getting our own place and go through with a winter wedding over Christmas break after all."

"That's still not a bad idea. I think we could do it. Rent is cheap enough around here.

We could get an apartment or a duplex somewhere between Troy and school. A lot of places base the rent amount upon your income. Let's look into it and see if we can qualify for a place. If we can, we can get the process started, save up some money to get married, and move in together. We can both work part-time to afford it, and we can still finish school."

"I'll put in applications around Troy to see what I can find for work. I heard they are looking for a waitress at the Golf Club Grille, the diner, and the cafe on Main Street. I may have a shot at one of them, at least."

"Great idea, sweetheart. I can't stand to be away from you. I'm ready for you to be my wife, have you by my side every day, and in my bed each night."

"That sounds amazing, my love!"

We finished watching the movie in one another's arms and then headed towards Troy so that Chad could take me home. We stopped along the way, of course, to take advantage of the heat that all of our teasing had built up. Chad turned down a side road. He parked the truck and laid me down on the seat. He took off my sandals, pulled my jeans and panties off, and tossed them into the floorboard.

"I want to taste you, sweetheart." His mouth clamped down on my bundle of nerves before I could draw in another breath. Colors swirled around us as pleasure began to build. I ran my fingers through his hair and writhed against him as I soared into climax.

"Ah! Yes, Chad! Please, don't stop! Oh, God! Yes!"

"That's it. Let go for me. You taste so good, sweetheart. You are so sweet, but I'm nowhere near done with you, Paisley." He sucked and nipped at my sensitive flesh as vibrant colors continued to swirl around us.

Chad's fingers found my little sensitive bud and began to circle it once again. He reached down and unfastened his belt and his jeans, then pulled them down. Then, Chad picked me up and sat me on his lap, so I was straddling him. I took him inside me and began to ride him as hard and as fast as I could. Chad squeezed my butt and then gripped my hips. He lifted me and slammed me down on him even harder. I moaned and screamed his name.

"Oh! Chad! Yes!"

Then, he lifted me and sat me on my hands and knees on the seat of the truck. He positioned himself behind me and seated himself inside me once again. He pulled my hips towards him as he continued to slam harder and faster into me. My whimpers, squeals, and screams of pleasure mixed with his moans and groans. A deep growl rumbled in his chest, and we soared together. Both of our bodies spasmed as an earth-shattering climax surged through us. Chad withdrew himself from me, and we both collapsed in the seat of his truck. The swirling colors disappeared as we came down from our bliss. We sat there, holding one another for just a while longer before he took me home.

If our plan worked out, it'd only be a few more months before we'd be heading to our place together after date nights like this one, instead of having to spend nights alone in our parents' houses. There'd be no need to sneak around to make love either. We'd be able to do so in the privacy of our own home. It kills me to have to be away from him. As I lay in my bed, I can only imagine how wonderful it will be to spend the night wrapped in his arms and wake up seeing his handsome face. I stared at my ceiling, thinking of Chad and how much I love him and need him in my life.

Chapter 13

Chad

Well, that settles it. I'm going to buy Paisley a ring, and propose to her the right way, as soon as possible. She'll be spending the day with my family tomorrow. I will be working the early shift at the marina. I have enough money in my savings account to buy her a beautiful ring and still have money left over to put toward getting a place together.

"I'm home, sweetheart. I have to be at work for the early shift in the morning, so I probably won't see you when you get here to spend the day with my family."

"I'm glad you made it home safely, my love. Would you like me to bring you something for breakfast on my way there? I'll be having breakfast with your family in the morning, but I'm coming through Troy on my

way to you. I don't mind grabbing you something and bringing it to you. Not to mention, I'll be able to see you for a few minutes before I head to your house. Your mom wants me there as long as possible before you come in from work. I guess they want to have me all to themselves for a while."

"That sounds amazing! Thank you, sweetheart. I'd greatly appreciate a sausage and egg biscuit and a medium coffee."

"Cream and sugar for your coffee?"

"Yes, please. I like my coffee like I like my mate; sweet, hot, and creamy."

"Hahaha! Sounds about right."

"Damn skippy! I've got the hottest woman alive as my mate. You're so hot, Paisley. I'm getting all hot and bothered again, just thinking about you."

"The feeling is mutual, I assure you. I miss you already, honey."

"I miss you too, sweetheart. We'll be together again before too long. We'll have our place and won't have to spend any more nights alone."

"I can hardly wait! Falling asleep in your arms is going to be so amazing. Just imagine those tingles soothing us to sleep after making love to the point of sheer exhaustion."

"Don't tease me, woman. I'm so turned on; I wouldn't put it past me to sneak into your window and take you again and again. I'd be exhausted at work tomorrow, but it'd be worth it."

"I wish we had powers like Molly does. We could just pop in and out without anyone even knowing we're gone."

"Maybe one day, they'll find something in the Ancient Texts to restore all of our powers. Maybe then, we'd have a chance of having at least one cool power."

"You've got one helluva power over me, Chad Greene."

"As do you over me, Paisley O'Riley."

"I'm so in love with you, Chad. I can't imagine life without you in it."

"Oh, Paisley. I'm so in love with you, too. I wouldn't want to live a life without you in it. As your chosen and bonded mate, I promise to keep you safe to my best ability, even if it means risking my life to save yours."

"I hope it never comes to that, but I'd protect you the same way."

"I know you would, sweetheart. Try to get some rest. You've got a big day tomorrow. I'm sure my siblings are going to try their best to wear you out. They are a rowdy duo sometimes."

"I can't wait to spend time with your family, Chad. They are already my family, you know. We are bonded now. Our lives are joined as one."

"Thank goodness! Could you imagine how unruly I'd be with 'the beast' inside me if we'd not bonded yet? The urge to bond would've eventually driven me mad with rage and aggression."

"I admit that I'm attracted and even drawn to that 'beast' inside you, but I'm not so sure you wouldn't have scared me away eventually, hahaha!"

"Nah, I think it would've been so prominent that your urge to bond with me would've taken over you, too. You would've *probably felt the need to satisfy 'the beast' and tame me like you're so good at doing."*

"I do enjoy taming that 'beast.' As a matter of fact, I can't wait to tame you again. We may have to find some time to be alone tomorrow night, too."

"As I said, don't tease me, woman. I may just take you up on that. Just don't let 'the beast' get too out of hand and hurt you in the process. I would never forgive myself if that happened."

"I know, my love. I know you'd be able to take back over if I wanted you to. I'd just have to tell you to go easier on me mind-to-mind. I trust you, Chad. I know in my soul and yours that you'd never hurt me."

"I'm glad you trust me so much, Paisley. You have more faith and trust in me than I've ever felt from anyone in my entire life, and that's really saying something, you know."

"You truly are wonderful, honey."

"Thank you, sweetheart, and so are you."

"I'm going to take you up on that idea to get some rest, though. I am pretty tired."

"Me too. I'll talk to you soon, sweetheart. I love you, Paisley. Good night and sweet dreams."

"I love you too, Chad. Good night and sweet dreams, my love."

I need to talk to Dad about this aggression I'm feeling getting stronger inside me. I won't tell him about bonding with Paisley or my fear of hurting her, but I will talk to him about the need to possess her and make her mine. There has to be more to it than the *urge* to bond. If it were just that, it'd be gone by now. I'll see if I can pull him aside tomorrow after work and chat with him in private. I don't want Paisley to overhear it because I'd rather be able to tell her myself if there's something wrong with me than for her to overhear it. I closed my eyes to tried to get some rest. All I could think about was the rising aggression of "the beast" inside me. I have to find a way to control it before it gets out of hand. I'm hoping Dad will have some sort of answer for me. Otherwise, I may have to get ahold of a copy of the Ancient Texts and find it myself. Surely, there's something in there about what I'm feeling and why. I finally drifted off to sleep with thoughts of Paisley running through my mind.

Paisley

My alarm went off bright and early at 6:00 a.m. I opened one eye just enough to find the alarm clock and turn off its buzzer. I stretched and headed into the bathroom to get a shower to wake up a bit more. I knew Chad would be awake by now, so I sent him a good morning message, mind-to-mind.
        "Good morning, my love. Did you sleep well?"

"Hey! Good morning, sweetheart! You're up awfully early. Yes, I slept very well, thanks to dreaming about my sexy woman."

"Hahaha! What a coincidence! I dreamed about you, too, sexy!"

"Hmm, imagine that. I can't wait to see you when you stop by the marina."

"Uh-huh. Sure. You're just ready for some breakfast."

"That has a tiny bit to do with it, but I'm looking forward to getting a few of those kisses of yours. I'm craving strawberries this morning, and the real thing doesn't even compare to you, Paisley."

"Well, I think I can bring some of those with me, then. I'm in the shower now and will be leaving before too long."

"Enjoy your shower, sweetheart, and I'll see you when you get to the marina."

"Okay, honey. I'll see you soon."

I finished getting ready, packed my day bag with my swimsuit, sunscreen, a towel, hairbrush, deodorant, and some perfume to freshen up with before Chad gets home. I left a message on the dry-erase board for my parents, letting them know I'd left for Chad's house. They know I'm going over there to spend time with his family, but it never hurts to let them know when I'd left and where I'd be just in case anything happened. I dropped the top on my MINI Cooper and drove into Troy to grab Chad some breakfast. I made sure to ask for enough cream and sugar for both of our coffees. It wasn't long before I was westbound with the top down.

I pulled into the marina and found a spot near the front door. I grabbed the coffees and Chad's biscuit and headed inside. A few guys were shopping in the convenience store when I walked in. One of them walked up to me and kept getting closer, trying to back me against a wall.

"Hey, there, pretty lady. What do we have here?"

"Just some breakfast for my boyfriend."

"Awe, well isn't that sweet. I wasn't expecting this, but I do believe I'll take it."

"Chad! Help! I'm in the store at the marina. My hands are full, and this guy won't leave me alone! He's trying to pin me against the wall."

"Oh, no, you won't! The only thing you'll be doing is leaving. Now!" A deep growl rumbled in Chad's chest as he grabbed the guy and threw him out the door.

The guy stumbled, regained his balance, and shouted at Chad, "You don't know who you're messing with, but you will soon enough!"

"Take your threats somewhere else," Chad shouted back at him. "Are you all right, sweetheart?"

"Yes, honey, I am now. My big strong boyfriend came to my rescue."

Chad wrapped his arms around me and kissed my lips. "I'll always come to your rescue, Paisley. You're my whole world now."

"And you're mine. Thank you for taking care of that guy. He was way too close for comfort."

"Any closer and I'm afraid to say what I would've done to him. I can't stand the thought of any man touching you but me, Paisley. It infuriates me to think about it. All I saw was red. 'The beast' inside me wanted to hurt him very badly."

"I know, my love. I sensed it. I felt the rage inside you."

"Just like I sense 'the beast' inside you when we make love. That's how I know you'll never hurt me. 'The beast' may be ferocious, with an appetite for rough sex, but it's also incredibly protective over me. I feel it, Chad. I'm not afraid."

"I'm just glad you're all right. I don't know what would've happened if he'd hurt you in any way."

"He didn't, though, because you were here to save me. Thank you, my love."

"You're welcome, sweetheart."

"Here, let's go sit down so you can enjoy your breakfast."

"Thank you for bringing it to me. You're the absolute best girlfriend I could ever imagine having. Thank goodness you're all mine."

We sat down at the counter, and Chad added the cream and sugar to his coffee. He sucked it down and devoured his biscuit. He really was hungry. Maybe I should've gotten him a second one.

"Still hungry, my love?"

"Nah, sweetheart. I'm full now. Thank you again for my breakfast. That hit the spot. I don't know why I was so hungry. I wasn't until

I felt the rage set in. Then, it was like I was ravenous all of a sudden. I've got to find out what's going on with this inner 'beast' thing. I wonder if my dad would know what's going on?"

"He just might."

"I hope he does. I was planning on talking to him after work. You may trust 'the beast' inside me, but I'm not so sure you should. I'm not even sure that I do."

"Don't make any assumptions just yet. It could be something with a perfectly good explanation. Maybe it's nothing more than you coming into sexual maturity, for instance."

"Very true. I'll talk to Dad today after work. I'll call him on the way home, so he'll be ready for our chat."

"I think that's a wonderful idea. Well, I suppose I'd better head that way. I don't want them to worry about me."

"Come on, sweetheart. I'll walk you to your car. I'd hate to know that douchebag is still out there waiting on you to walk out alone."

Luckily, the guy had left, but Chad's hackles were still standing up on the back of his neck. He was hyper-alert. I sensed it and felt his uneasiness. Chad opened my car door for me and gave me a searing hot goodbye kiss. I stepped inside, and he closed my door.

"Please be careful, sweetheart. Let me know when you get there safely, so I won't worry."

"I promise I will. I want you to be careful and stay safe too, honey. I worry about you too, you know."

"Yes, I know. I sense you too. I know when something's off. That's how I knew to get to you, even before I heard you calling out to me. I was down at the docks. I started running the second I felt you becoming uncomfortable."

"Thank you again, honey. I appreciate you coming to my aid."

"I told you I'd protect you with my life. I mean it, Paisley."

"I know, Chad. Thank you, but I hope it never comes to that. I'll see you when you get home, my love."

"I love the sound of coming home to you. I can't wait until the day that I'll be coming home to you at our place."

"I know, honey, me too. It's going to be so wonderful!"

"Agreed. You'd better get going, though, or I'll keep you here with me all day."

"Hahaha! Okay, I'll see you soon, my love."

I cranked my car and drove out of the parking lot towards Chad's house. The radio is blaring my favorite playlist from my phone, the sun is shining, and the wind is blowing through my hair. It is going to be a beautiful day at the lake. I can't wait to spend it with Chad's family. I already know I'll love them. I just hope they love me too.

I pulled into their driveway a few minutes later, and Tabby ran out to my car to help me bring in my bag.

"Hey, Paisley! I'm so happy you're here!"

"Hey, Tabby! I'm glad your mom invited me over."

"We've wanted to get to know you since we found out you were Chad's chosen mate. I thought for sure it'd be Angie, but then again, I'm happy it's you instead."

"Well, between you and me, I'm happy it's me too."

Tabby giggled and said, "Come on! Mama's got breakfast going. It'll be ready in a few minutes."

The smell of bacon, eggs, and french toast greeted me as Tabby opened the door for us to go inside. Chad's mom, Shannon, was scraping a heap of scrambled eggs into a large bowl.

"Hello, Paisley! Thank you so much for coming to spend the day with us. We've been waiting on this day all week."

"Thank you for inviting me. I've been looking forward to it too."

"Chad's told us so much about you, we almost feel like we already know you, but we still wanted to have the day with you all to ourselves. Trevor had to go out on a quick call, but he's just pulling into the driveway now."

Shannon didn't even look out the window. She just knew he was there. She sensed him. I love being able to sense Chad. It makes the distance between us seem not so far apart.

Trevor walked in and headed straight for Shannon. He wrapped his arms around her from behind and nuzzled her neck. Most bonded, chosen mates remain in love for all eternity. Seeing them together like that reminds me of my parents and the loving bond they share. Mom and Dad are always affectionate. There has never been a lack of love in our home.

"I sure hope you're hungry, Paisley," Trevor said. "Shannon has whipped up quite the spread this morning."

"Oh, I am. Everything looks and smells delicious! Thank you again for having me over today."

"You're practically part of the family. You're welcome here anytime. You make sure Chad doesn't hog you all to himself and brings you around more often, all right?"

"I'll try to keep him in line, Mr. Greene."

"Call me Trevor, or Dad, if you want. I already consider you my daughter-in-law."

"Thank you. It feels good to know you want me here, and that I'm welcome. I was worried y'all wouldn't like me because I'm not Angie. I know they were together for a long time."

"Yes, they were, but we, well, Trevor and I have known about you much longer. We just couldn't tell him or anyone else until fate stepped in and awakened your connection. We wanted y'all to find one another and fall in love naturally, as we all have with our chosen mates in our family for generations."

"I'm glad we did. I'm so very deeply in love with Chad. I'd had a huge crush on him for years but had given up when I'd thought he was in love with Angie. I moved on and fell in love with Max, or at least I'd thought I was in love with Max. Now that Chad and I have fallen in love, I know what true love is."

"We couldn't agree more. You don't know how badly we hoped it would happen sooner, but we couldn't be happier that it's finally happened for you two."

"Shannon here has been humming the wedding march since Chad told us your connection awakened."

"Hahaha! I'm looking forward to our wedding too. I've been having dreams about our wedding just about every night. I never was the kind of girl to put that much thought into finding 'the one' and getting married. I always just went with the flow, and if something happened, great. It not, no biggie. Now, all of that has changed. I can't wait to become Chad's wife and change my name to Paisley O'Riley Greene."

"Oh, I'm so happy I could cry. I'm gaining such a wonderful daughter-in-law!"

"I think so too." Trevor said, "Well, let's grab our plates and dig into this fabulous breakfast before it gets cold. We can tell Paisley stories about Chad's childhood and show her some home movies and plenty of embarrassing photos afterward."

"Is that why you wanted me all to yourselves with him at work? Oh, he's going to be so mad. Hahaha! I love it!"

"I'm sure he suspects that is just what we'd planned to do with you. We've been threatening to do so all week," Shannon said.

"He told us that you'd find out eventually, and for us to have fun, but not too much fun at his expense," Trevor said.

I laughed and said, "He's such a good sport."

"He is a great kid," Shannon said. "I think we did a pretty good job of raising him."

"Yes, you sure did. I definitely could've done much worse when I picked my chosen mate, that's for sure."

"Well, we already know Chad. So, tell us all about you, Paisley," Shannon said.

I didn't know where to start, so I started as far back as I could remember. I told them about my family, my favorite things, hobbies, interests, and a few of the things I dislike. That list is super small anyway. I've always tried to be easy going and even easier to please. They took turns telling me about themselves too.

Chad's siblings are pretty awesome. Tabby is growing into a beautiful young lady. She has Chad's black hair and the same amber and honey-colored eyes but favors her mom. Tabby's chosen mate is a lucky fellow, whoever he may be. Garrett looks like Chad's mini-me, but with his mom's light brown hair and green eyes. He has a great personality too. He's so down to earth and carefree, yet has a silly streak that'll have you laughing at any given moment.

Chad's mom walked over to a bookshelf and retrieved a stack of photo albums. They were serious about taking me down memory lane with Chad's childhood photos. Oh boy, this should be interesting.

"Oh, honey?"

"Yes, sweetheart?"

"I'm about to take a stroll down memory lane with your mom and a huge stack of photo albums."

"Oh, no."

"Oh, yes."

"Hahaha! Have fun, but just know that I will get to do the same thing with your mom and all of your childhood photos someday too."

"Ugh, so true. I'm sure she can hardly wait."

"I'm sure my mom has been waiting to do this with you my whole life."

"She has known about our connection since then, huh?"

"That she has. I still don't know how they kept everything a secret for so long."

"Me either, but I'm so glad the cat's out of the bag."

"You and me too, sweetheart. I'll be home in a few short hours. Have fun. I love you and can't wait to see you."

"I'm having a blast so far! I love you too, and can't wait to see you either."

"Come on over here and have a seat next to me, Paisley. I have so much to show you."

"I'll bet Chad was such cutie when he was little."

"Oh, he sure was, but I'm quite biased. See for yourself."

Shannon and I went through every single album. I think I fell even deeper in love with Chad than I ever thought was possible. I can also imagine us starting a family together someday. Someday further down the road, but definitely someday. He truly was a precious little boy.

There were several pictures of him playing various sports throughout the years. He's always been so athletic and excelled in every sport he played. There were lots of trophies lining the shelves in the family room. Most of them were Chad's. He played baseball, football, and basketball. His little brother, Garrett, is following right in his brother's footsteps, excelling in the same sports. Their sister, Tabby, is a skilled gymnast and loves cheerleading as well.

I enjoyed going through the photo albums with his mom. Shannon and I had already formed a mother-in-law to daughter-in-law bond. I felt as though I was being welcomed right into their family with open arms. She even set up a camera on a tripod to take some new photos to add to the album. She and I took a few shots together, as well as a few pictures with everyone else. She said we'd take more when Chad got home. She wanted to document the moment I was welcomed into the family from the very beginning but had to wait for obvious reasons.

She had pictures of Mama and her together while they were pregnant. Those were hidden in a separate photo album with other photos of Trevor and Daddy when they worked together. I'd have never guessed they were all close friends back then. They'd had to separate us and conceal their friendship so Chad and I would be brought together by fate. I do wish that we'd been brought together sooner, but I can't complain, because at least we are together now.

Garrett and Tabby were getting restless and wanted to go swimming. So, we all put on our swimsuits and went down to the water. Shannon brought her camera, and we all took turns cannonballing and diving off the top of the boathouse. We took so many photos of all of us being silly and having fun together. We were still swimming when Chad pulled in on one of their jet skis.

"Hey, sweetheart! Oh, my! You are a sight for sore eyes in that bikini! Wow!"

"Hey, honey! Why don't you go put on your swimming trunks and join us?"

"I think I will. I want to talk to Dad first, though. Is he here?"

"Yeah, I think he went inside to grab some cold water bottles. You may be able to catch him before he comes back out."

"I'll be back shortly, sweetheart." Chad leaned down and pressed his lips to mine in a brief, but searing kiss.

"I'm looking forward to it, my love."

Chapter 14

Chad

I hurried up the hillside to the house. I need to talk to Dad in private. I have to tell him what was going on inside me and see if he can answer my questions.

"Hey, Dad, where are you?"

"I'm in the kitchen, son."

"I'm glad I caught you. I need to talk to you about something that's been bothering me here lately. I'm hoping you can help me."

"What is it, son? You can talk to me about anything; you know that. If I don't have any answers for you, you know I'll do anything and everything in my power to find them."

"Thanks, Dad." I took a deep breath and sighed. "Well, as you know, Paisley and I are already eighteen. The *urge* to bond is setting in and is getting stronger each day."

"That's natural, Son. You're chosen mates. The *urge* is just going to get harder to fight as time goes on."

"Yes, I get that, and I find myself fighting it harder and harder all the time. I know we should try to stay away from one another to keep from completing our bond, but I can't stand to be away from her for very long."

"I wouldn't say you should avoid spending time together. That could prove to be quite painful for you both. You'll crave one another's closeness and will need to be near one another for the sake of your sanities."

"Why is that?"

"Being away from one another for too long can begin to drive chosen mates a bit crazy once their connection awakens."

"I'm already going crazy, Dad."

"Tell me what's going on. It may just be increased hormones now that you've reached sexual maturity, and it could be something else entirely. Either way, I'll need details to know how to proceed."

I know I can't exactly give my dad all of the details, like the fact that Paisley and I have already completed our bond, for example. However, I need to tell him exactly how I feel when 'the beast' inside me takes over. "Well, I sometimes feel like there's a savage 'beast' inside me."

"What do you mean, and when do you feel this way?"

"It feels like someone else is inside me, Dad. Someone aggressive, possessive, overprotective, and even full of rage at times. It happens when I'm with Paisley. When we touch or kiss, or when I hold her in my arms. I've also felt it when other guys have tried to touch her or get too close to her. It seems like all I want to do is possess her and make her mine. I know the *urge* will make me want to complete our bond, but it seems much more primal, more aggressive than that."

"Well, I have to be honest with you. I had a feeling you'd be next in line to experience this."

"Experience this, what, Dad? Why am I feeling this way?"

"You come from a long line of Royal Guardians. Our bloodline was chosen to protect the Royal Family, and ours of course, at all costs. 'The beast' inside you, as you call it, is making you feel this way because the Royal Family is currently without your protection. Molly and Toby are to become our next Queen and Prince Consort of our people. Now that the connection with your chosen mate has awakened, she is without proper protection as well. She must also be protected at all costs. You are to become the new leader of the Royal Guard, but you've not had any training, and you're not prepared to take on this responsibility just yet. Your training must be underway at once. You and I will be spending a lot more time together so that you're fully prepared. I'll call Taggart to assist me. It appears that Molly won't be the only Nymph in your generation with powers, after all. This 'beast' you feel inside you also comes with great power."

"So, let me get this straight. I'm supposed to be the Royal Guard's new leader, and I'll have great power? What great power?"

"Your power is one of perception. You'll feel danger coming before it draws near. In time, you'll see a vision of impending danger. You'll know how to thwart it beforehand, so you can react in time to protect your charges. This power was granted to our bloodline centuries ago when our original kingdom was raided. The first Royal Guardian, our ancestor, who protected the Royal Family and got them to safety, was granted this power from the Ancients. It would then be passed through his bloodline for all eternity. This is a great responsibility, Chad. Our people will be counting on you."

"So, how do I control this 'beast' inside me so I don't accidentally hurt Paisley? I fear that most of all. I would never forgive myself if I ever hurt her."

"We'll have to begin your training immediately and move up your wedding ceremony to occur as soon as possible. The need to possess her should ease after you two are wed and your bond is completed. Your need to bond with her will override any other need you are feeling until then. Your training will also ease that feeling as well because you'll be more prepared to step into your new responsibility."

"How am I going to protect Toby and Molly? Will Paisley and I have to move in with them?"

"No, Son. You will be required to live near them, though, so you can get to them at a moment's notice if need be. Molly will be able to summon you to them if you are too far away, but the closer you are to them, the easier it will be to protect them. You'll have to travel with them to Kilchoman, and anywhere else they need to travel around the world. Paisley may have to go too, so you can continue to keep her safe as well. If something happens to you, Tabby and then Garrett will inherit the power and will have to step in, but I'd rather not think of such a thing. You can do this, son. I have so much faith in you and will be here to guide you along the way."

"About the wedding... Paisley and I had briefly discussed a winter wedding over Christmas vacation since we are both eighteen. We'd need somewhere to live together afterward, and neither of us makes enough money to sustain a place of our own just yet or pay for a wedding for that matter."

"Let us worry about that. Everything will be just fine. Our family has plenty of money to take care of that. All you and Paisley will have to do is keep the utilities paid for and food on the table. Your job at the marina should bring in enough to do that until you fully take on your role for Molly and Toby. Then, your earnings will come from the Royal Family entirely."

"Thanks for talking with me, Dad. I do feel a little bit better about 'the beast,' but I admit I'm worried about taking on such a massive responsibility of being the leader of the Royal Guard. How many other guards will there be?"

"There will be several. They will be named before too long as well. They will be coming from all over the world, once Molly and Toby are wed, and their commencement ceremony is held. The Royal Guard will also have elder members such as Taggart and myself. Don't worry. You won't be alone, my son."

"You said the power was passed through our bloodline. Did you ever have it?"

"All of our powers have been dormant for a long time. I was the leader of the Royal Guard after my father retired, but neither of us ever had the power. We've passed the training down from one generation to the next, just in case the power did come back to one of us at some point in time. You, Chad, are the first in our bloodline to have this power in centuries. It's possible that your power awakened when Molly's did."

"What do I do now, Dad?"

"Go and enjoy the rest of the day with our family and your future bride. We'll begin your training first thing in the morning. You'll need your rest. Training begins at 0500 hours. That's 5:00 a.m. for civilians."

"Ouch, that's going to hurt. Hahaha!"

"It builds character. Hydrate, eat well, and rest up kiddo. You're going to need it." Dad chuckled under his breath and walked back outside with a cooler full of bottled water and ice.

I headed upstairs to change into my swimming trunks and flip flops. I grabbed a towel from the hall closet and headed down the stairs. I reached the bottom and realized I'd forgotten my phone in my room. I felt "the beast" inside me begin to panic. I walked into my room and looked out my bedroom window just in time to see Paisley do a cannonball off the top of the boathouse. I watched the water where she went in, waiting for her to emerge.

"Paisley? Sweetheart? Come up." Nothing. No response. *"You have to come up for air."*

Something is very wrong. She isn't coming back up. She isn't answering me. I reached out for her soul to sense her. She's unconscious! No! No, no, no! She's drowning! I can't let her die! I ran to the dock as fast as my legs would carry me, and dove in after her.

The water is murky. I can't see anything. I had to use my hands and feel my way around. I searched and searched. Nothing. I came up for a quick breath and went back down again. Nothing. I can't find her. My heart is pounding in my chest, and I'm panicking more than I ever have in my entire life. I took another deep breath and went down again. My precious Paisley is missing. Her life is dwindling. I have to find her before it's too late. I have to. I can't lose her. I just can't. I have to keep searching. I came up for yet another breath and went back down.

My hand just happened to run through Paisley's hair. I frantically felt around for her body and pulled her up to the surface. I lifted her for Dad to pull her out of the water. He laid her on the dock so that I could climb up with them. She was already turning blue. No! God, no!

"Mom! Call Molly! We need her! Now! She has to save Paisley. I can't lose her! Not now, not ever!"

Dad started doing CPR on Paisley, trying to get her to spit up the water and breathe again. She isn't responding. He kept going, refusing to stop. It isn't working. We are losing her. My sweet Paisley is dying right in front of me, and there is nothing else I can do to save her. My heart is pounding in my chest while hers remains still. If only I could do something, anything to make her breathe again. I sat beside Dad and held her hand while he continued to do CPR.

"She's not answering! Pick up, Molly! Answer your phone! Finally! Molly!"

"Hey, Mrs. Greene. How are you?"

"There's no time! We need you at our dock! Now! Paisley did a cannonball off the top of the boathouse and hit her head on something. She took in a lot of water before Chad got to her. Please, Molly! We need you to come and help her! Please, don't let her die, Molly!"

Molly and Toby appeared not even a split second later. Molly laid her hands on Paisley, and water began spurting from her mouth. We rolled her on her side, and she started coughing and gasping for air.

"Paisley, sweetheart, take it easy. You're all right now. You're safe, my love. I've got you. Molly, I think she may have hit her head on something down there in the water. There's blood in her hair. Would you mind checking it out too? Please?"

"Sure. I don't mind at all." Molly placed her hands on Paisley's head. "She's got a concussion. It's minor. I can heal her, but she may still feel its after-effects for a little while. Keep her awake for a few more hours. Make her take it easy and ensure she drinks plenty of fluids."

"Thanks, Molly. I owe you. I don't know what I'd have done if I'd lost her."

"Well, thankfully, we don't have to find out this time."

Paisley had stopped coughing and tried to speak. "Molly."

"Easy now, sweetheart."

"I'm fine, at least, I will be. Thank you for saving me, Molly."

"Chad pulled you from the water. His mom called me. I got here as soon as I could. Mr.

Greene was doing CPR on you when I got here to take over."

"Oh, Chad. Thank you, my love, and thank you too, Trevor and Shannon."

"I was worried, sick! I was afraid I wouldn't find you until it was too late if I was able to find you at all."

"I-I'm so sorry. I don't know what I hit down there. We'd jumped off the top quite a few times before then. I didn't think there was anything down there to hit."

"No more jumping off into the water anymore. Promise me! I can't lose you, Paisley."

"I promise."

"That goes for all of you. The current from the dam can move boulders the size of vehicles and carry fallen trees pretty far. It's not too outlandish to think that a log could be carried here. I don't want to think about that happening again, but with a worse outcome."

"Well, I guess we should go," Molly said.

"Thank you again for coming to help us, Molly and Toby. I don't know what I'd have done if you hadn't come."

"You're welcome. I'm just glad we were able to get here in time."

Everyone agreed not to jump off of the top deck into the water ever again. Toby and Molly popped back to wherever they were before. My family went inside to give Paisley and me some alone time together. I held Paisley in my arms as though it was the last time I'd ever hold her again.

Paisley

Life is so precious. I'd taken so much for granted in my short eighteen years. I was having fun and enjoying a beautiful Saturday in one moment, and nearly died in the next. I would've died if Chad hadn't have found me. I can't imagine the panic and fear he'd felt.

As I sit here on his family's dock in his arms, I can't help but think what would've happened if I'd died here today. We aren't just chosen mates anymore; we're bonded mates now. I was reckless with not only my own life but with his as well. Sure, I was only having some fun with his family, but none of us considered that there could be anything dangerous down there.

"I was so scared, Paisley. I was afraid I'd lost you. I called out to you mind-to-mind, but you didn't answer me. Then, I reached out to your soul to sense you. You were unconscious. I knew right then you were drowning and would die if I didn't find you. I panicked. I knew I had to keep looking for you. I had to find you. I would've never given up— never."

"I'm so sorry, my love. I wasn't thinking of how risky it was."

"I love you so much, Paisley, but I'd never really realized just how much until I'd nearly lost you forever. You are my everything. I don't want to live in a world without you in it."

"I love you too, Chad. More than life itself. I promise to be more careful. I'll never do anything stupid like this again. I'm so, so very sorry, my love."

"It's all right, sweetheart. If you only knew how many times I've jumped off the top of the boathouse, you'd probably yell at me. None of us knew there was anything down there until today. Hell, it may not have even washed in until just recently. Everything happens for a reason. Maybe this was meant to show us just how precious life is and that we have to protect and look out for one another."

I made a vow to myself right then and there. From here on, I will do everything in my power to avoid taking unnecessary risks. This life isn't just about me anymore. I have to consider what my choices will do to Chad now too. I nuzzled closer into his chest and squeezed him tighter.

Chad

Paisley's accident solidifies the need to keep her safe. I can't let anything like that happen to her again. Between today's accident and the incident at the Derby, I'd say that the love of my life is more than just a little accident-prone. No wonder I feel so overprotective of her. It's time to tell Paisley about my conversation with Dad.

"Sweetheart?"

"Yes, my love?"

"There's something I need to tell you. I talked to Dad about 'the beast' inside me."

"What did he say?"

"He said it has to do with a great responsibility that was passed down to me through my bloodline."

"What is it?"

"I'm next in line to become the new leader of the Royal Guard."

"That's wonderful and quite an honor. I don't understand what that has to do with you feeling like there's a 'beast' inside you, though."

"Well, it has to do with not being prepared to take on the responsibility and the need for it. Molly and Toby aren't as protected as they should be. That alone leaves me feeling unsettled inside. Now, add in the fact that I can't protect you as I should, and it makes it even worse. This responsibility came with power too."

"Power? Like Molly's?"

I explained everything to her the best way I knew how. I told her about how I will eventually be able to see danger coming and put a stop to it before it comes to pass.

"That's amazing!"

"I think that's why I was able to sense Angie's intention to start a fight in the hallway that day. I felt very protective over you before I even saw her coming. Before that, I'd felt protective over you at the Derby when you'd fallen, and our connection was awakened. Angie was verbally attacking you, and I stood up to her in the car on the way to The Alley. Dad thinks that my power was activated with Molly's powers. Otherwise, it's been dormant in our bloodline for a very long time."

"So, where does all of this leave us?"

"Dad thinks it's a good idea to move our wedding to Christmas break as we'd talked about earlier. He said it would help with the feeling I've had to possess you. Before you ask, no, he doesn't know that we've already completed our bond. He said that our wedding and completing the bond would ease that feeling. That, and the training I'll have to go through with him and your dad."

"Do we have to move in with Toby and Molly once they become Queen and Prince Consort? What about going to school and pursuing a career? I'm sorry for berating you with questions. I'm sure you have as many questions of your own, if not more, that are still unanswered."

"No, it's okay, sweetheart. We don't have to move in with them. We do have to live close to them, though. That way, I will be able to save them if I need to. We'll also have to go out of the country with them when they travel for meetings, training at Kilchoman, and anywhere else they have to go. As for school and a career, I could get a degree in antiterrorism with a minor in engineering.

Then, I could help design security measures to put in place to keep us all safe in case something big does happen. As far as making money goes, Dad said the Royal Family would pay me for my services, and that we'd be more than well taken care of."

"What about a place to live?"

"Dad said to leave that to him. He and Mom will take care of that for us. Our family served the Royal Family for a very long time, and has the resources to get a place for us around here near Toby and Molly."

"So, does this mean we are getting married in a few months?"

"Yes, it does. If that's okay with you."

"That's perfectly fine with me, my love."

"I'm going to buy you a ring. I want to make our engagement official as soon as possible."

"Oh, Chad, I'm so happy! I can't wait to marry you."

"I can't wait to marry you either, sweetheart."

There's no way I'll make it to a jewelry store in time after work tomorrow. My best bet is probably going to be a shopping trip tonight. I'll either have to cut my date with Paisley short or take her with me to pick out her ring. I know some women dream of being taken to a jewelry store to pick out their ring, while others like to be surprised. Angie is the kind of girl who'd love to pick out her ring, while Paisley is the kind of girl who would be happy with anything I chose for her. I could give her the option and see what she decides to do, though. That way, she won't feel like I deserted her for our date tonight.

"About our date tonight... Would you mind if we postponed it? Something's come up, and it's really important."

"Of course, my love. What is it? That is if you don't mind me asking."

"It's nothing bad, I promise. It's a surprise."

"Oh, all right. I won't worry then."

"I still don't want you to have to drive home, so we will get you and your car home safely."

"I'm feeling much better, but I understand your concern. Thank you, honey."

Paisley and I joined the rest of my family back at the house. I pulled Mom aside to talk to her about my plans for the evening. "Hey, Mom? Can I talk to you for a few minutes?"

"Sure, Son, what's on your mind?"

"I'm ready to buy Paisley an engagement ring. I talked to Dad earlier. I wasn't sure if he's told you yet, but Paisley and I will be getting married over Christmas break."

"Oh, how wonderful! When were you thinking of buying her ring?"

"I was thinking of going after supper tonight. Would you still like to go with me?"

"I'd love to. Have you thought of how you want to propose?"

"I was thinking of proposing with all of our friends and family members there somehow, or maybe somewhere special just the two of us. To be honest, I'm open to suggestions. What do you think would be romantic and special? I want to make it memorable so that we can tell our kids, grandkids, and their kids about it for many centuries."

"That's the one question everyone wants to know. 'How did he propose?'"

"Exactly! So, would you mind helping me plan the proposal too?"

"I'm sure we can come up with something special. When are you planning on proposing?"

"As soon as possible, but I'd like to talk to her dad first, of course. I want to do this the right way and ask for her hand. I'll be seeing him tomorrow morning for training. I may slip in that conversation as well."

"I wish you the best of luck. Although I doubt you'll need it. Trevor and Taggart have been waiting for you two to get together since you chose one another. You should have seen them. They looked like a pair of giddy schoolboys. They were so happy about you two becoming chosen mates. They celebrated for the longest time."

"Oh, yeah? Hahaha! That's awesome! I honestly do love Paisley, Mom."

"I know you do, Son. How could you not? She's beautiful, sweet, and she's so much fun to be around. Not to mention the whole chosen mate thing. You can't help falling in love with her."

"I'm thrilled y'all like her. It means a lot to both of us."

"We don't just like her. We love her. She's a perfect fit for our family. You did very well choosing her."

"Thanks, Mom. Do you mind if she stays for supper? It's still early, and I'd like to be able to stay with her a little while longer, especially after the accident. I'll take her home, so she doesn't have to drive. If you don't mind following us in her car, you and I can go shopping from there."

"I don't mind at all. That sounds like a wonderful plan."

Paisley stayed for supper, and Mom and I took her and her car home. She'd already told her parents what happened at the lake, so they continued to keep a close eye on her for the rest of the evening just in case.

Mom and I headed to the jewelry store. On the way, we brainstormed ideas for the perfect proposal. We came up with a dinner proposal, a secret party proposal, a hot air balloon ride, and a picnic at Morrow Mountain. I decided on the secret party idea, so we could all celebrate together. Mom and I are planning everything for next weekend. Any further out than that may be a bit rough for everyone to keep a secret.

We finally arrived at the jewelry store and were greeted by the staff. We were then led to the loose diamond counter to pick the perfect diamond. I chose a one-carat, marquise-cut diamond. Then, we looked at settings. One of her favorite colors is rose gold, so that narrowed it down just a bit. There's one set that caught my eye over the others. It's an elaborate design that resembles delicate lace with tiny, twinkling diamonds on top. Her wedding band is a rose gold, chevron-shaped, half-infinity band, with channel-set diamonds. It fits perfectly alongside the engagement ring. The jeweler set the stone in the setting while I picked out my band. Mine is a rose gold band with channel-set diamonds. It will go splendidly with hers. I finished the paperwork, paid for my selections, and we headed home.

Mom was on the phone during the entire trip. She's making arrangements for the surprise engagement party. She called all of our friends and family members and invited them. She even swore them to absolute secrecy not to tell Paisley or even hint anything to her about the plan. This is happening. I am going to officially propose marriage to the love of my life.

Once we arrived back at home, I told everyone good night and went upstairs to shower and go to bed. Dad had warned me that I'd need to be rested for my training. I just hope I can live up to his expectations. There's a lot at stake if I fail. I can't let that happen.

Chapter 15

Chad

I woke up early and reported for my first training session. Training with Dad and Taggart was no joke! They put me through the wringer! We started with a three-mile run, then calisthenics, and finished off with hand-to-hand combat. They told me that one mile of running is nearly equal to one minute of a physical altercation. They also said that training while fatigued would condition my body to keep going instead of tiring out during a fight. Survival is paramount. I must survive and protect my charges as well as my loved ones.

I would never forgive myself if anything happened to them. I focused my efforts on my training regimen, turning to Dad and Taggart for advice, paying attention to everything they had to teach me, and applying it when instructed. I pulled Taggart aside when training was finally over.

"Sir Taggart, may I have a moment of your time?"

"Sure, but why so formal?"

"I have a crucial question to ask of you. As you know, Lady Paisley and I are chosen mates. I'd like to formally ask for her hand in marriage. May I have your blessing to marry Lady Paisley?"

"Why, Sir Chadwick, I thought you'd never ask. Of course, you may. Lady Fiona and I are quite pleased with your match with our Lady Paisley. We've been waiting for your connection to awaken for so very long."

"Thank you so very much, Sir Taggart. You don't know how much having your blessing means to me. I plan to marry Lady Paisley over Christmas break. We have a lot of preparation to do for the wedding, but I am more than ready to care for her and protect her with my life."

"Let's hope it doesn't come to that, but I can rest easy, knowing that she will be in good hands."

"I pray that I never let you down. I am asking Lady Paisley to marry me on Saturday, during a gathering at our house that evening. I'd very much like for you and your family to be there."

"We wouldn't miss it for the world."

I feel better knowing I have his blessing. An invisible weight has lifted from my shoulders. Nymphean parents don't always approve of their children's choice of mates. I'm very thankful that our parents do approve of our connection. Our future family gatherings will be more pleasant that way. Paisley and I will eventually be starting a family of our own. I hadn't thought about it until now. We will hopefully have a few years together before that happens, but if it should happen sooner than later, the child will be a welcomed blessing whenever he or she makes their entrance into our lives.

I am determined to keep my word to Paisley's father to care for her and protect her. I continued to pour everything I had into my training. Yet, no matter how hard I trained over the next few days, it still hadn't lessened my appetite for Paisley. I still craved her nearness, her touch, her scent, the taste of her on my tongue. The *urges* I feel inside for her, my need for her still grows, as does our connection. I can feel our bond growing stronger with each passing day. My need for her and the inability to satisfy that need has been part of my drive for training as hard as I have. I can feel that unsatisfied need turning into aggression as it's poured into my training. I don't know if it's working or not, because it's only been a few days. I just know that the training alone isn't enough to calm "the beast" inside me. I need her, too.

Seeing her at school is not nearly enough. I've resisted the *urge* to take her in my truck during lunch, for fear of getting caught. We got lucky the first time. Who's to say we won't get caught the next time. I know we have to be more careful, but not having her these last few days is taking its toll on me. Thank goodness it's Thursday, and there's no football practice tonight. I'll still have my evening training session with Dad and Taggart, though.

Paisley is coming over tonight with her dad so that we can see one another. Maybe they'll allow us to spend some time studying together after my training is over. Tonight's session will involve Paisley. I'll have to apply what I've learned so far to save her from an attacker in various scenarios. I hope that I'll be able to protect her and rescue her in real life if something like that ever happens. The same goes for Molly and Toby once they become my charges.

We went through each scenario slowly at first, and then at full speed. Taggart was the attacker. It felt bizarre to have to fight him since he is my future father-in-law, but he showed me no mercy. A real attacker wouldn't, so when it was game on, it was game on. We went so hard that I think Paisley was worried we'd hurt one another a few times. We didn't, of course, but we came pretty close. I wasn't giving up, though, no matter what. I wanted to show them that I was getting the hang of it and that I'd kill for her if I had to. I'd even die for her if that's what I had to do.

Once our training session was finally over, Paisley and I went down to the dock for some alone time. We sat on the edge, dangled our feet in the water, and held one another close. This was the closest we'd been all week. Having her this close just made me want her closer. I dreaded her leaving to go home.

"Take a drive with me, sweetheart. I'll take you home if your dad wants to leave before we get back. I need you. I can't fight it too much longer."

"Oh, Chad. I'm so glad it's not just me. I've been going crazy! At least you have your training and football to keep you busy. All I've had is my homework. I need you so badly it hurts."

"What are we waiting for then? Let's go."

"Oh, I'm so in."

We went inside and told everyone we were going to grab a bite to eat together in Troy, and that I'd have her home by her curfew time. We were on our way in no time flat. She scooted closer to me and fastened the center seat belt around her. She nuzzled her head into my chest, placed her arm over my thigh, and gave it a gentle squeeze. The spark and tingles coursed through us, making it even more difficult to wait any longer for what we both craved from one another. I pulled onto the first turn off I could find, parked the truck, and sat the seat back as far as it would go.

I pulled her into my arms and kissed her deeply and passionately. I sucked and nipped at her luscious lips, and our tongues twirled. I undressed her in a hurried fit of flying clothes, and then made short work of mine. I laid her down on the seat and leaned over her. A low growl rumbled in my chest. I spoke to her mind-to-mind as I breached her warm, wet center.

"Mine."

"Oh! Yes, Chad. I'm all yours, and you're mine. All mine."

We took from one another and gave to one another as we made wild and passionate love, again and again. Our energy mixed and swirled within our bodies. Vibrant colors swirled with flashing lights as we soared into each climax together. We laid on the seat of my truck, and I held Paisley tight to my chest. I love the feel of her body and her soft skin against me. I lightly stroked her back and ran my fingers through her hair. We came down from our bliss together, and just enjoyed the closeness of our naked bodies, and the tingles that coursed through us.

I had missed having her close like this. Everything felt right in the world with Paisley in my arms. I never want to let her go. If only I could hold her like this all night, and wake her with a kiss in the morning. I'd make love to her once again before we had to face the day. Maybe someday soon, but for now, I have to make sure she gets something to eat, and get her back home before her curfew. I kissed the top of her head, and she looked up at me. Her glowing tanzanite eyes bored into my soul. She took my lips in a tender kiss and parted them with her tongue. I savored the tangy sweetness of her flavor in her kiss, letting it linger on my tongue. She slowly broke the kiss and sat up.

"Honey? As much as I hate to say it, we should probably get ready to go."

"Yeah, I know we should, sweetheart, but I hate having to let you go."

"We don't have to wait too much longer. We'll be married in a few months. Then, we won't have to say goodbye each night. We can simply kiss each other goodnight, and hold one another in our bed, in our home."

"Got any plans on Saturday?"

"No, not at the moment. I was hoping we could do something together, though."

"Good. I'll pick you up at 5:00 that evening. I've got to work the early shift at the marina, and then I have a training session. I'll shower and swing by to get you afterward. Sound good?"

"That sounds wonderful. I can hardly wait. Just what are we going to do, anyway?"

"Don't you worry about it. It's a surprise."

"Um, okay. What should I wear, anything specific?"

"Hmm. Maybe a sundress? You always look gorgeous in anything and everything you wear. You're gorgeous with nothing on, too, though."

"Hahaha! Thank you, my love."

We reluctantly got dressed, headed into town, and stopped for a couple of hotdogs and potato wedges. All of the tables and booths were full. There were kids around our age piling in from the Junior Varsity football game at the Montgomery County High School. I'm guessing they won, judging the energy of the crowd. I pulled Paisley in closer to my side. She smiled sweetly at me and nuzzled into my chest. We snagged a booth in the back, just as our number was called. Paisley went to sit down, and I grabbed our tray at the counter.

On the way to our booth, I recognized a familiar face in the crowd. It was the guy who'd tried to manhandle Paisley at the marina. I felt a low growl rumble deep in my chest. "The beast." I quickly sat down in the booth with Paisley without making eye contact with him. Maybe he won't recognize us, and we can eat in peace and leave. Paisley spoke to me mind-to-mind. She sounded worried.

"What is it, my love? I sensed 'the beast' stirring."

"It's nothing, sweetheart. Don't look or draw any attention to you or us. The guy that tried to put his hands on you at the marina is over there. I don't think he's recognized us."

"Oh. Okay. I won't. Do you want to take this to go?"

"No, we are fine, right where we are. Let's just enjoy our supper. We won't stick around any longer than that. I'd almost hate to think about what I'd do if he tried to touch you again."

We devoured our meals and walked briskly to my truck. I was on edge the entire time. "The beast" had me on hyper-alert, adrenaline-pumping, heart-pounding, hackles raised, and eyes darting from one person to another. I had to get Paisley out of there. Something was off, and neither "the beast" nor I liked it one bit. I haven't learned to hone in on my power to know exactly what has me on edge, but something tells me it has to do with being near that guy again. I can't put my finger on it just yet, but it isn't good.

I took Paisley home but took a longer way around, so I could make sure we weren't being followed. I can't wait until I can be with her all the time so I can protect her. I'm not taking any chances with her life. She is much too precious to allow something to happen to her.

The following day was a typical school day, but with an away game afterward. Luckily, it wasn't too far away. Molly transported Paisley there so I could be near them if something happened. Toby led our team to another victory, but I couldn't put my all into the game like I usually had in the past. My guard is still up. I can't get past the thought of how that guy had irritated "the beast" last night. There is something dangerous about him, and I am damned determined to find out what he is up to as soon as possible. Dad told me there might be threats against the Royal Family and ours too, but I hadn't counted on anything so close to home so soon. Maybe he will have some insight on any recent threats or perhaps some kind of intel gathered by the Royal Guard's Security Team.

"Dad, may I borrow some of your time? I've got an uneasy feeling I want to talk to you about."

"Sure, Son. You know you can tell me anything."

" Thanks, Dad. It all started when Paisley brought me some food to the marina last Saturday. Some guy tried to manhandle her. I felt 'the beast' stir inside me and came to her aid. I threw the guy out of the marina's convenience store. He made some kind of threat as I kicked him out. He said, "You don't know who you're messing with, but you will soon enough!" We saw him again last night when we stopped in Troy for a bite to eat. I felt 'the beast' increasingly irritated by his presence. I don't think he saw us, but we didn't make it a point to draw attention to ourselves either. We ate quickly and got out of there. I don't know what he's up to just yet, but something's sinister about him."

"Well, there are rival Nymphs here, that aren't exactly keen on living under a monarchy. They believe the Royal Family and all noble bloodlines should be eradicated and the power of authority to be given to the commoners. They don't want to have to live by Nymphean laws. They see our race as being superior to humans. They want to be able to tell all the humans what we are and eventually control them as the gods they see themselves to be. I expected they were close, but we hadn't heard they'd gotten this close. I'm glad you told me, Son. We have our work cut out for us. It could be only a matter of time before they strike."

"So, you're telling me that guy is a Nymph like us?"

"It's possible. I definitely wouldn't rule it out just yet. Have you felt anything else, or seen any visions?"

"No, not yet. I'll keep you in the loop if I do."

"We need to continue working on your training. There may be something in the Ancient Texts about how to hone in on your abilities. We will need more insight on how to strengthen them and develop the ability to see visions of future events. I'll make a few calls, do some research, and see what I can find out before your next training session. I'll also talk to Taggart and have him to look into possible local threats and radical groups as well."

"Thanks, Dad. We may need to begin bringing in other members of the Royal Guard, depending on how big of a threat we're facing. Not going to lie, I'll accept all the help we can get."

"I agree, Son. We can't afford to take risks with the Royal Family's lives or ours for that matter. Do you think you can manage training before and after your shift on Saturday?"

"It'll be rough, I'm sure, but I'll do my best."

"You always do."

I woke up early on Saturday morning for my training session. Taggart was bursting at the seams by the time we arrived.

"I'm glad you could make it, gentlemen," he said. "I've found some information about who we're up against. They call themselves The Liberation Force. They have been slowly and silently boosting their numbers in our area since word got out about Molly and Toby's abduction. They figured if two nobodies could abduct Molly and Toby, they'd have no trouble striking against us."

"How many have joined them?"

"From what our source was able to uncover, they are about two hundred strong as a whole. There may only be around fifty in our area. With their capabilities, even fifty would be problematic."

"Any information about the guy we encountered at the marina and the burger joint in Troy?"

"Yes, our source seems to believe he is Eric Berman, the son of Micah Berman, The Liberation Force's leader."

"No wonder he was so cocky. What's our plan, or is there one?"

"Well, we don't exactly have one as of yet. All we can do is boost our numbers and remain vigilant for the time being. An official threat has not been issued. We do need to keep a close eye on them to stay at least one step ahead."

"How many Royal Guards can we get here within the next twenty-four hours?" I asked.

"As many as one hundred if necessary," Taggart said.

"I think we should make the call and get them here pronto," Dad said. "The Royal Family will need all the protection we can offer. The rest of the Nymphean nobles will need protection as well. Send guards to each of their homes to ensure their safety."

"I'll make the calls immediately. Go ahead and start your warm-up routine without me, and I'll be back shortly." Taggart stepped away to make the calls and rally the Royal Guards.

Dad started me off doing calisthenics and stretching to loosen up my muscles and prepare for today's session. He said that training will continue to gain intensity from here on. I have to be ready for an attack at any given moment. The Ancient Texts revealed a ritual that could be conducted to help me tap into my visions. High Priestess Arren's successor has not been named. So, there is no one to perform it at the moment. I'll just have to learn how to tap into it on my own. The Ancient Texts did recommend focusing on the intuition as I begin to feel it rising within me. I haven't felt "the beast" in that way since seeing Eric Berman in Troy. Although, the absence of that particular feeling didn't mean that I could relax. It could merely be the calm before the storm.

Taggart returned, and my training began. Today's lesson was more hand-to-hand combat. Dad said I've improved on my reaction time and the power behind my strikes. They taught me how to channel my energy into specific body parts accordingly, so I didn't tire out as quickly during a fight. I can direct a small amount of energy into my legs for stability and kicks, and another amount into my arms and hands for a powerful strike or to block an attack. We have no idea when our enemies will strike. I only hope I'm ready and able to protect those I love when the time comes.

Chapter 16

Chad

Mom has outdone herself with the engagement party. All of our friends have agreed to attend, and the back yard is decorated with flowers, tiki torches, and strands of white lights. There is also a spread of delectables that she and Tabby have been preparing all day. They made a fresh fruit and vegetable tray, various cheeses and crackers, deviled eggs, sandwich trays, and cupcakes. They even made a batch of sparkling punch for the occasion.

Although I know Paisley will say yes, I'm more nervous now than I have ever been in my whole life. We are already bonded mates, after all. I'm doing my best to hide it, though. Paisley will sense it if I don't tamp it down. I've rehearsed what I'm going to say to her over and over again. The ring is safely secured in my pocket, awaiting its presentation to the woman I love. My palms are clammy, my pulse is racing, and I feel a bit jittery. Our friends are starting to arrive. They each express their excitement and offer their congratulations. I excuse myself and let them know that I'm on my way to get her. Everyone knows that this is our engagement party, except for Paisley. She thinks this is just a small family get-together. Everyone should be there by the time I get back home with her. I only hope I can continue to hide my nervousness from her and act normal, so I don't give away the surprise before it's time to pop the question of the evening.

I arrived at her house promptly at 4:55 p.m. Her parents and little brother have already left early to "go grocery shopping." They will already be at the party when we arrive. I took a deep breath, gave myself a moment to regain my composure and try to calm my nerves. Then, I jumped out of my truck, walked up to her door, and rang the doorbell. Paisley answered the door, wearing the cutest floral sundress I've ever seen her in. She had a white cardigan shrug over her shoulders and a pair of white, kitten-heeled sandals. Her hair was half up, half down, with delicate tendrils framing both sides of her face. All I can do is stand there speechless, as I drink in every detail and commit them to my memory. Today is a day I want to remember for the rest of my life.

"Well, say something. Earth to Chad."

"Wow! You look amazing! You've rendered me speechless."

"Awe, thank you, honey! You're mighty handsome yourself."

"Thank you, sweetheart. Are you ready to go?"

"Absolutely!"

I held out my arm for her to take, and she looped her arm through mine. The spark and tingles began to surge through me and instantly soothed away my nervousness. Paisley is mine, now and forever. This proposal is going to be a piece of cake. I know exactly what to do and what to say. I'm ready to make our engagement official in front of all of our family members and friends. Well, not all of our friends. Angie respectfully declined the invitation, but I understand why. Angie said she is happy for us and wants to be here, but she's not entirely ready to face it head-on just yet.

I opened the passenger door of my truck and helped Paisley inside. Once I was inside, I backed out of her driveway and headed home. My plan is now in full bloom. We talked, laughed, and sang along to the radio the whole way there. I treated it like it was just another family get-together. Paisley's eyes grew wide as we pulled up to my house.

"Why are there so many cars here?"

"I invited all of our friends and family members here tonight."

"Oh, how wonderful! I had no idea they were all coming too."

"Well, come on. Let's go inside."
I jumped out of the truck and headed around to her side to help her out. We walked inside hand-in-hand. The spark and tingles surged through my arm and settled deep in my chest. The warm feeling they imbibed was soothing and reassuring. Everyone was waiting for us inside when I opened the door. Everyone greeted us, shouting, "Surprise!"

"Chad, what's going on here?" Paisley asked.

I stepped in front of Paisley, took the tiny ring box from my pocket, opened it, and dropped to one knee. I took her left hand in mine and smiled up at her. The spark and tingles surged between us. Paisley's eyes begin to glisten with tears, and her hands began to shake. Some of our friends and family members started snapping pictures with their cell phones throughout the room, while others began recording videos of the proposal.

"Lady Paisley Rose O'Riley, you are the most beautiful woman I have ever seen. Your beauty radiates from within your soul and from your heart of gold. I feel your soul calling out to mine, as mine calls out to yours. You are my chosen mate, soulmate, the love of my life, my everything. I love you more and more each day and will continue to love you with every fiber of my being for the rest of my life. Lady Paisley, you light up my world each time you smile. Even the most beautifully composed symphony cannot compare to the sound of your laughter in my ears. I want to be the one to make you smile and laugh each day from now until the end of time. I want to build a life with you and raise a family of our own. Lady Paisley, will you do me the honor of becoming my wife and bonded mate for all eternity?"

"Yes! Yes, Sir Chadwick, I absolutely will!"

I took the ring out of its box and placed it on her left ring finger. Then, I stood, wrapped my arms around her, and spun her around as I kissed her lips.

"Lady Paisley, my love, this isn't just an ordinary family get-together, as you've probably guessed by now. It's our surprise engagement party."

"I can't believe you put all of this together!"

"I wanted to make the proposal special. I knew you'd want our families and friends here to celebrate with us. With your permission, I'd like to go ahead and set our wedding date. How do you feel about December twenty-first? We could have our wedding during the Winter Solstice."

"I think it's perfect! I'd marry you tomorrow if I could."

"I know you would, sweetheart. I feel the same way. I just want our wedding day to be perfect—a dream come true for both of us."

"It will be my dream come true as long as I'm marrying you."

"Paisley, my beautiful fiancé. I wouldn't have it any other way."

"Good, because I'm never giving up this gorgeous ring!"

Everyone laughed and wiped the tears from their eyes and faces. Then, everyone began hugging us and offering their congratulations.

"Thank you all for being here to share this special moment with us tonight. This was quite a surprise. I'm so happy! I'm finally going to be Lady Paisley O'Riley Greene."

"I cannot wait to make you my wife, sweetheart. I've been ready to marry you since the day we discovered our connection awakened. Our love story is only just beginning. I cannot wait to see what our future holds."

"Me either. I'm ready to begin my life with you, my love."

"Everyone, please eat, drink and be merry. Let the engagement party begin!" We all enjoyed the food, the punch, and dancing in the beautifully-lit back yard. The party was a huge success! Paisley and other members of our friends and families kept admiring her ring throughout the evening.

"Do you really like it, sweetheart?"

"I love it! I couldn't have picked a more perfect ring myself. I love the details in the rose gold and all of the sparkle! It's breathtaking!"

"Not as breathtaking as you are in my eyes."

"You are such a charmer, Chad Greene."

Paisley stood on her tip-toes and wrapped her arms around my neck. I pulled her closer to me and whispered in her ear. "You are the only woman I ever want to charm for all eternity."

"Well, I suggest you'd better keep it up and kiss me."

"Your wish is my command, my love."

I leaned down and pressed my lips to hers. I traced her bottom lip with my tongue, and her lips parted. I deepened the kiss, and our tongues swirled and danced together. I relished in her sweet and tangy flavor on my tongue that I craved every day, always wanting more, needing so much more. I can't help but think about how much I want to take her. "The beast" inside me began to stir. A low growl rumbled in my chest.

"I need you, Paisley. I need you so badly!"

"I can feel how badly you need me. I can sense "the beast" inside you. I want to satisfy you in every way possible."

"What do you think about taking a walk with me now that it's all over?"

"How can I possibly resist you, Chad?"

"Good. I'm so glad, sweetheart, because I don't know how much longer I can wait to have you again."

Just then, a throat cleared behind Paisley, followed by a feminine giggle. We broke the kiss and turned to find Molly and Toby standing there.

"Oh, hey! Sorry. We kind of got carried away with one another."

"We noticed. How's that *urge* to bond treating you?" Toby asked.

"Dude, it's seriously killing me."

"We know how you feel, buddy. It's no laughing matter, that's for sure. It will only get stronger from here."

"Don't remind me. It's already physically painful."

"Look at it this way. You only have a few more months to go, and you and Paisley can complete your bond on your wedding night."

"This is very true. How are you holding up, by the way? I know yours and Molly's connection has been awakened a lot longer than ours has. How are you two able to remain so calm and composed?"

"Mind over matter. We force ourselves to think of and do other things to keep us occupied. The busier we are, the less time we have to think about the *urge* to complete our bond."

"That makes sense," Paisley said. "You two have been quite busy here lately."

"Yes, we have," Molly said. "Between school, homework, practicing with my powers, learning the ropes of becoming Queen and Prince Consort, and working at the Brody's ranch, we don't have much free time at all."

"Yeah, I've been trying to stay busy myself. With school, working at the marina, football practice, football games, and training sessions with my dad and Paisley's dad, I haven't had much time with Paisley either. The longer I'm away from her, the more I need to be with her. Staying busy isn't exactly working for me."

"I'm not as busy as you guys are, Paisley said. "All I have going on is going to school and doing homework. I've been contemplating getting a job as a waitress at one of the local restaurants to earn some extra cash and have something to do while Chad is busy."

"You never know. It may work for you. At least you two will be able to bond on your wedding night in a few short months. We have to wait until after graduation to get married and complete our bond." Toby said.

"Ouch. I'm sorry you have to wait so long."

"We will survive somehow because we have to. What other choice do we have?" Molly said.

"Very true."

"Well, we just wanted to congratulate you on your engagement. We hate to leave so soon, but we really should get going. I need to get up pretty early to go practice my powers tomorrow in Kilchoman."

"Please be sure to take a security team with you. We've gotten word about a group of anti-monarchal radicals who want to eradicate all of the Nymphean Royalty and noble bloodlines. My training is progressing, but I still haven't been fully trained to help protect you as your personal guard and leader of the Royal Guard."

"We promise we will," Toby said. "I have faith in you, Chad. I know you'll be up to the task before too long. You've got great mentors to show you the ropes."

"That, I do."

"Congratulations again on your engagement and upcoming wedding. We are so very happy for you both," Molly said.

"Thank you. We are truly excited about our future together." Paisley said and kissed my cheek. Molly and Toby held one another close, smiled, and disappeared into thin air. "I don't know if I'll ever get used to that," Paisley said with a giggle.

"Well, we've got plenty of time for that. Molly and Toby are going to be a pretty big part of our lives, you know."

"Yeah, but the way I see it, they already are. I adore Molly and Toby. I'm honored that they welcomed me into the group the way they did. I didn't exactly have many friends before all of you helped me at the Derby. People weren't mean to me or anything, but everyone just kind of disregarded me altogether as though I didn't exist."

"I'm sorry, sweetheart. I wish I had known."

"It's all right. I know how jealous Angelina was back then. I never saw any girls hanging out with your group at all unless she was one of Angelina's friends. I'm surprised she was so open to Molly joining the group when she came along."

"She didn't exactly give her a warm welcome. Once she realized Molly wasn't interested in me, she slowly started warming up to her."

"I do hope Angelina is okay. I know she said she's happy for us and wishes us the best, but I still worry about her. She and I were just starting to get close before our connection awakened. I miss my friend," Paisley said and looked down at her feet.

"Angie is going to be just fine. She just needs time to herself to allow her broken heart to mend. She'll come back around in her own time." I tilted Paisley's chin up to look at me once again. "Hey, enough about all of that. Tonight is about us. I want to celebrate us and our future together and give you a little taste of what's to come."

Paisley's eyes began to glow, and the lights sparkled within them. "How did I get so lucky to have you? I've loved you from afar for so long. I was afraid I'd never know your love in return. I finally feel as though my soul is complete."

"I'm the lucky one, Paisley. I wish our connection had awakened much sooner, so I could've returned your love before now." I cupped her face in my hand and tenderly caressed her cheek with my thumb. "I'm just glad I have the rest of eternity to make it up to you, and I fully intend to do just that. Come on. There's something I'd like to show you."

"More surprises? Count me in!"

I took Paisley's hand in mine and led her down the path to the dock and boathouse. Once inside of the boathouse, I locked the door behind us. I stepped onto the pontoon boat and reached for Paisley's hand, and helped her inside. I untied the ropes from the dock and slid into the captain's seat. I turned on the engine and the lights on the boat and eased it out of the boathouse.

"Where are we going?" Paisley asked.

"You'll just have to wait and see."

I drove the boat out into the open water and continued out to one of the islands with a dock. I slowly pulled up to the dock and cut the engine. I tied the ropes to the dock and opened one of the storage compartments on board. I removed a large throw blanket, spread it out on the pontoon boat floor, and laid out the seat cushions around the edges. I then sank onto the blanket and patted the spot beside me for Paisley to join me. She just smiled and fell into my arms.

"Now that I have my beautiful fiancé all to myself, what on earth am I going to do with her?"

"Hmm... I'm sure you can come up with something."

I wrapped my arms around her and pulled her closer. I gazed into her eyes in the moonlight and lowered my mouth onto hers. Her soft, plump lips opened for me, and our kiss deepened into a heat of passion. I broke the kiss and trailed more kisses down her jaw, to the sensitive skin on her neck. I slid her cardigan off of her shoulders and kissed each inch of skin as it was exposed. A soft moan escaped her lips as I kissed my way down to her chest and cupped her breasts in my hands. I reached behind her and slid the zipper of her dress down. I eased the straps over her shoulders, then past her hips, and finally over her shapely legs. Her flawless skin seemed to nearly glow in the moonlight as she lay there in her strapless bra and matching thong.

I sat back and drank in the sight of her in the moonlight. "Paisley, sweetheart, you are by far the most beautiful sight I have ever laid eyes on."

"Thank you, my love. You're much too far away. I need you."

I smiled at her, slowly unbuttoned my shirt, and tossed it aside with her dress. Then, I unfastened my belt and my slacks, stepped out of them, and tossed them with the rest of our clothes. I leaned over her and captured her lips with mine once again. Her hands were in my hair and caressing my back while my hands roamed over her breasts and then down lower to the lace of her thong. I playfully traced her panty line just below her navel with my fingers.

Paisley broke the kiss, lightly panting. "Please, Chad. Touch me."

"Like this?" I slid my hand into her panties and gently caressed her sensitive bundle of nerves within. The spark and tingles surged into her sex as she writhed against my hand.

"Oooooh! Yes! Just like that," she whimpered.

I slowly trailed kisses down her body and unhooked the center closure of her bra. I took one of her aroused buds into my mouth. Paisley's back arched, and I heard her moan as I sucked and lightly nipped at her flesh and continued to rub her bundle of nerves. I moved on to the other, sucked it into my mouth, and teased it with my teeth. Paisley's soft moans and whimpers were all the encouragement I needed. I withdrew my mouth from her breast and trailed kisses lower and lower until I'd finally reached her panty line. Her peppery arousal is mouth-watering. I crave her flavor on my tongue. I hooked my fingers into the sides of her thong and gently pulled it off of her. I trailed soft kisses from her ankle, up the inside of her leg, and up to her sweet, wet center. I flicked my tongue against her and felt her shudder. I pressed my hands against her thighs and continued to tease her sensitive flesh with my tongue. Her sweet and tangy flavor lingered on my tongue, and a low groan rumbled within my chest.

"I can't get enough of you, Paisley."

"Oh, Chad! Please don't stop!"

"Your wish is my command, my love."

I sucked and nipped and swirled my tongue inside of her again and again as she writhed against me. Her fingers were in my hair as I savored and devoured her.

"Please, Chad, I'm about to… "

I licked upwards and swirled my tongue around her bundle of nerves, and her back arched once again. She let out an even louder moan than before. I sucked her sensitive flesh and inserted two of my fingers inside her tight channel, probing in and out. Colors swirled around us as her pleasure began to build. I increased my suction on her sensitive bud. Her muscles tensed and spasmed around my fingers as her climax washed over her. I sat back on my knees and slid my boxer briefs off. Paisley's gaze traveled over my body, and she bit her bottom lip as my hardness sprang free.

"I need you, Chad. Please make love to me. I need to feel you inside me and feel your energy mixing with mine."

"I couldn't resist you if I wanted to."

I leaned over her once again, and she wrapped her legs around my waist. I ran my hands over her thighs and gripped her butt as I thrust deep inside her. A low groan rumbled in my chest as I breached her tight, warm center. Paisley moaned my nam as the spark jolted between our bodies. The tingles pulsed and seemed to vibrate at our joining. I felt "the beast" stir inside me. I can feel it begging to take over, to ravish Paisley, and take everything she was willing to give it. I focused my will power on containing it. I wanted to make love to her the way she deserved. I would not be rough with her tonight. No, I wanted to love her tenderly and passionately.

I leaned over her and softly kissed her lips as I began to move my hips. I broke the kiss and placed tender kisses along her neck and back up to her luscious lips. I sucked her bottom lip into my mouth and traced it with my tongue. Our kiss deepened, and Paisley began to move with me in perfect rhythm. I rested on my elbows, and Paisley raised her arms over her head to find my hands. She laced her fingers with mine, pressing our palms together. I felt my energy flow through my body and into Paisley as her energy flowed through her and into me. I stopped kissing her long enough to look into her eyes.

I felt my eyes begin to glow as I bared my soul to her. Her eyes began to glow, as well. Our souls joined one another, and I felt how genuinely pure our love is. Bright, psychedelic colors swirled around us, and lightning seemed to flash within its cyclone.

"Paisley, I love you with everything I am. Look inside me and feel my love for you as I feel your love for me."

"I feel it, Chad. It's the most wonderful feeling in the entire world."

"My love for you grows stronger and stronger every single day. Soar with me, Paisley."

"Ohhhh! Chaaaaad! Yeeeeees!"

Our bodies shuddered and spasmed as our climax rippled through us. I rested my forehead on hers as we both laid there panting. Once our breathing and our pulses had slowed, I lowered my mouth to hers once again. I still wanted more of Paisley. "The beast" always wanted more. I sat back on my knees, pulling her on top of me. I wrapped my arms around her and held her close as I continued to thrust into her. Paisley began to rock her hips along with my rhythm as her nails dug into my back. Her moans and sighs were music to my ears. I wanted more. I wanted to hear her shout my name once again. I wedged one hand between our bodies and began to massage her sensitive bundle of nerves. Her moans grew louder as I increased the pressure along with the tempo of my thrusts inside her. Colors swirled around us as her muscles tightened around me once again.

"Shout my name, sweetheart. I want to hear my name on your sweet lips."

"Chaaaaad! Yes! Please don't stop!"

Both of our bodies spasmed again as another climax sizzled through us. I wrapped my arms around Paisley and held her as close as I could get her, and slowed the tempo to a stop. I laid my cheek against her chest as our breathing and pulses slowed back to normal. I laid her back onto the blanket and continued to hold her. She laid her head on my chest and draped her leg over mine. We held one another and gazed up at the stars, relishing in the moment we had alone with one another.

"Sweetheart, it pains me to say this, but we should probably get back before everyone misses us."

"You're right, my love. Let's go."

We got dressed and headed back to the party. No one even realized we'd left. They thought we'd just gone down to the dock for a while. The younger kids were running through the yard with sparklers, Max was laughing with my dad and Taggart, and our mothers were already planning the wedding. We overheard them mentioning various venues, menu items for the rehearsal dinner, flower arrangements, and other decoration ideas. They have been looking forward to our wedding since the day we chose one another, a little over eighteen years ago.

It wasn't much longer before the party dwindled, and everyone was ready to go their separate ways. The younger kids were getting sleepy, and the adults didn't want to leave too late. Deer and drunk drivers would be coming out soon. They didn't want to take any chances with either on their trips home.

Paisley went home with her family, to save on fuel and me having to risk getting in too late. I missed her the moment she left my embrace. The void I feel in her absence is nearly overwhelming. I'm so glad we will be getting married in a few months. I don't know how much longer I could bear being away from her like this otherwise. I need to have her with me. The pain of being apart is maddening. "The beast" inside me is unsettled when we are apart. I can feel its uneasiness. It's restless and longs for her as I do. I reach out to her with my soul to sense her. She has arrived home safely and is walking inside her home now.

"Paisley, sweetheart?"

"Yes, my love?"

"I know you haven't been gone long, but I miss you so much."

"I miss you too, honey. I wish we had our own place."

"I know, sweetheart. I do too. We will, though, very soon. I need you near me. This distance is killing me. I hate letting you go each night. 'The beast" inside me does too. It's restless."

"I know the feeling all too well. I crave you, Chad. It's a craving that never fades, no matter how much time we spend together, it never seems to be enough."

"I know all about cravings, Paisley, believe me. I have craved you from the moment we realized our connection had awakened. I was ready to make you mine as soon as possible."

"Oh, Chad! I love you so much! Thank you for being so wonderful. I'm so lucky to have you."

"I love you too, Paisley. You're no luckier than I am, I assure you. You're the wonderful one in this relationship. You love me and accept me for who I am, 'the beast' inside me, and all of my flaws. I couldn't ask for anything more than that."

"You are perfect in my eyes, my love. You and that 'beast' of yours."

"Thank you, Paisley. You're perfect in my eyes too. Try to get some rest, sweetheart. We will be together soon and won't have to spend any more nights alone."

"All right, my love. I'll try. You do the same. Good night and sweet dreams. I love you, honey."

"Good night and sweet dreams to you too, sweetheart. I love you too."

Chapter 17

Paisley

It's been just over a month since our engagement party. Chad and our fathers have been training every night through the week and every Saturday, either before or after Chad's shift at the marina. They've even brought in a few of the elder Royal Guards to assist in his training. His grandfather is one of them. Chad had thought his grandparents were killed in a car accident with a drunk driver when he was younger. It just so happens that they have had to move around a lot over the years. People get suspicious of us after being in one place for too long. We don't age after thirty-five, after all. Chad's grandparents had kept in touch with his parents all these years.

Now that Chad and his siblings know about their heritage, their grandparents have decided to move back to the area under different names. His grandfather has been an excellent resource for Chad and has helped prepare him for his new role. While he still has a lot further to go in his training, he is learning so quickly. I'm proud of him and all he's doing to protect us all.

Me on the other hand, I'm a bit worried, but not for our safety. I'm concerned because my cycle is late. I realized too late that I'd missed my birth control pill the day of my accident at Chad's house and the day afterward due to still having a bit of a concussion. Not good, indeed. I spoke to my doctor in confidentiality. She told me to take two pills that day and two on the following day to get back on schedule. I did as she'd said, but I'm afraid that I could still be pregnant. I don't want Chad to worry, but I need to tell him. He deserves to know one way or another. I'm afraid of what he will say or how he will react when I tell him. I sent him a message mind-to-mind.

"Chad, my love?"

"Yes, sweetheart? What's up?"

"I know you're probably busy right now, but what do you think about getting out for a date later tonight?"

"I'm in! I miss you so much! This training has taken a lot of our alone time away from us, and I'm so sorry."

"I understand, and I don't blame you, honey. I miss you too."

"I'll shower after training and pick up as soon as I can. I cannot wait to see you, Paisley. I have been craving you like crazy!"

"That sounds fantastic, my love. I'll be ready and waiting for you to get here. I love you, Chad."

"I love you too, Paisley."

Well, I suppose I'll tell Chad during our date tonight. Our connection allows us to know how the other is feeling at any given moment. I need to find a way to relax. I don't want to alert him to my suspicion or how worried I am. I decided to take a nap so that I can share my energy with Chad on our date. I know how grueling his training is and how exhausted he is afterward. I'll do anything to help him restore his energy and ease the soreness from his muscles.

He has begun to put on more muscle mass since his training started. He was sexy before, but oh, my! He is super sexy now. Several other girls at school have noticed and have tried to come between us. It didn't work out so well in their favor. Chad ended up hurting quite a few feelings, but they have finally backed off and have accepted that he and I are engaged and will be getting married soon.

Chad picked me up at 7:00 p.m., and we went to grab some food together at the Golf Club Grille. It is so wonderful to see him and spend time with him. We went for a drive after our meal so we could have some much needed alone time.

Chad pulled off the road into the Uwharrie National Forrest Trailhead and drove a bit further away from the road before parking his truck. He turned the lights off and slid the seat further back. We undid our seatbelts and undressed as quickly as we could. He picked me up and sat me upon him, seating him deep inside me. The sparks and tingles were so intense after not making love the last few weeks that I nearly climaxed as soon as they hit my sex. We made love in a hungry fit of passion and need. I had missed him and craved him so much that I felt I was going insane. He felt the same way. "The beast" inside him was longing to be unleashed. I sensed it stir inside him.

"Let it out, Chad. 'The beast.' I need you to ravish me. I've missed you so much. Take me, Chad. I submit to you and 'the beast' inside you."

"Are you sure, sweetheart?"

"Yes, honey. I'm sure."

"Good, because I'm going to take you—hard."

Without another word, Chad picked me up and laid me on the seat. "The beast" was unleashed. He entered me once again and kept his promise. He took me harder and faster than he ever has, holding my hands above my head as he pounded into me again and again. Vibrant colors and flashing lights swirled around us as our energy flowed between our bodies. We soared higher and higher into our climax. Pleasure washed over us in the most intense wave of tingles as our bodies spasmed together as one. Chad collapsed and rolled us so that I was now lying on his chest. We laid there in silence for a few more minutes, just relishing in the tingles coursing through us in soothing waves. I know I have to tell Chad about being late, but I'm not quite sure how. So, I just eased my way into it.

"Chad?"

"Yes, sweetheart?"

"How do you suppose things will be once we're married?"

"Everything can only get better from here, my love. We won't have to sneak out to make love anymore for one thing."

"Yeah, I know that, but I was referring to being married in our senior year of high school. Will people look down on us or judge us for being married so young?"

"They may, but we can't let that get to us. Humans don't understand our love and our bonds. We'll just laugh it off and tell them they are just jealous of our love. It's clear that a lot of them already are."

"I guess I'd be jealous too if I were them. I do find it sad that there's a chance they'll never know a love like ours in their whole lives. They don't even have as long to live with their lovers as we do with ours, either."

"While that could be true, that's just part of being human versus being Nymphean. I know

all of this is still pretty new for both of us, but I
am so glad I'll be able to spend my eternity
with you."

"I feel the same way about you, honey. I'll
admit, I've also been thinking about what it'd
be like to start a family with you. How will our
children look? Will they look more like you,
more like me, or a mix of us both? What will
their personalities be? Will we make good
parents and be able to give them the lives they
deserve?"

"Hahaha! Easy, sweetheart. We will be the
best parents we can. Our children will be
smart, funny, a bit spunky, and will be
beautiful. I want to start a family with you too,
but I wouldn't complain if we can have a few
years with just the two of us, so we can be
better prepared for our children when they do
come along."

"What if they come along sooner than that?"

"Then, they will be the greatest blessing I
could ask for."

"I'm glad you feel that way."

"Paisley, you are my everything. Raising a
family with you will be the greatest
accomplishment of my life."

"Do you really mean it?"

"I really do."

"Good, because I think I may be pregnant." I
instantly felt my pulse quicken, and I began to
panic. Chad placed his hand on my tummy,
cradling the spot where our child could be
growing and developing as we speak.

"Paisley, are you sure?"

"I haven't taken a test yet, but my cycle is late. I've been on my birth control for so long that I haven't been late since right after my cycles began. I missed two pills, though. The first one was the day of my accident at the dock. The second one was the following day when I still had a bit of a concussion."

He held me in his arms, still cradling my tummy, and kissed my forehead.

"Sweetheart, did I hurt you when we made love?"

"No, honey, you didn't. You were amazing. I'd tell you if you had."

"Okay. Good. So, you're sure you're okay?"

"Yes," I giggled. "I'm perfectly fine, my love. Are you okay? I just dropped the ultimate bomb on you."

"Paisley, sweetheart, I'm more than okay. You carrying my child would be the most wonderful news I've ever gotten. How soon can we know for sure?"

"Well, I'm only a few days late. A home pregnancy test may be able to tell us for sure by Wednesday if I haven't gotten my cycle by then."

"All right. Well, let's plan on getting a test and finding out for sure before we start jumping to conclusions. Oh, Paisley, if you are carrying my child, you're going to look so cute with a baby bump."

"So, you're not mad or upset?"

"Sweetheart, no. Why on earth would you think I'd be mad or upset if we created a life together? I mean, sure, I had hoped that our children would come a little later on, but that doesn't mean I'm disappointed in the least little bit. It just means our parents are going to kill us when they find out that we completed our bond before we were married."

"Yeah, I thought about that too. What if we just eloped? We could tell our parents that we couldn't fight the *urge* to bond and 'the beast' inside of you any longer. We could also say that we conceived a baby on our wedding night. We could still have a real wedding ceremony for all of our friends and families in December. I may not be showing by then if I am pregnant. We could call the magistrate and get married at the courthouse with Molly and Toby as our witnesses."

"Paisley, I'd marry you right this instant if I could. Let me check online and see what I can find out about applying for a marriage license."

"Okay, let's see what the Internet says."

Chad took his phone out of his pants pocket and began searching the Internet. "According to the site on US Marriage Laws, there's no waiting time or blood tests required in our county. We can go and apply for it at the Register of Deeds office. All we need is our driver's licenses, birth certificates, social security cards, and sixty dollars. The soonest I'd be able to go with you would be Thursday. I don't have football practice, but I do have training with our dads. I have a bit of time in between school and then, though. We can buy a home pregnancy test Monday or Tuesday night during our study session before then, so we'll know for sure. If we are expecting a baby, we will go to the Register of Deeds office, apply for a marriage license, and get married as soon as possible. You'll also need to be under the care of an obstetrician to make sure you and our baby are healthy for the whole pregnancy."

"Wow, you are taking this so much better than I ever imagined. I love you, Chad!"

"I love you too, Paisley. I'll do anything and everything in my power to take care of you and make sure you know just how much I love you. You asked me how I felt about all this. How are you feeling about possibly having a baby so soon?"

"Honestly? I'm excited, scared, and anxious all at the same time. I'll be as big as a barrel at graduation. Maybe I should see if I can do home schooling for the second semester. That way, I won't have to face any mean jeers from anyone at school, and no one will have to know. I'll stay out of public and only go out for my doctor's appointments. I can conceal the pregnancy under the graduation gown a lot better than in a pair of jeans and a t-shirt."

"We can talk about all of that when the time comes, sweetheart. No need to worry yourself with that just yet. If it just so happens that you're carrying our baby, you'll have my full support no matter what you decide."

"Oh, Chad, you are so wonderful! Thank you."

"Nothing to thank me for, sweetheart."

He tilted my face up to his, tenderly kissed my lips, and licked over my bottom one with his tongue. I parted my lips for him, and our kiss deepened. He rolled on top of me, and we made love once more, savoring one another in the moonlight before heading back and parting ways for the night.

The next few days came in a blur. I still hadn't gotten my monthly cycle. So, Chad and I went to a drug store in another county during our study session Tuesday night. I woke up Wednesday morning before my alarm clock even had a chance to go off. I hadn't slept well in days, worrying about the pregnancy test. The moment of truth had finally come.

I took the pregnancy test out of my backpack and headed into the bathroom. I read over the instructions and took the test. I sat the test on the counter and waited. Time seemed to stand still. Each minute dragged on for what felt like forever. I checked the test after the suggested time had passed. The digital screen said one word. Pregnant.

I sat down on the edge of the tub, and silent tears began to fall down my cheeks. My heart is pounding in my chest, I feel the color draining from my face, and I began to hyperventilate. I'm carrying Chad's baby—our baby. This isn't the kind of news that should be given over the phone, in a text message, or even mind-to-mind. Although, I'm sure he can sense how I'm feeling right now. Our connection leaves nothing to the imagination. I'll tell him in person the first moment we have alone. Our lives are about to change forever.

I wrapped the pregnancy test in toilet paper and hid it inside my backpack to show Chad before I disposed of the evidence. Then, I continued to get ready for school, as though nothing had changed. It's just another typical Wednesday morning. I just have to focus on right now and not worry about what happens next. I just have to take things one step at a time. First, I'll take Caden to school. Then, I'll get ready to tell my bonded mate that we will be parents in about eight months or so. No biggie, right? Yeah. Right.

I remembered the things Chad said about having a baby right now. It still doesn't lessen the anxiety I'm having about telling him about my confirmed suspicions. How am I supposed to act normal, as though nothing has changed? I have a small life form growing inside me. One that was created in love and passion. One that will be cherished and loved from now throughout the rest of our lives. I just hope that I'll be the mother this little one needs and deserves. I made a promise to myself and my baby that I'll do my very best to be that and so much more.

"Good morning, sweetheart. Are you okay?"

"Good morning, honey. Yes, I'm okay."

"Did you remember to take the test?"

"Yes, I did."

"And? How did it go?"

"I'd rather talk to you about it in person, face-to-face, and mind-to-mind."

"Paisley, the suspense is killing me. I didn't sleep at all last night, thinking about you having to take the test and face the result alone. I just want you to know that we will make great parents, whether it happens sooner or later. I'm more excited than ever to start our lives together. If a new baby is a part of that right off the bat, then I can hardly wait to gaze into his or her eyes for the first time."

"Well, I'm not giving anything away just yet. You'll have to wait a little while longer."

"How long are we talking?"

"However long it takes to steal away a private moment together."

"Okay. I am at your mercy, sweetheart. Please don't keep me waiting too much longer."

"I promise I won't, my love. I love you, honey. I'll see you soon."

"I love you too, sweetheart. I'll see you then."

I put the finishing touches on my makeup and headed downstairs. Mama had made pancakes for breakfast. Caden was already digging into the stack and filling up his plate.

"Mmmmm! Those pancakes look and smell great, Mama!"

"Thanks! You'd better grab them while you can before your brother devours them all."

"Yeah, Paisley. You'd better hurry up. They're delicious!"

"Well, if you insist. I suppose I can't pass up Mama's pancakes."

"You're looking a little pale, sweetie. Are you okay?"

"Yeah, I'm fine. I may be a little dehydrated. I'll be sure to drink more water today and see if that helps."

"Okay. Well, let me know if it doesn't, and I'll make an appointment with your doctor."

"Thanks, Mama. I'm sure I'll feel better once I wake up a bit more. I didn't sleep that well last night."

"Oh? Is something troubling you, sweetie?"

"No. Not that I can think of."

"Okay. You can talk to me about anything. I was your age once, you know."

"Yes, Mama. I know that. Thank you."

"Caden, did you even chew those pancakes, or did you just inhale them, Son? Hahaha!"

"What? I'm a growing boy," he said with a huge grin. "That, and they were delicious. Thanks again, Mama."

"You're welcome. Brush your teeth and fix your hair. You still have a cowlick in the back from your pillow."

"Yes, Mama."

I spread peanut butter on each pancake, drizzled a little bit of melted butter and warm maple syrup on top, and savored every single bite. I've always enjoyed putting peanut butter on my pancakes, but it tasted so much better today for some reason. It seems like all of my senses are slightly heightened—my senses of smell and taste in particular. The tanginess of the orange juice, the syrup's sweetness, and the creaminess of the peanut butter all seemed more intense than usual. Could the growing baby in my womb be causing heightened sensations? Surely not.

I finished the rest of my breakfast, thanked Mama again, and headed upstairs to brush my teeth and grab my backpack from my room. Then, I bounded downstairs and went out to my car to wait for Caden to come out. He came out a few short minutes later and tossed his backpack into the back seat. We fastened our seatbelts and were off to school. I dropped Caden off at his school and headed to mine.

Chad was waiting in the parking lot when I pulled into the spot next to his truck. He walked around to my door, opened it, and took my hand to help me out of my car. He instantly pulled me into his arms and buried his face in my hair.

"Please don't make me wait any longer, sweetheart. I can't take it anymore."

"Look at me, Chad." He pulled back just enough to gaze into my eyes.

"The test was positive. I'm pregnant. We're going to have a baby!"

His eyes lit up and seemed to dance with pure joy. *"REALLY?! Oh, Paisley! I couldn't be happier! I love you so very much!"*

"I love you too, Chad! I'm happy too, but I'm also pretty scared. Are we ready to do this?"

"I know, my love. I'm scared too. We will get through this together. We may not be ready right at this very instant, but we have a little while before our baby is born. We can do everything in our power to get ready for him or her to arrive."

"What would I ever do without you?"

"I have no idea, but luckily, you won't have to find out. I'll be here with you every step of the way. Come on, let's get to class."

I feel like I am walking on air with Chad holding my hand and smiling down at me. He truly is happy about our baby. I was worried that he wouldn't be. I can imagine that most guys his age would've taken the news a lot differently. I'm so thankful that this isn't the case. Everything is going to be just fine. *We* are going to be just fine. Chad walked me into my homeroom class just as the bell rang.

"I'll be back to walk you to class in a few minutes, okay?"

"That sounds wonderful, my love. Thank you."

He gave me a hug, placed his hand on my tummy, and kissed my forehead before turning to walk down the hallway to his homeroom class. I must've been daydreaming because I hardly realized the bell had rung for the first period. Chad was waiting for me outside of the classroom. He took my hand in his, and we walked together to our Chemistry class. Chad kept beaming his gorgeous smile at me throughout the entire course.

"I still can't believe you're carrying our baby. I can't stop smiling."

"Oh, honey. Neither can I. I can't help but think about how we're going to break the news to everyone, especially to our parents."

"I'm going to call around and see if I can find a Nymphean priest that'll be available tomorrow after school. If I can, we'll talk to Toby and Molly. We'll meet them all at the courthouse, and our marriage will be official. Our parents will have to understand. We can still have a more public wedding in December, but I want to be already married before we announce the pregnancy news."

"What about rings? Don't we need wedding rings for the ceremony?"

"I already have them. I got our wedding rings when I bought your engagement ring. They are safe in my room."

"So, are we going to keep our marriage a secret for now, or are we going to tell our parents the truth about everything?"

"I think they may take the news better if we get married, then tell them the truth about it all. We'll explain everything. Both of our dads know about 'the beast' feeling inside me because of my new power and responsibility. My dad told me that the best way to help control it was to complete our bond. I could just tell him that 'the beast' took over, and we

ended up completing our bond sooner than expected."

"Yeah, I think it would be best to be open with them about it. We'd still have to live separately for now until we can get our place."

"Dad told me that he and Mom would line up a house for us near Toby and Molly's house. I think the one a few houses down from their land is for sale. I'll look into it and see if we can go ahead and get it before someone else does. Molly"s mom is a realtor. Maybe she can help as well."

"I'll look into home school as well. I don't exactly want to be waddling down the halls between classes."

"I'd gladly walk you to each one and kiss you and your tummy in front of everyone. I'm not ashamed of you or our baby. Our baby was made with love. I'm not going to let anyone treat us or it any differently."

"I know, honey, but I think I'd rather be at home. I've heard pregnancy isn't always easy for our kind. I could have a miscarriage in my first trimester if I don't take it easy."

"All right, sweetheart. I'll support your decision either way. I just want what's best for you and our baby."

"Thank you, honey. So do I."

The rest of our classes went on as usual, only with Chad checking on me a lot more frequently to make sure I am okay in my "delicate state." It is still too soon for morning sickness. That may not begin for a few more weeks. Chad is already pretty protective over me, but now that he knows about the baby, he's even more defensive. I know he loves and wants this baby as much as I do. He places his hand on my tummy every time I see him.

Chad and I grabbed some sandwiches, chips, and bottled water from the cafeteria and headed out to his truck in the parking lot. Chad made a few calls while we ate. There is one Nymphean priest available to meet us directly after school tomorrow. We called the Register of Deeds office and had them pull certified copies of our birth certificates so they'd be ready for tomorrow. We'd have access to all documents needed for our marriage license and certificate. Now, all that was left to do was to ask Molly and Toby to be our witnesses. We still had a little bit more time left of our lunch period, so we headed back to the quad to find them. They were still sitting there at the table. Max had already gone to his next class.

"Hey, Molly. Hey, Toby. Could we talk to you two in private for a few minutes?" I asked.

"Sure," Molly said. "What's up?"

"Well, the thing is, Chad and I, we're eloping."

"What? When?"

"After school tomorrow. We'd like you both to be our witnesses."

"Are you sure this is what you want to do?" Toby asked. "What brought this on?"

Chad and I looked at one another and smiled. "Well, what we're about to tell you must stay between us. Please promise us that we have your word."

"Yes, of course," Molly said.

"We won't tell anyone. We promise," Toby said.

"Thank you," Chad said. "The truth is, we've already completed our bond. It happened not long after our connection awakened."

"Then, something else happened," I said. "We just found out this morning that we are expecting a baby."

"Ohmygosh! How exciting," Molly said in an excited whisper. "Have you told your parents yet?"

"No. You two are the first to know. We wanted to go ahead and be married before we told them."

"What about the wedding in December?"

"We will still have that ceremony," Chad said, "but the only ones who will know that we are already married will be you two and the priest."

"When are you going to tell your parents?" Toby asked.

"After we are already legally married."

"Are you going to finish school?" Molly asked.

"Yes, I'll be doing the rest of my school work from home next semester, though. I don't want to waddle through the hallways between classes with a big pregnant belly. It's not because I'm ashamed of being pregnant, though. I'd just rather be on the safe side in case there are complications."

"I understand completely," Molly said.

"You and Chad have our full support," Toby said.

"Okay, so, you'll meet us at the Montgomery County Courthouse in Troy after school tomorrow?"

"Absolutely. We wouldn't miss it for the world."

"Thank you both so very much."

"That's what friends are for."

The bell for the third period rang a few minutes later, and Chad walked me to class as always. He tilted my face up to his and placed a gentle kiss on my lips while no one was looking.

"I'm only a silent message away if you need me," he said, mind-to-mind.

"Thank you, honey. I'm sure I'll be just fine. I haven't had any fainting spells or nausea yet."

"I'll come running the minute you do. I thought I hated being away from you before we knew about the baby, but I really hate being away from you now."

"I know the feeling. I never want to leave your side." He reached up and cupped my face with his hands.

"It won't be too much longer, sweetheart. We'll have our own home together soon. I may do my studies at home with you next semester as well."

"What about basketball? I know how much you love playing and were looking forward to getting a college scholarship."

"You and our baby are far more important than basketball. I'll make more

than enough money working for the Royal Family to go to college without a basketball scholarship."

"Are you sure you want to give up playing basketball?"

"Yes, I'm absolutely sure."

I nodded, and he kissed my forehead. A moment later, he reluctantly let me go and walked me to my desk like he always does. The rest of the day went by as any other day would. Chad walked me to my last class and then waited to walk with me to my car before he went to football practice. Then, I went to pick up Caden from school and went home to wait for my study date with Chad.

We went for a drive to get some alone time while we went over the lessons for the week and prepared for the upcoming unit test. I quizzed Chad while he drove. Then, he had me recite my upcoming speech that was due on Friday. Our study sessions were starting to pay off. I was beginning to get the hang of being in front of an audience with his advice, and he was gaining a better understanding of Chemistry and Biology. We do make a great couple; not that I ever had any doubts about that. I love Chad Greene with all that I am. I'm so ready to begin our lives together. Tonight is the last night that I will legally be Paisley Rose O'Riley. Tomorrow, I will become Mrs. Paisley O'Riley Greene.

Chapter 18

Chad

I can hardly wait to get to Paisley as the last bell rings, releasing us from school for the day. I walked her to her car, and we said our goodbyes. Then, we each picked up our siblings from school and took them home before heading to the courthouse. I needed to get the rings and my social security card anyway. That's not something I just carry around in my wallet. I keep it locked away in a fireproof safe in my room where our wedding rings are now.

I was only home long enough to grab everything I needed and kiss Mom on the cheek. She knows my usual schedule, so she didn't ask where I was going. I'm glad she didn't because I hate lying to her or Dad, for that matter. Not telling them about the most recent events felt like I'd betrayed them, but I couldn't tell them. Not just yet. Certain things needed to be taken care of first. Paisley and I will find a way to break the news to them all when the time is right, but for now, the current situation is still our little secret.

I stopped by Paisley's house to pick her up, and we headed straight to the courthouse. We arrived just in time. The priest walked up the steps to the main entrance as we were pulling into a parking spot. I gave her a searing-hot kiss and told her I love her. I hopped out, opened her door for her, and helped her out of my truck.

We walked inside and followed the signs to the Register of Deeds office, paid for our copies of our birth certificates and the marriage license, and filled out the application. Then, the clerk gave us the marriage certificate for the priest to fill out after the ceremony. We then headed to one of the open courtrooms, where the priest, Molly, and Toby were waiting for us. We handed the priest the certificate, and he began the ceremony without any questions or further ado.

"We are gathered here today to unite Lady Paisley Rose O'Riley and Sir Chadwick Owen Greene into the sanctity of marriage. Who gives this woman to this man?"

"I, Prince Tobias Sylar Brennan and Princess Molly Isabella Hendrix, do so on behalf of her parents, Sir Taggart O'Riley and Lady Fiona O'Riley."

The priest continued with the traditional Nymphean wedding ceremony as I took Paisley's hand in mine and gazed into her eyes. The time had finally come for us to recite our vows to one another.

"I, Sir Chadwick Owen Greene, in the name of the spirit of God that resides within us all, by the life that courses within my blood and the love that resides within my heart, take thee, Lady Paisley Rose O'Riley, to my hand, my heart, and my soul, to be my chosen one. To desire thee and be desired by thee, to possess thee, and be possessed by thee, without sin nor shame, for naught can exist in the purity of my love for thee. I promise to love thee wholly and completely without restraint, in sickness, and in health, in plenty and in poverty, in life and beyond, where we shall meet, remember, and love again. I shall not seek to change thee in any way. I shall respect thee, thy beliefs, thy people, and thy ways as I respect myself. I pledge my eternity to you."

"I, Lady Paisley Rose O'Riley, in the name of the spirit of God that resides within us all, by the life that courses within my blood, and the love that resides within my heart, take thee, Sir Chadwick Owen Greene, to my hand, my heart, and my soul to be my chosen one. To desire and be desired by thee, to possess thee, and be possessed by thee, without sin nor shame, for naught can exist in the purity of my love for thee. I promise to love thee wholly and completely without restraint, in sickness, and in health, in plenty and in poverty, in life and beyond, where we shall meet, remember, and love again. I shall not seek to change thee in any way. I shall respect thee, thy beliefs, thy people, and thy ways as I respect myself. I pledge my eternity to you."

Molly handed our rings to the priest, and he began the ring ceremony. The priest then gave them to us to place on one another's fingers.

I removed Paisley's engagement ring, placed her wedding ring on her finger, and stated, "With this ring, I thee wed. My eternity belongs to you." I replaced her engagement ring, where it fit together with her new wedding ring.

She then placed my ring on my finger and stated, "With this ring, I thee wed. My eternity belongs to you."

The priest then said, "By the powers vested in me, I now pronounce you husband and wife. Sir Chadwick, you may now kiss your bride."

I took her into my arms, gently dipped her, and placed a romantic kiss on her lips. Toby and Molly cheered and applauded as I broke our kiss and brought Paisley back upright. Everyone signed the marriage certificate, and we delivered it to the Register of Deeds.

Paisley and I were legally married, and our child would be born into a legitimate marriage. We need to schedule Paisley a doctor's appointment to make sure she and the baby are healthy. Then, we'll figure out a way to tell our parents without causing them to resort to murder. I'd thought about telling them at a private dinner, just the six of us plus one unseen guest, of course.

Paisley and I hid our wedding rings from everyone. No one knew we'd gotten married. Paisley did go to the social security office to change her name. It would take a few weeks for her new card to come in the mail. We'd have told our parents about our news by then anyway. We wouldn't want them to be blindsided when the card comes in the mail addressed to her new name.

We were able to get Paisley an appointment the following Thursday, right after school. The days leading up to her appointment flew by. Nothing seemed out of the ordinary. She said she hadn't felt any differently; no morning sickness, fainting spells, or extreme fatigue as of yet. I picked Paisley up and drove her to her appointment so we could be there together.

The doctor had requested a blood test, so we stopped by the lab before checking into the OB/GYN clinic for her appointment. We only waited a short time before the nurse called her name. My palms were sweaty, and I was feeling anxious. We were lucky that the OB/GYN she would be assigned to was Nymphean like us. Dr. Addison had overseen both of our mother's pregnancies and had delivered us both when the time came.

"Lady Paisley and Sir Chadwick, I presume. I was wondering when I'd be seeing the two of you. Your parents were so excited about your future bond. I hadn't heard of an official wedding ceremony, though."

"Well, we were married in a private setting—very private. We haven't informed our parents. So, we'd appreciate your confidentiality. We are planning on telling them soon."

"I understand. You have my word as your doctor. Now, Lady Paisley, let's review your blood test, shall we?"

Dr. Addison confirmed Paisley's pregnancy and estimated that she was about six weeks pregnant. We conceived our baby on August ninth. He or she will be due on May sixteenth. Dr. Addison prescribed some prenatal vitamins for Paisley to take and gave her a few different sites to research, so she'll know what to expect during her pregnancy and answer the questions she'll have along the way. She also did an ultrasound while we were there. We got to see our little bundle of joy for the first time. Dr. Addison recorded the baby's size and took a few screenshots for us to take with us. We requested three to give one to each set of parents and keep one for ourselves.

I'm already so in love with our baby. I can't help but touch Paisley's tummy every time I am near her. Dr. Addison told us that we would find out the baby's sex in another four to six weeks. I'm so excited! I can hardly wait to meet him or her. We will need to find other expecting couples once we learn its sex to find our baby's chosen mate. I wonder who its parents will be, if we already know them, or if they will be from somewhere else in the country or even across the world.

Paisley and I organized a private dinner the following Saturday evening for our parents at her house. Molly and Toby will be watching our siblings at my home. So, we can have the time we need with just us and our parents. I don't know how this will go, but we are hoping for the best outcome possible.

Molly popped in and took Caden to my house Saturday evening. She and Toby ordered pizzas for everyone and had found a few movies on Netflix for the kids to watch. With our siblings taken care of, it was time for Paisley and me to get started on dinner. We made lemon-peppered Cornish hens with glazed baby carrots, a fresh garden salad, and a gallon of sweet tea. Our parents should be here shortly.

Let's hope this goes better than expected because it can go a few different ways. They could be ecstatic about becoming grandparents, or they could be furious with us for not waiting until after graduation. Either way, there wasn't much that could be done about it now. Paisley and I are married, we have completed our bond, and are expecting our first child.

I placed the ultrasound pictures into cards and envelopes for both sets of parents. Paisley set the table with plates, glasses, cutlery, and tapered, non-drip candles. Paisley's parents arrived first and were already asking questions about what this was all about. We simply told them that we would explain everything after all of the guests had come.

Once both sets of parents were present, we gathered around the table and took our seats. Everyone enjoyed the meal we'd prepared and had also enjoyed being together as two families about to be joined in a marriage they had no idea had already occurred. It was officially time to tell them our news. I spoke up and addressed everyone to get the ball rolling.

"I'm sure you all are wondering why we have asked you to have dinner with us tonight. Paisley and I have a couple of significant announcements to make."

"We already know you're engaged and your upcoming wedding date. What other announcements could you have?" Fiona asked.

"Well, there are two announcements we'd like to make. The first one is that Paisley and I are already married."

"What? What do you mean you're already married?" Taggart asked, with rage washing all over his face.

"Calm down, babe," Fiona said as she placed a hand on his arm to calm him down. "I'm sure there's an excellent explanation as to what brought this on."

"As I'm sure you all know, I've inherited the responsibility of becoming the Leader of the Royal Guard. Along with that responsibility came great power. I feel as though there is an overly protective 'beast' inside of me. My dad's idea to control 'the beast' was to marry Paisley and complete our bond as soon as possible. Although we had planned on waiting, that didn't necessarily happen. I felt 'the beast' inside of me getting stronger each day as our connection grew stronger. We both decided it would be best to elope and gave in to the *urge* to bond." I handed each set of parents their envelopes.

"What are these," Mom asked.

"Please, go ahead and open them," Paisley said.

Our mothers opened the envelopes with cautious hands, and tears began to fall.

"Chad, Paisley, is this some kind of joke?" Taggart asked.

"No, this is no joke. We are having a baby," Paisley said very softly. "We just found out. Our baby is due on May sixteenth."

Taggart is furious. "Do you realize what you've done? You've ruined your life, Paisley! What about your dreams of going to school and making a life for yourself? Have you thought about that and how a baby fits into that?"

"Daddy! There was always the possibility of us getting pregnant after our wedding in December. Things just happened a bit sooner than we'd planned. I've decided to finish my senior year at home so that I can take it easy. I want to be able to do what it takes to have a healthy pregnancy."

"So, we're going to be grandparents?" Mom asked.

"Yes, Mom. You are. We are keeping the baby news just inside our families for now, though. We'd also like to continue with the wedding plans in December."

"Those aren't exactly bad ideas. I think they sound pretty feasible," Fiona said.

"What about a place to live? Have you thought of that?" Taggart asked.

"Dad said he'd be able to help us out with buying a house. There's a house a few lots down from Toby and Molly's. We'd like to try to buy it. It would keep us near them so I can properly protect them as the Leader of the Royal Guard."

"Yes, I did say that. Well, I suppose I have a few phone calls to make to see which realtor represents the owner. I'll call CeCe tomorrow and get the process started. You two are going to need somewhere to live sooner than later. Especially since you've bonded and conceived a child, it'll be worse for you two to be apart than ever before. Speaking of which, I'd say congratulations are in order. I know I can speak for us all when I say that we would've preferred you waited a bit longer for all of this, but there's a baby on the way to consider now. Congratulations, Chad and Paisley. I don't know about the rest of you, but I'm personally looking forward to holding my grandchild."

"So am I!" Mom said. "I agree that we all would've rather you waited, but we can't turn back time. All we can do now is help you prepare for your new baby the best we can. It may take a few months to buy the house. As for temporary living arrangements, we could make the basement into your own living space for now. There's a full bathroom down there, as well as a living room set. It's got enough room to put a bed down there too. There's no kitchen, but you're more than welcome to share ours."

"Thank you so much! Are you sure I wouldn't be imposing? Chad and I could just continue living separately until we can get into our own home."

"Nonsense! You two will lose your minds being apart. Especially Chad. I'm sure his protective instincts will get even stronger now that you're carrying his baby. You two should move in together sooner than later."

"Thank you so very much! I really do appreciate it. I'll admit, it has been difficult to be away from one another these past few weeks."

"Then, it's settled. You can move in as soon as possible. We'll even come and help you pack up and get you all settled in. You shouldn't be lifting anything heavy or overdoing it anyway."

"I can't thank you enough, Mom and Dad. This means more to us than you know."

"Think nothing of it. It's the least we can do to get you two off to a good start."

Well, that went much better than I'd expected. Everyone was hugging, and tears of joy were flowing. My parents headed home after dinner, and Paisley and I took care of the cleanup. I wasn't ready to say goodbye to Paisley just yet. She had just turned on the dishwasher and was drying her hands with a dishtowel. I swept her into my arms and crushed my mouth onto hers. The spark and tingles coursed through us and lit my insides on fire. She opened for me instantly, and our tongues swirled together in a heated dance of love and passion. She whimpered as I broke the kiss. Her tanzanite eyes were glowing when she opened them to look into mine.

"I'd like to take my wife for a drive so I can have her all to myself. What do you say, Mrs. Greene?"

"How can I say no to that? I'd love to have some alone time with my husband."

We told her parents we were leaving, and I helped her into my truck. She slid into the center seat, and I hopped in after her. I turned onto Highway 109 and headed for the Uwharrie National Forest. There wouldn't be anyone there at the trailhead, and we'd have plenty of privacy. Paisley kissed my neck and nibbled and sucked on my earlobe the whole way. My bulge is pressing against the zipper of my pants and is now throbbing. I felt "the beast" stir inside me. I needed to be inside of her. Now.

I turned into the small parking area deep enough that my truck wouldn't be seen from the road and turned off the ignition. I unfastened our seatbelts and crushed my mouth to hers. The spark of the kiss sent tingles coursing through us. I undressed

Paisley as quickly as I could and laid her on the seat. The tantalizing scent of strawberries and her peppery arousal wafted into my nostrils. I had to taste her. I lowered my mouth onto her and licked along the slit of her wet folds. A soft whimper caressed her luscious lips, and I felt her fingers in my hair.

"Damn, you taste so good."
"Please don't stop."
"I hadn't planned on it. At least, not until you beg me to."

I plunged my tongue into her tight channel and licked upward to her tiny bundle of nerves, and circled it. Her back arched, and she writhed against me. I inserted two fingers into her channel as I licked, sucked, and teased her sensitive flesh. Colors began to swirl around us, and her muscles began to grip my fingers as her pleasure began to build. Her fingers left my hair and went to the firm buds of her breasts. She pinched and twisted them, heightening her enjoyment. Her skin began to flush, and her body spasmed.

I slid my tongue down and into her once again, so I could savor her juices. I have to keep the baby in mind. I shouldn't be rough with her like I have in the past. Her skin is flushed and glistening with sweat. My God, she is so damned beautiful.

"Chad, I need you. I need you inside of me."

Her sweet plea caused my already engorged bulge to swell even more. I sat up and unfastened my pants. I slid them and my boxer briefs down to my knees. Paisley sat up and straddled my lap. A low groan rumbled in my chest as she sank upon me, impaling herself onto my hardness. The spark and tingles at our joining were so intense. My hips instinctively thrust upwards, plunging into her. I placed my hands on her hips and held her there. The tingles seemed to pulse and heighten the pleasure.

"Your pace, sweetheart. I don't want to hurt you or the baby. Although, I do want to hear you moan and call out my name. There's no one out here to hear us."

She simply nodded and touched my cheek with her hand. She leaned down and took my mouth as she began to ride me. "The beast" inside of me longed to take control, to turn her onto her hands and knees and take her fast and hard. I can't let it take over. I have to maintain control. I used all of the willpower I could muster to tamp "the beast" down. I broke the kiss, trailed kisses down her neck, and leaned her back so I could suck on her gorgeous breasts. I slid my hand to her sex and circled her bundle of nerves. Paisley gripped my shoulders and began to pick up her pace as her muscles tightened around me. Colors swirled around us once again. I was nearly on the verge of spilling into her. I slid my hands up her body and along her arms to her link her hands with mine. Flashing lights joined the swirling colors as our energy combined and swirled within our bodies. Paisley tilted her head back and called out my name. Wave upon wave of orgasmic spasms crashed over us and surged through our bodies.

We sat there, panting in ragged breaths as we came down. Paisley leaned forward and laid her head on my shoulder. I wrapped my arms around her and held her as close as I possibly could. I gently stroked my hands up and down her silky smooth back and whispered into her ear.

"I love you, Paisley Greene. I love you more and more every second, and I love our child too. I never want to hurt either of you. I didn't hurt you when we made love, did I?"

"I love you too, Chad Greene. No, you didn't hurt either of us."

"Good. That's why I wanted us to make love at your pace. I couldn't bear the thought of losing control and hurting either of you. As much as I hate the thought of having to say goodbye, we should probably get you home before it gets too late."

She nodded against my chest and climbed off my lap to get dressed. Once we were both fully clothed, we headed back to her house.

"What do you think about going to pick out a bedroom suit tomorrow?"

"That sounds like a great idea. I'm ready to move in with you, so we won't have to part like this ever again."

"I'll pick you up first thing in the morning, and we'll be there as soon as the furniture store opens."

"I'll start packing my things tonight then. I'd
like to be all settled in as soon as possible. I
don't have a whole lot to pack and move; just
mainly my clothes. We'll be able to get
everything in one trip."

"Do you need any boxes?"

"No, I have a few storage totes I can use.
They'll work just fine."

"I'll stay and help you pack if you'd like."

"Thank you, honey. I'd appreciate that."

We walked together to her door and went
inside to start packing her things. My cell
phone started ringing. It was Mom.

"Hey, Mom. What's up?"

"Are you still with Paisley?"

"Yes, Mom. She's right here. Do you need to
speak to her?"

"No, I just wanted to let you know that your
dad and I have moved your bedroom suit down
to the basement. Have Paisley pack an
overnight bag, and y'all come on home."

"Thanks, Mom. Will do. See y'all soon."

"Well, it looks like we won't have to pick out
any furniture just yet. Mom and Dad just
moved my whole bedroom suite into the
basement for us. She said for you to pack an
overnight bag and for us to come on home."

"Really? That's wonderful! We can come
back tomorrow and get the rest of my stuff
then."

"So, what can I do to help you pack?"

"Nothing, honey. I'll only be a few minutes. I
just need my makeup bag and the rest of my

toiletries, a change of clothes for tomorrow, and something to sleep in.”

“You know, the basement door locks from the inside. You don’t have to sleep in anything if you don’t want to. I always sleep naked anyway.”

“I like the sound of that.”

She packed her bag, we told her parents and little brother goodbye, and headed home. I was finally going to spend a whole night with my wife in my arms.

Paisley

Chad and I arrived at his parents’ house a short time later. We hugged them and thanked them for allowing me to stay with them until we could move into our own home. Then, we headed into the basement to get ready for bed. Chad locked the door behind us, and I put my shower items in the bathroom. Chad came up behind me and wrapped his arms around me. He nuzzled his face into my neck.

I turned around and took his face into my hands, forcing him to look at me. “Chad, look at me. I may be pregnant, but I’m not a delicate flower. While I agree it may not be a good idea to get too rough, I trust you not to hurt us. I trust you. You're strong enough to remain in control of 'the beast' inside of you."

"You really do trust me and have that much faith in me, to not hurt you, huh?"

"Yes, my love. I do. I fully submit to you and 'the beast' inside of you. Take me, Chad. I'm all yours."

I felt his bulge harden as he pressed himself against me. I looked into his glowing amber eyes and slid my hand over the massive bulge. His chest rumbled with a low groan. His eyes were now blazing with fire and desire. His gaze never left mine as he reached into the shower and turned it on.

"Get undressed. Quickly."

I grabbed the hem of my shirt, lifted it over my head, and tossed it into the clothes hamper. I unsnapped my bra and slid the straps over my shoulders and off of my arms. Chad had already stripped completely and was standing in the bathroom's doorway.

"Faster, Paisley, or I'll rip those clothes off of you myself."

I shuddered in excitement, and I felt searing heat rush through my body and settle in my sex. I quickly shed the rest of my clothes and stood bare before him. His blazing eyes traveled over my body and then locked with mine. He stalked closer to me like a tiger stalking its prey. He cupped my sex in his hand and slid two fingers into my channel. The spark and tingles hit my sensitive flesh, and I trembled under his touch.

"Mine."

"Yes, my love. All yours."

The heel of his hand pressed against me as his fingers plunged inside me. My knees nearly buckled, but he wrapped his other arm around me and crushed his mouth to mine in a searing hot kiss. Colors began to swirl around us as pleasure pulsed through me.

"That's it, Paisley. Let go for me. I'm going to take you in that shower. I won't be gentle. I'm going to fuck you. Hard and fast."

Just hearing his voice speak those words in my mind evoked another climax, and I spasmed around his fingers once again.

"In the shower. Now."

I sensed that "the beast" was stirring inside of him and had become restless from Chad suppressing it earlier. I did as I was told and stepped into the shower. The warm spray poured over me. Chad stepped in behind me and turned me to face him. He knelt in front of me and put my leg over his shoulder. He looked up at me once more and buried his face in my sex. Colors swirled around us once again in a psychedelic cyclone as another orgasm spasmed through me. Chad stood, picked me up, and sat me down onto him. He pressed me against the cold shower wall and pounded into me just as he'd promised. I couldn't suppress the moan from escaping my lips as he thrust into me.

"Yes, Chad. Fuck me just like that. Take me. Hard. I want 'the beast,' and I want it now."

Chad's eyes burned into mine, and I felt my eyes burning into his. I wanted him to unleash "the beast" and take me. I knew he'd never hurt our unborn child or me, but I also wanted him to dominate me and take me, to sate "the beast" inside him. An almost feral growl rumbled in his chest. "The beast" is unleashed. Excitement coursed through me, and goose flesh erupted all over my body. Chad's thrusts became more powerful as he slammed into me over and over and over. Colors swirled as I felt my muscles clench around him. I was not prepared for the intensity of the climax that crashed over me.

"Chad! Oh, my God! Yes, yes, yes!"

"Soar with me, Paisley. Mine. Mine!"

I climaxed harder than I ever had before. I was light-headed, and every muscle in my body was weak. My knees buckled underneath me when Chad sat me on my feet. I slid down the shower wall and sat there, catching my breath, with my head between my knees.

"Oh my God, Paisley! Are you all right?! Oh, God! I hurt you. I lost control, let "the beast" out, and I hurt you. What have I done?"

"Shh... No, honey. I'm all right—just a little light-headed. I've never climaxed that hard. That's all. I'm okay, and the baby is okay. You didn't hurt us. I promise."

"You're sure? I will never forgive myself if I hurt either of you."

"Yes, I'm sure. You didn't hurt either of us. I'd tell you if you did, but you didn't."

"Oh, thank God. 'The beast' I felt it take over. I should have never lost control like that, not with you being pregnant. It was irresponsible of me. I won't let it happen again. I won't give in to it again."

"Chad, I told you that I wanted 'the beast,' remember? I wanted you to take me hard and fast. That was so intense! I loved it!"

His expression lightened. He slowly shook his head and smiled at me.

"You are incredible. Do you know that? You never cease to amaze me. I love you so much. Please stop me next time if I ever get too forceful. I never want to hurt you or our baby."

"I trust you, Chad. You won't hurt our baby or me. You need to believe that in yourself. I don't believe that even 'the beast' would allow you to hurt either one of us. It is protective over us after all."

"Deep down, I know you're right, but still. I don't want to risk it. I need you to stop me if I lose control and get too rough."

"I like rough, but I promise to stop you if you go overboard."

"Thank you. That's all I ask."

Chad helped me stand and lathered my hair with my shampoo. He massaged my scalp with his strong hands and then turned me so that the water rinsed out the suds. Then, he rubbed the conditioner into my hair, making sure to get it to the ends. Again, he helped rinse everything out. I returned the favor for him. He bent his knees and leaned his head back to allow me to reach. Then, we lathered each other with body wash. He seemed to worship every curve and crevice of my body. I traced every line and ridge of muscle on his hard body and rinsed him with the shower wand. Chad turned the water off and reached outside the shower for two clean towels. He wrapped one around me, patted the water from my body, and did the same for himself.

We brushed our teeth, and Chad carried me in his arms to the bed. Our bed. The covers were already turned down. He laid me down gently and climbed in beside me. He pulled me closer to his side, and I laid my head on his chest. I draped my leg over him, and we drifted off to sleep.

We were so tired that we didn't move all night. We were in the same position the following morning as the sunshine lit up the room from the double doors that led down to the lake. I still couldn't believe that I had stayed the whole night with Chad, my husband. Although that's exactly what he is to me now, and I'm his wife, it still sounded surreal. I gazed up at his handsome face. His eyes are still closed, and his long, dark eyelashes are resting upon his chiseled cheeks. He is so incredibly gorgeous, and he's all mine. I hope our baby resembles its father, with his dark hair and blazing amber and honey-colored eyes.

I gently caressed his chest, running my fingers through the spray of dark hair, and circled his coppery-brown buds. They responded to my touch, and a slight smile crept upon his lips.

"Good morning, sweetheart. How did you sleep?"

"Good morning, honey. I slept better than I think I have my whole life."

"Same here. Having you in my arms made a huge difference. I hated being away from you and sleeping alone when I needed you right here with me."

"Trust me. I know all too well. I think even our baby knew we were too far apart."

"Speaking of the baby, we should probably get some breakfast. That baby needs proper nourishment so he can grow up nice and strong like his father."

"What makes you think it's a boy? We could be having a little girl, you know."

"I don't know. That's the first time I've thought about our baby being a boy. It's like something just came over me that it's a boy."

"Hmm. I'll be happy either way, but you may be right. Before you woke up, I was thinking about our baby resembling you with your dark hair and the same colored eyes."

"We should probably start thinking of baby names before too long."

"Yes, we should. He'll need a good strong name for sure. We could make him Chadwick Owen Greene, Junior, and call him CJ for short. Or, we could name him after our friends, Toby and Max."

"I like both of those options. Although, I think Toby and Max would feel honored if we named our son after them."

"Great idea, honey. He'd be Tobias Maxwell Greene, or maybe we could use their middle names and name him Sylar Austin Greene. Now, let's get some breakfast. It's time to feed our growing boy."

I sat up, started to get out of bed to get dressed, and follow Chad upstairs to the kitchen. That's when it hit me—my first bout of morning sickness. I ran as fast as I could to the bathroom and knelt in front of the toilet. I didn't have anything in my stomach, but that didn't seem to matter. I threw up until I was all I could do was dry heave. Chad knelt beside me, held back my hair with one hand, and rubbed my back with the other. He tried to soothe me as best as he could, but the nausea was just too much. He brought me a glass of water. I took a small sip. It felt so good going down my throat but came back up as soon as it hit my stomach. I felt awful. I finally got a break from throwing up and was able to follow Chad up to the kitchen. His mom, Shannon, was already milling about and was cooking breakfast. The smell of bacon wafted into my nostrils, and my stomach turned once again. I barely made it to the trash can in time.

Chad's mom gasped and came to my side immediately. "Oh, you poor thing. Morning sickness, huh?"

I tried to answer her between heaves but could only nod.

"I remember that all too well. Saltine crackers will help a little bit, well that and plenty of water. I always had the worst morning sickness if I waited too long to eat something. It was so bad. I had to set alarms to wake myself up in the middle of the night to eat a few crackers just to have something on my stomach."

I took a few steadying breaths in and out. Chad handed me a cold washcloth. It felt so good on my face. His mom gave me a few saltine crackers and a bottle of water to see if I could keep it down. They helped a bit, but I still felt queasy.

"How long is this supposed to last?"

"Oh, sweetie. I'm afraid it can last on into your second trimester. When did it start?"

"Just this morning."

"I'm afraid this is just the beginning then. I had it from the time I found out I was pregnant until about the fourteenth week. That was the first sign I had that I was pregnant, other than being a few days late. Our cycles are always haywire anyway, so I didn't think anything of it until the morning sickness hit me."

"Does it last all day?"

"It can. Every woman's pregnancy is different. Each one of my pregnancies was different. I hardly had any morning sickness at all with Tabby, but I stayed sick with the boys for months!"

I guess I'll have to keep a box of crackers and bottled water in my backpack to snack on between classes. At least this school semester is halfway through. It'll be over just before

Christmas. I'll finish my schooling from home so that I can take it easy. I want to do what's best for my baby.

"Well, Chad and I both have had the feeling that this baby is a boy, but we won't know for at least another month."

"Trust me. You'll know before the doctor can confirm it."

"How?"

"You'll sense it. Your maternal instinct will tell you. You may already know. If you already have a feeling it's a boy, then it probably is." She smiled at me and returned to the stove to finish cooking breakfast.

I guess those Greene boys are dead set on making their mothers sick during pregnancy. It looks like saltine crackers and bottled water are going to become staples of my new diet. How am I going to hide them from everyone at school to keep them from figuring out our secret? I'm sure the cat will be out of the bag soon, whether we want it to or not. I'm not ashamed of being pregnant by any means, but I'd hate to start a trend among the humans and other Nymphs our age.

We aren't well prepared, but we are better off than some young adults would be in our situation. Our noble status in our community does have its benefits. Our families have served and protected the Royal Family for many years and were compensated quite generously. Chad is to become the next Leader of the Royal Guard. Our baby will be very well protected.

I took Shannon's advice. I ate some more saltine crackers and stayed as hydrated as I could. I even set the alarm on my phone to wake up in the middle of the night, so I could eat a few crackers to stave off the sickness. It wasn't foolproof, but it did help some. Sneaking crackers and water between classes and trying not to show any difference in behavior was harder than I thought.

I was starting to feel more and more easily fatigued. I chose to nap while Chad went to football practice and his training with our fathers. We studied together afterward for a little while, but the baby growing inside me was draining my body of energy and nutrients. Chad and I made love and connected the Nymphean way to share energy at least once a day to help maintain my energy levels.

It was beginning to affect him too. I was taking more energy than I was able to give him. His training and football practices weren't easy on him, but he was getting stronger still. I think "the beast" inside of him helped with that. As Chad grew more powerful, so did "the beast." His keen instincts continued to develop, as well. He was beginning to have dreams at night of things to come. Some of his nightmares are so intense that he thrashes and kicks in his sleep and sometimes awakens in a cold sweat. He won't talk about them, no matter how many times I ask. He says he doesn't want to worry me and cause any stress to me or the baby. He may not want to upset me by telling me, but

I'm still worried nonetheless. I can sense how concerned and how bothered he is by his dreams. Whatever is coming cannot be good.

Chapter 19

Chad

Everyone is dressed to impress, in evening gowns, tuxedos, glitter, and glamour. The venue is packed with Nymphs from all over the world—Royal Council members, nobles, world leaders, politicians, and commoners alike. Dad approached me, smiling, and pulled me in for a hug.

"This event is going so smoothly, and it's all thanks to you and your security efforts. The Royal Guard has never been more prepared, more trained, or more equipped with the best technology money can buy than they are now. I'm so proud of you, Son."

"Thanks, Dad. I couldn't have done it without you and Sir Taggart."

"We would never set you up to fail, Son. You had it in you the whole time. Your instincts are so very impressive. We just helped you develop them further. We owe our families' safety and the safety of the Royal Family to you."

A voice came through on my earpiece. "Sparrows are ready to fly." That meant that Molly and Toby were about to enter the venue. I hurried to their private quarters to escort them.

It's showtime. "I want a status check from each checkpoint and perimeter guard. ASAP."

The guards began rattling off their statuses one after the other. Everything was going as planned. We'd rehearsed every detail multiple times on a tabletop model. Then, it had been practiced over and over until it was second nature. Everyone knew their positions and their responsibilities by heart, but still, something had my hackles standing on end. Something felt off. Maybe it's just nerves. Then, it hit me like a freight train—a premonition.

There were bombs set to detonate all around the venue. No one would make it out alive with that amount of explosives. I alerted all of the guards on the standby response force to conduct an immediate evacuation. We had to get everyone out. Now! I grabbed Molly and Toby and told them about my vision. Molly transported Toby and their parents to safety and returned to help as many others as possible, but it was too late. By the time she had returned for another group of people, the bombs had begun to detonate. I pushed her out of the way and shielded her with my body as best as I could when another bomb detonated. She put an air shield around us and kept the debris from collapsing on top of us.

More explosions went off on the other side of the venue, filling it with fire, smoke, and falling debris. There are bodies strewn all over the floor. People are crying, screaming, and running, trying to find a safe exit. All exits are blocked. Everyone is trapped. How did we miss the bombs in our security checks? We had gone over everything with a fine-toothed comb. Someone we trusted in the security detail had to have done this. How else could we have missed this with all of our security measures? Then, I heard it. A scream rang out across the venue. A scream from a voice I recognized— Paisley.

"Where are you, sweetheart?"

"Chad, I'm... near the... ladies' room... at the... far end... of the venue."

"What happened, sweetheart?"

"The ceiling... collapsed. Please, get... out of here."

"I'm not leaving without you. I'm coming for you, sweetheart."

"Molly, It's Paisley! She's hurt! I have to get to her!"

"I don't know if we can, Chad. We don't know if there are any more bombs, or where they're set to detonate. It may not be safe to get to her."

"I have to try, Molly. Please, get yourself out of here. We can't lose you. You're too important to our race. I'll go to Paisley."

"No, I'm not leaving. She may need me to heal her, Chad. If you're going, I'm going with you."

"I'm on my way, my love. Stay with me."

"Chad, please... hurry... I don't... know how much... longer I can... hold on. It hurts... so much."

We ran, dodging falling debris and jumping over piles of bodies and rubble. I sensed her nearby, but couldn't see her. She is hurt. Badly. I reached out to her soul. Then, there she was. Her arm was jutting out from under rubble that had fallen on top of her. We didn't have much time. I was losing her.

"Molly, you have to try to help me get this off of her!"

"I'm trying!"

"Try harder! She's slipping away!"

The debris on top of Paisley started to move. Molly was straining, but she was doing it. She had commanded the air around us to push against the rubble and lift it off of Paisley. I scooped her into my arms and laid her out gently, so Molly could release the debris and heal her. Her body is mangled, and she's lost so much blood. Molly knelt beside her and placed her hands on her.

"Chad, her injuries are quite extensive. I'll do my best, but I'm not sure I have the energy to heal her completely."

"Please, Molly." I cried. "Please, help her. I can't lose her."

Molly's hands began to glow, and then so did Paisley. Her whole body was glowing, while Molly poured her healing energy into her. Paisley's eyelids began to flutter. It was working. I could sense her getting stronger, but by very little.

"Paisley, sweetheart, can you hear me?"

"Yes, my love... I can... hear you, but... I don't... think Molly can... save me... this time."

"Please, hang in there. Don't leave us. I need you. Our son needs you."

Blue sparks surrounded Molly as she began to absorb energy from all around us. She needed more energy to heal Paisley. Paisley weakly squeezed my hand.

"It's not... working... I'm slipping... away, Chad... I'm dying... I'm so... sorry... Tell our son... I love him... I love you, Chad."

"I love you too, Paisley. Don't you dare leave me! Hold on, please, hold on!"

Just like that, her life faded from her frail body. Molly had tried, but couldn't save her. Molly broke down beside me, her body shaking with uncontrollable sobs. Her injuries were too significant to repair. My precious Paisley, my chosen, bonded mate, was gone. I held her lifeless body in my arms, sobbing and screaming.

Chapter 20

Chad

"NO! No, no, no! Oh, God, no!" I screamed and sat up in bed. I am covered in sweat, my whole body is shaking, and I'm hyperventilating. Paisley woke up next to me and placed her hand on my shoulder. I turned and held her in my arms, rocking and sobbing into her hair.

"Shh. It's okay, honey. I'm right here. Everything is okay. It was just a dream."

Nightmares and night terrors are coming more and more frequently. It's always the same nightmare but with more details each time. People are screaming as explosions and fires erupt, and smoke fills the venue. Injured, unconscious, and dead bodies are strewn across the floor. Paisley! Oh, God. My precious Paisley. I can't lose her. I have to protect her and our child. I have to protect everyone. I have got to find a way to keep the nightmare from coming true. I haven't seen enough of it to know what happened or how to prevent it. All I know is that people I love and care about are in danger. I have got to stop this tragedy from occurring. But how?

The Royal Wedding and Commencement Ceremony are scheduled for July fourth and fifth. I need to address the Royal Council. I should brief the Royal Family immediately so that they can call an emergency meeting with their council. I'll need to talk to Dad and Sir Taggart as well. Maybe we can come up with a plan together. I have to figure out a way to keep everyone safe. There just has to be something we can do. I can't let this happen.

I made all of the phone calls and set up an immediate meeting at my house. Molly brought everyone within a matter of minutes. Everyone's nerves are on edge because they all know about my power of perception. I hadn't divulged the details of my nightmares just yet. I am sure it will cause everyone to worry when they learn what I've seen. Everyone took a seat in our living room, and I began the meeting.

"As you all know, I have asked you to come tonight due to a series of dreams I've recently had. While I still can't tell when or where it takes place or how it comes to be, I think you all should be made aware of it. If it were a one-time weird dream, I might not have thought anything of it and dismissed it as such, but the dream has been repeated for the last several nights, giving more and more details each time. I cannot tell if it occurs at the Royal Wedding or the Commencement ceremony. Either way, many people's lives are in grave danger."

The reason I don't suspect that it occurs during the Autumn Equinox or Winter Solstice celebrations is that Paisley had already given birth to our son in all of my dreams. She'd told me to tell him she loved him. I couldn't inform the council about our unborn child because we had decided not to go public with the pregnancy until after the formal wedding ceremony during the Winter Solstice, while we are on Christmas break from school.

"What have you seen so far?" Dad asked.

"I've seen multiple explosions, with fire, smoke, falling debris, people running and screaming, and injured people lying on the floor, unconscious or maybe even dead."

"Where does the location appear to be before the explosion? You mentioned falling debris. What kind of building is it?" Prince Consort Michael asked.

"I couldn't quite make it out. A lot of people were gathered there for some sort of event. Everyone was dressed in formalwear."

"Well, that could have easily been either the Autumn Equinox, Winter Solstice, the Royal wedding, or the Commencement ceremony then." Queen Regent Cecelia said. "Should we make the calls to cancel the celebrations?"

"I'm not so sure just yet. If I can prevent it from happening, we may not have to cancel anything. I just have to figure out who is behind it, when and where it takes place, and why."

"Is there enough time for that? The Autumn Equinox is only days away," Prince Consort Michael said.

"We are not nearly as prepared as we should be," Dad said.

"I think we should cancel the Autumn Equinox Celebration, or at least postpone it until we can be more prepared," Queen Regent Cecelia said.

"Dad, Sir Taggart, have either of you gotten any reports of possible threats or any hostile forces moving into the area?"

"There are a few families in the area, as you know, who call themselves The Liberation Force. They don't exactly agree with the Royal Family or with having a monarchy at all. I suppose they may be planning something, but to our knowledge, they've never hinted to resulting in acts of terrorism or violence."

"Unless... well, never mind," Queen Regent Cecelia said.

"No, what is it, CeCe?" Prince Consort Michael asked. "Anything is worth looking into; even if it may seem insignificant at the time."

"There were reports of those families in the area when my father was killed during the bank robbery. I just wonder if the two are connected, or if it was purely coincidental?"

"There's no way to know for sure, but I do think we should increase our security measures in the meantime," Dad said.

Sir Taggart spoke up and said, "Sir Chadwick's training isn't complete, but he has advanced rather quickly. I think it'd be a great idea for him to be with the Royal Family at all times until we can get a handle on what his premonition means."

"We live right across the lake. Princess Molly can summon me to her in an instant. How are we going to get around the school day? We don't have classes together."

"Let us work that out," Prince Consort Michael said. "You all will more than likely be doing your classwork from home for a while. Your safety is paramount. That goes for all of you, not just for Princess Molly and Prince Tobias."

"The Autumn Equinox Celebration Ball will be postponed in the meantime. We cannot take any chances," Queen Regent Cecelia said.

We all began making plans and sharing ideas on how to prevent my premonitions from coming to fruition. Royal Guard security details flew in from all over the world. I had figured that doubling the security would stop the dreams from occurring, and thus, stop the disaster from happening. Yet, the nightmares still came. Nothing has changed. We are all still in danger. There could always be someone working on the inside, but who? Surely no one in our circle would do such a thing. All of the

Royal Guards will be screened to ensure there are no ulterior motives.

With all of the new security measures in place, we are all well-protected but still on edge. We have no idea who is plotting against the Royal Family, but we have to find out. Too many lives will end if we don't. We got to work on the screening process immediately. Annalise O'Malley, a trusted family friend of the Royal Family from Kilchoman, just happened to be a psychoanalyst. Annalise was the best in her field. Princess Molly and I brought her in once everything was finalized. The interviews and screening process hadn't brought forth anything suspicious so far, but we weren't taking any chances.

Not one Royal Guard member was allowed anywhere near the Royal Family until their interview and screening were complete; they were deemed safe and not a potential risk. The process took weeks to complete, even while working around the clock to screen each guard.

The Autumn Equinox Celebration Ball was finally upon us. Royal Council members, their families, and other Nymphean people came from worldwide to celebrate. Everything was going on without a hitch: no security breaches, no other premonitions, and no weird feelings.

A small orchestra began playing, and couples paired off for the Nymphean Waltz. Ballgowns in an array of colors swirled, twirled, and glided around the Atrium's ballroom. I walked up to my beautiful wife and extended my hand to her.

"May I have this dance, milady?"

"Yes, you may, milord."

She placed her hand in mine. The spark sent tingles through my arm, igniting a fire inside me that burned only for her. I led her onto the ballroom floor to join the other happy couples. I then gathered her into my arms, and we began to glide into the Nymphean Waltz.

"You are a magnificent dancer, sweetheart."

"Thank you, honey. Mama taught me when I was a little girl. She said I'd need to know how to dance when I grew up. For the life of me, I couldn't imagine why I'd need to learn ballroom dancing at the time, but now, I'm glad I did."

"You are quite a vision to behold, Lady Paisley. I'm the luckiest man in the world to have you in my arms."

"I'm even luckier to be the man to take you to his bed."

"I'm the lucky one, my love."

When the dance ended, I escorted Paisley to her seat and kissed her. She became fatigued easily these days, and I didn't want her to overdo it. I did my rounds and found Princess Molly and Prince Tobias. I requested that Dad and Sir Taggart do inner and exterior perimeter checks and asked all guards for their status checks. Each one took their turn reporting that their tasks were completed and that he or she was all secure. Our security measures were holding up at the moment. Everyone is enjoying the festivities and are none the wiser. Only the Royal Family and Royal Council members knew of my premonitions. If others had known, it might have caused a bit of hysteria and anxiety regarding the festivities. It may have prevented them from attending the event at all. After seeing my premonitions, I can't say I would've blamed them, myself. Although I hadn't gotten any weird feelings or more premonitions, I was still a little uneasy about being here with Paisley.

Dad came up to me and reported that all was secure after his perimeter check, as did Taggart. I requested them to do the checks randomly twice an hour. I must ensure that no one has the opportunity to install any explosives or infiltrate the venue. There are Royal Guards at each entrance, spread throughout the venue and around the inner and outer perimeter. No one is getting in without being seen by someone. All avenues of approach are thoroughly covered with 360-degree coverage. As the event continued, I kept my head on a swivel. I can't let my guard down, nor can I afford to. I am staying close to Paisley, Toby, Molly, and the rest of our family members while conducting my security duties as the Leader of the Royal Guard.

Couples are gradually beginning to take their leave as the event's festivities come to an end. Perhaps our increased measures worked in our favor, or maybe this isn't the event from my dream after all. Either way, I am glad that this evening hadn't ended in tragedy. All I want to do is get everyone home safely.

I sent Paisley home with my parents because I still had work to do, and she needed to rest. Once everyone left, the security teams and I swept the venue to ensure it was cleared out. I congratulated the teams for a successful evening, thanked them for their support and loyalty, and released them for the night.

Paisley was waiting up for me when I finally returned home. She had taken her hair down, showered, and is now wearing a soft, cotton pajama set. Her baby bump is hardly noticeable for anyone who doesn't know she is pregnant, but I notice. I have become very familiar with her body and adore that baby bump as much as I do her. I can't help but place my hand on it each time I'm near her. I know it is still too early to feel the baby move, but that isn't why I'm drawn to it. It is because of the love I already have for the baby growing inside—my son. I know it's a boy; not only from my vision but deep inside, I just know.

I drew her into my arms and pressed my lips to hers. Sparks and tingles surged through us. I licked along the crease of her lips, and she parted her beautiful lips for me. Our tongues danced and twirled with one another just as we had on the dance floor earlier in the night. Our connection is undeniable. We know one another on a level so deep and are so in tune with one another that we don't have to ask what the other desires. She knows when "the beast" stirs within me and exactly what it demands. She submits to it and satiates it without question. She craves "the beast" within me as much as it does her. There's no denying her the satisfaction she craves, not that I ever would or even could.

"Make love to me, Chad. I need you. Now."

"Nothing would please me more, my love."

Her hands slid under my tuxedo jacket and slid it over my shoulders. I tossed it onto the back of the oversized chair and removed my bow tie and vest. Paisley immediately started unbuttoning my shirt. Her tanzanite eyes are glowing brightly and burning with her desire for me. My arousal hardened further, straining against my zipper. I removed my shirt and made short work of my trousers and boxer briefs, allowing my hardness to spring free. Paisley trailed kisses down my chest and even lower. God, she will be my undoing.

"You're wearing way too many clothes. Strip for me."

She quickly obeyed, and I laid her on our bed. The scent of her arousal is the most delightful aroma in the world. My mouth watered. I licked my lips and brought them to her sex. Her sweet and tangy flavor of strawberries slid over my tongue. I gently thumbed her sensitive bundle of nerves. Her breathing became ragged as she writhed against me and twirled her fingers through my hair. Colors began to swirl around us as her pleasure began to build.

When her spasms subsided, I crawled over her and plunged deep inside her. Her body welcomed me and squeezed even tighter as I moved. Her fingers trailed up and down my back, and colors continued to swirl around us. Her nails dug into my flesh as her body began to spasm beneath me. I increased my tempo to heighten her pleasure each time I plunged deeper inside her. I held her hands and pressed our palms together as lights flashed within the colorful cyclone spinning around us. I felt my energy blending and mixing with hers. She needed my energy for our baby, and I was more than willing to pour as much as I could into her.

I felt the climax pulse through my whole body as I released inside her. We were both breathing heavily, completely sated with bliss. I pulled her to my side, and she laid her head upon my chest. I lightly caressed her arm as her breathing slowed, and we both fell asleep in each other's arms.

Chapter 21

Paisley

The Autumn Equinox Celebration Ball was a great success. Everyone seemed to enjoy themselves, and there was no terrorist activity. Thank goodness. Chad is still on edge about the upcoming celebrations, but with as much time as we have to prepare, we should be able to figure out what needs to be done to prevent his premonitions from coming true.

The Royal Guard's training regimens have gotten so much more rigorous than they were before. It's even expanded to encompass multidimensional security. There are bomb detection teams, emergency response force teams, undercover secret service teams, K-9 handlers, IT gurus, and weapons specialists. Chad has been learning each role and getting to know each unit so that he knows every single team member. As their leader, they need to know and trust him as much as he needs to know and trust them.

He comes home late each night from his daily activities and still has to keep up with his schoolwork. I know "the beast" inside of him helps him keep going. It's driving him onward when he feels like giving up, but even "the beast" has its limits. I make sure that I nap when I can, after I do my homework, to help him with his as much as possible when he comes home. Not to mention, I want to be rested enough to share my energy with him when we make love.

My next appointment with Dr. Addison is this afternoon. We should be able to officially find out the baby's sex. We feel that it's a boy, but the blood test will determine if our suspicions are correct. Molly wanted to be the one to get the results and throw us a gender reveal party, but we have decided that we'd like to be the first to know. We'll still throw a gender reveal party for our family members and friends. If it is a boy, we've decided to name him Sylar Austin Greene, after Toby's and Max's middle names. We haven't even talked about girl names because we just have that strong of a hunch that it's a boy.

We've been able to conceal my pregnancy from everyone outside of our family and close friends, but it hasn't been easy with as bad as my morning sickness has been. I'm worried that the baby isn't getting enough nutrients. I've started drinking protein shakes and eating fresh fruit after my stomach settles, but some things still turn my stomach. Just the smell of some foods is enough to turn me into a puking mess. If my morning sickness gets any worse, I may have to have an IV put in my arm to get fluids into my body. Dr. Addison said that would be the next step. I want our baby to be healthy, so I'm willing to do anything to ensure he gets what he needs.

We arrived at Dr. Addison's office a few minutes early. Dr. Addison said her last appointment was canceled. So, she had time to do another ultrasound for us to see our baby. She confirmed that we both are healthy, and our baby is growing strong; despite my morning sickness and the inability to keep much of anything down. The blood test confirmed our suspicions were correct. We are having a boy! We are so happy! Now, we just have to start the search for his chosen mate. We still have plenty of time, but I don't know where to start. Is there some kind of secret group that Nymphean women join when they get pregnant so that they can get together? I'll have to ask Mama and Shannon. I'm sure they'll know something. They found all of their children's chosen mates, after all.

Chad is such an attentive husband and father-to-be. He takes such great care of me. He always makes sure there are crackers and a bottle of water near the bed to help lessen my morning sickness. He also holds my hair back when I do get sick, gets me a cold washcloth and a bottle of water, and prepares my toothbrush so that I can brush my teeth afterward. He is even more protective over me now than ever before. I'm sure "the beast" inside of him has a little bit to do with that as well as the baby growing inside of me. He's even growled at a few of his family members a time or two. He is always asking if I'm okay, if I need anything, and volunteering to do things to keep me from overdoing it. I'm worried that he's overdoing it too.

We are all still doing our schoolwork from home and may continue to do so throughout the remainder of the school year. Chad, Max, and Toby are still going to football practice and football games, Angie is still going to cheerleading practices and cheering at the games, and all of our younger siblings are still able to do the same with their sports activities. We have disguised security details with us everywhere we go. Chad is almost always on duty. His earpiece and radio are never too far away. He says he has to be ready for anything at any given moment.

They've gotten word that The Liberation Force has been watching Molly and Toby a bit more closely. The Royal Guard has built profiles on the vast majority of its members and has been tracking their activities. They haven't tried anything just yet, but it's only a matter of time before they do. They have been holding gatherings and private meetings. Chad says he and his Royal Guards will be ready for them. I hope it doesn't come to that, but I'm glad they are prepared in case it does.

The Winter Solstice Celebration Ball is just around the corner. Our wedding planning is still well underway. I'm so excited! Our wedding will be the opening event for the ball! Molly will be my maid of honor, and Angie and Tabby have agreed to be my bridesmaids. Toby is Chad's best man, and Max is his groomsman. Caden is the ring bearer, and Max's little sister, Alyssia, is the flower girl. Molly, Angie, Tabby, and Alyssia will be wearing different dresses, but in the same shade of rose gold. That way, the girls can pick their favorite style that works best with their body type. So, they'll be able to wear their dresses for another occasion someday, instead of having them wasting away in their closets. Mama and Shannon picked out their dresses too. Their dresses are the same color as the other girls. All of the girls picked dresses that look less like bridesmaid dresses and more like evening gowns. The wedding is to be held right before a ball, after all. Everyone is going to look spectacular!

My dress is a soft, A-line style, with a sweetheart neckline and white lace over blush-colored satin. The back has multiple spaghetti straps that criss-cross on my upper back and corset strings at my lower back that will accommodate my figure if my baby bump is showing more by then. It was the first dress I tried on. I tried on a few others to see how different styles fit, but my mind kept going back to that one. I knew the moment I slipped it on that it was "the one" because my eyes filled with tears of joy. All of the girls had tears streaming down their faces too.

Our wedding and the Winter Solstice Celebration Ball will be held at a mountain resort in Sevierville, Tennessee. The whole resort has been reserved to accommodate the guests in attendance. Chad has been taking trips there periodically with Molly, Toby, and the Royal Guards to conduct training. They have been surveying the area to ensure they know all escape routes and avenues of approach. I know the event must be adequately secured, but I hope Chad will enjoy our wedding as well. His nightmares have returned. He hasn't wanted to talk about them, and I'm beginning to worry.

One of Chad's observation teams set up outside of The Liberation Force's meeting locations. They set up listening devices and recorded the meeting. They stayed in place long enough for all of the members to leave, so their cover wouldn't be blown. Chad received the call that they were all clear and needed to rendezvous with him to pass on the information they received. They said it was urgent and that a meeting needed to be called immediately. He placed a call to Molly and Toby to begin transporting every one of importance to a safe house in Kilchoman. We were all there together in a matter of minutes.

Chad played the recording on a speaker system so all could hear it. The Liberation Force's leader began the meeting, and its officers each reported their findings. A plan had begun to assault us during the Winter Solstice Celebration Ball. They have acquired enough explosives, guns, and ammunition to wipe the whole resort off of the map. The council members voted unanimously to move the celebration to another location and keep it under wraps until just before the event. This may be enough to prevent The Liberation Force from attacking. If not, we will need to be prepared to fight.

The Winter Solstice Celebration Ball will be held within the original Nymphean Kingdom in Kilchoman. Molly has agreed to travel there and use her powers to help resurrect and restore the kingdom. The Ancient Texts hold the power to protect its entrance once again. The Liberation Force members are Nymphean, which would mean they'd be able to enter under the old spell, but Molly has stumbled upon an even more potent spell. This spell will detect one's intentions and deny entry if they intend to cause harm.

The first day we transported to the kingdom was a total culture shock for me. Molly used her power to light the sconces, lights, and torches around the kingdom. My skin erupted in goose flesh the instant I looked around inside of the vast emptiness. Witnessing the destruction the kingdom had faced all those years ago was soul-shattering. I nearly wept for the many Nymphs that lost their lives on that terrible day. Their bodies are long gone, but their presence can still be felt within the kingdom's walls. If you listen, you can almost hear their screams, the clashing of swords, and the swoosh of arrows flying through the air.

"Are you all right, Paisley?" Molly asked.

"Yeah, I'm all right. I can feel them. They're all still here."

"Yes, I feel them too. Their energy is still here, all around us. They fought bravely so that our future generations could live on. They will never be forgotten and will live on as heroes in our history."

"I can only imagine what they went through. The horrors they faced and the pain they suffered."

"It was a great loss, indeed. We will prove ourselves to be worthy of their sacrifices and make this kingdom whole again. It will be safe for all Nymphs who come here."

"Do you think we will ever move back into the kingdom?"

"It's a possibility. If the kingdom proves to be the safest option for our people to thrive, then that option will be forwarded to our people. It is up to them to decide if they'd like to move here. We can do our best to modernize it and bring in the technology it needs to compete with the modern world."

"What about you and Toby? Will you be moving here?"

"If our people inhabit the kingdom, it will need the Queen and Prince Consort here with them."

"So, that means Chad and I will need to be here too, since Chad is the Leader of the Royal Guard and your personal guard, right?"

"Technically, yes, but if the protection spell works, we'd be safe here either way. I'd be able to summon you and Chad to me if needed. You and your families are more than welcome to live here if you choose. If you want to remain outside of the kingdom, you can. That decision would be for you and your families to make."

"Thank you, Molly. I appreciate that. I'll talk it over with Chad and our families. We may take you up on the offer to move here. I want our families to be safe. I can't stand to think of our children being in danger."

"I agree. Toby and I will be having a family of our own someday too."

"You are going to make a fantastic Queen to our people, Molly. I know I can't do much to help in my delicate predicament, but I'd like to help as much as I can."

"Well, let's get down to it, shall we?"

Since then, Molly, Toby, Chad, myself, all of our friends, and security details, of course, transport to the kingdom in Kilchoman every day to begin the restoration. Molly has also cast a spell on the entrance to ensure we are safe. There's no way to know if the magic is intact, though, because we all have pure intentions here. All we can do right now is continue readying the kingdom for the celebration and hope for the best.

Chad's IT team has been hard at work, incorporating state of the art technology into the kingdom. The walls are lined with thousands of doors to residences. There are tunnels throughout, leading to more homes, a marketplace, and a huge banquet hall. The throne room is large enough to be a ballroom itself, but the formal ballroom is located just off the banquet hall.

The majority of the residences won't be ready for occupants to move into before the Winter Solstice. Still, quite a few of them may be prepared by the time Molly and Toby's wedding and commencement ceremonies come. They may need to be used as hotel rooms for the guests. A few of them have been restored, though. Those few residences have been reserved for the Royal Family, our family, and all of our close friends and their families. The Royal Guards also have their quarters restored so they can keep us all safe. Chad and his guards have also repaired the war room and security headquarters near the Royal Family's residence tunnel.

The kingdom will be breathtaking for the Winter Solstice Celebration Ball. Our wedding decorations have been brought here little-by-little each trip. The ballroom and banquet hall look amazing! I'm so excited! Our residence has been fully restored and furnished. We will be staying there for our wedding night and honeymoon.

The decorating is done, and guests have been transported from all over the world. My family is with me in my quarters, along with Molly, my maid of honor, and my bridesmaids and flower girl. We are all primping together for the big day.

It's time to begin. The guests have taken their seats. Chad, his best man, and his groomsmen are all in place. The music is starting to play. Daddy is waiting for me outside of the wedding suite. He's ready to walk me down the aisle and give me away. Tears fill both of our eyes as I open the door and take his arm. He spun me around to get a good look at me.

"Lady Paisley, sweetheart, you are an absolutely stunning bride. Sir Chadwick is a fortunate man."

"Thank you, Daddy. Our baby and I are lucky to have him too."

"As much as I wish you two would've waited to bond and start a family until now, I'm excited about meeting my grandson."

"We can't wait to meet him either. I'm nervous about finding his chosen mate, though. Where do I even start?"

"I'll admit, we had it pretty easy when we found yours and Caden's mates. I'm sure you and Chad will find your son's chosen mate in due time. We can talk about that later. There are a lot of people waiting on us out there, kiddo. Are you ready?"

"Yes, let's do this. Thanks, Dad."

All of the girls lined up and began making their way, one-by-one down the aisle, taking their places at the front of the ballroom. The flower girl and ring bearer walked in just ahead of Daddy and me. The wedding march began, and we made our entrance. Chad's eyes linked with mine, and he sent me a message mind-to-mind.

"Sweetheart, you are breathtakingly beautiful."

"Thank you, my love. You're mighty handsome yourself."

"We are gathered here today to unite Lady Paisley Rose O'Riley and Sir Chadwick Owen Greene. Who gives this woman to this man?"

"I, Sir Taggart O'Riley, and her mother, Lady Fiona O'Riley, do."

The priest continued with the traditional Nymphean wedding ceremony as Chad took my hand in his and gazed into my eyes. We recited our vows to one another as we had at our first wedding ceremony.

"I, Sir Chadwick Owen Greene, in the name of the spirit of God that resides within us all, by the life that courses within my blood and the love that resides within my heart, take thee Lady Paisley Rose O'Riley, to my hand, my heart, and my soul, to be my chosen one. To desire thee and be desired by thee, to possess thee, and be possessed by thee, without sin nor shame, for naught can exist in the purity of my love for thee. I promise to love thee wholly and completely without restraint, in sickness, and in health, in plenty and in poverty, in life and beyond, where we shall meet, remember, and love again. I shall not seek to change thee in any way. I shall respect thee, thy beliefs, thy people, and thy ways as I respect myself. I pledge my eternity to you."

"I, Lady Paisley Rose O'Riley, in the name of the spirit of God that resides within us all, by the life that courses within my blood, and the love that resides within my heart, take thee, Sir Chadwick Owen Greene, to my hand, my heart, and my soul to be my chosen one. To desire and be desired by thee, to possess thee, and be possessed by thee, without sin nor shame, for naught can exist in the purity of my love for thee. I promise to love thee wholly and completely without restraint, in sickness, and in health, in plenty and in poverty, in life and beyond, where we shall meet, remember, and love again. I shall not seek to change thee in any way. I shall respect thee, thy beliefs, thy people, and thy ways as I respect myself. I pledge my eternity to you."

Caden handed our rings to the priest, and he began the ring ceremony. The priest then gave us the rings for us to place on one another's fingers.

Chad removed my engagement ring, placed my wedding ring on my finger, and stated, "With this ring, I thee wed. My eternity belongs to you." He then replaced my engagement ring, where it fit together with my wedding ring once again.

I then placed Chad's ring on his finger and stated, "With this ring, I thee wed. My eternity belongs to you."

The priest then said, "By the powers vested in me, I now pronounce you husband and wife. Sir Chadwick, you may now kiss your bride."

Chad took me into his arms and kissed me once tenderly and then again so passionately that I felt lightheaded afterward. All of the wedding guests seemed to disappear. It felt as though we were the only two people in the room. My dream wedding had finally come true. I was wrapped in the arms of my soulmate, my chosen, bonded mate, Chadwick Owen Greene. Our baby is growing in my womb as we speak, and we will be beginning our life together here in the original Nymphean Kingdom. How much more perfect could our lives be?

A few throats cleared behind Chad. I suppose our kiss had gone on a bit longer than we realized. We broke the kiss, and everyone laughed.

The priest spoke up once again and said, "It is my honor to present to you, Sir Chadwick Owen Greene and Lady Paisley O'Riley Greene."

The crowd erupted in applause, whistles, and cheers of congratulations as we hurried down the aisle to the banquet hall. We took our places at the entry doors to receive all of our guests as they filed in. Molly, Toby, the Queen Regent, and the Prince Consort joined us. Once everyone had taken their seats at their tables, the Queen Regent and Prince Consort took the stage to welcome everyone to the wedding reception and Winter Solstice Celebration Ball.

"Prince Consort Michael and I would love to thank you all for joining us this evening for the wedding of Sir Chadwick and Lady Paisley. It is both my pleasure and an honor to announce the happy couple for their first dance. Sir Chadwick and Lady Paisley, the floor is yours."

The orchestra began playing the Traditional Nymphean Waltz, and we glided together in the space that was left open for a dance floor. Once our dance was over, everyone stood and applauded us, and we took our seats. The Queen Regent took the stage once again.

"Thank you for your beautiful and graceful representation of the Traditional Nymphean Waltz. The Traditional Nymphean Waltz has been the first dance of chosen mates since its creation. You two are beautifully matched and will no doubt share an even more beautiful eternity. Prince Consort Michael and I wish you an eternity of love and happiness. Please join us all in congratulations to the happy couple and in celebration of the Winter Solstice Celebration Ball."

The meals were brought in and served to each guest. Then, the wait staff joined us all in the celebration. Everyone thoroughly enjoyed their meals. It was now time for us to cut the cake. We both took hold of the knife and cut a slice from the cake. We each took a small piece of it and fed it to one another. No, we didn't smash it into each other's faces. We had that discussion beforehand. This was neither the time nor the place for such a thing. We agreed to do so once we'd changed out of our elegant wedding clothes and were all alone.

One of the caterers took over and sliced the cake for the wait staff to pass around to all of the guests. After the cake, the ball was underway. The guests were dressed in ball gowns and tuxedos. Each gentleman's tuxedo had matching colored vests and ties to match their ladies' gowns. The orchestra played an array of music, and couples whirled and twirled around and around the ballroom floor. There were other noble couples there, who were also expecting parents. Four of them were expecting female babies. One of them could very well be our baby's chosen mate. We changed out of our wedding attire and into something more comfortable. The four couples expecting female babies met with us in our private residence after the ball.

Sir Glenn McLeod and his wife, Lady Yasmine McLeod of the Dalriadan clan of Scotland, were the first to try. Lady Yasmine and I exposed our bellies and stepped close to one another until our bellies touched. We held hands and waited for our babies to reach out to one another. I felt my baby stir within my womb. His tiny little hand pressed against my belly. There was no spark. Our babies aren't chosen mates, after all. We thanked them for trying and bid them a good night and a safe trip home.

The next couple was Lord Vincent Carlisle and Lady Hailey Carlisle of the city of Carlisle in the county of Cumberland, Scotland. Lady Hailey and I repeated the process, but still no spark. Chad and I thanked them as well and bid them safe travels.

The third couple to try was Lord Patrik Murphy and Lady Lora Murphy of Leinster, Ireland. Lady Lora and I bared our bellies and tried yet again to establish a connection between our unborn son and their unborn daughter. Again, there was no spark felt. We had one couple left to try.

The fourth and final couple at the Winter Solstice Celebration Ball was Duke William Lismore and Duchess Leona Lismore of the Isle of Islay, Scotland. Duchess Leona and I bared our bellies, stepped closer and closer until our bellies touched. We held hands and waited for our little ones to reach out to one another. I felt my son's hand press against my stomach yet again. I closed my eyes and prayed that this is his chosen mate. My prayer was answered with a spark. It was as strong as the spark that Chad and I feel when we touch. We all hugged one another and exchanged our contact information. It's a good thing that Chad and I would be moving here to the original Nymphean Kingdom in Kilchoman, on the Isle of Islay. They also agreed to move into the kingdom once it was ready to be inhabited. We decided to allow our children to grow up together instead of waiting until later to reunite. We bid them good night and wished them a safe trip home. They didn't have far to go, but we still wished them well. Our families will be joined someday, after all. Chad and I are looking forward to getting to know them and their daughter.

It was such a magical night. We didn't want it to end, but then again, we were ready to begin our official honeymoon. Molly was improving her transportation skills and could travel with more people than before. She had already started taking everyone home. Our close family and friends were still lingering around. We were bursting at the seams to tell them we'd found our son's chosen mate. Everyone wanted to know who she is and where she is from, but we had elected to keep that information solely between us.

Molly took Max and his family home first. They had an early morning at the ranch and needed to get going. She returned and transported Angelina and her parents, as well as her own family home. When she returned, she was frantic and had her family with her once again.

"We have to stay here!" She screamed. "Our homes are gone! They're up in flames! There's nothing left!"

"What? What do you mean?"

"Chad's home and ours are both in flames! Someone set them on fire while we were celebrating here. I have to go and get Max and his family and make sure they're still safe."

Toby and Chad both spoke up at the same time. "I'm coming with you."

"I can only take one of you since Max's family is coming back with me," she said.

"Chad, you go with her," Toby said. "Your training is far more advanced. Protect her and get back here safely."

"I fully intend to."

"Let's go. There's no time to waste."

Chad

We arrived at Max's ranch amid a battle. The Liberation Force was trying to set everything ablaze while Max's family was fighting for their lives. I immediately went into action and lunged for the attacker that was fighting Max. Molly went to work using her powers to put out the existing flames with water. One of the attackers started running towards her. I knocked out Max's attacker and broadsided the one heading for Molly. I took him off of his feet. The air was knocked out of him on impact. He laid there gasping for air. I put him in the sleeper move, and he was out of the fight for a while.

Another blaze started in the barn. The horses were trapped inside. Their panic was evident. Their cries could be heard all over the ranch. Molly focused her energy toward them and quickly put out that fire. Max's mom, Jessica, was on the ground fighting off an attacker of her own. Max came up behind him and pulled him off of her. He then threw the guy against a tree. The sound of the man's bones snapping crackled in my ears. He was not getting up anytime soon. Max's dad was fighting off two other attackers, while two more were stalking toward his siblings, Thomas and Alyssia. Max and I rushed them first and took them out of the fight. We sent Thomas and Alyssia to Molly. She'll be able to protect them with her powers better than we can at the moment. We then went to help Jason, Max's dad. He was holding his own but was tiring out from fighting off his two attackers. Max and I joined him in the fight, and the last two attackers went down. The damage was done before the battle was over. Their family home was burned beyond repair, and their barn was charred, and the animals were severely injured. Molly went to work, healing them the best she could. Once the animals were treated, we apprehended the attackers and called the sheriff's department and the fire department. Fire trucks came to finish putting out the flames, and the attackers were taken to the county jail.

Molly was crying and holding Max's siblings close to her. The destruction that she'd seen tonight was too much to bear. Max's family farm was gone. Her family's home was gone. The house that she and Toby were having built was even burned down. There was nothing left. She looked at me with fear and sadness in her eyes.

"Chad, we have to go and get Angie and her family. I took them home too. I can't get Angie on her phone. We have to go now. I can't leave Max's family here. They aren't safe here anymore. None of us are."

"Take them back to the kingdom. Max and I will stay here and wait for you to return. The animals will need to be taken to the kingdom as well. Thank goodness you can get there and back in a matter of seconds. The sooner, the better."

Molly took Max's mother and siblings to the kingdom. Jason stayed behind with us, so he could help out if there was indeed trouble at the Simpson's place too. Molly returned a moment later and gathered up as many animals as she could. It took a few trips to get them all, but once they were all safely transported to the kingdom, she transported us to Angie's home.

The scene there wasn't much better than the one at the Brody's ranch. The house was on fire, Angie was being held at gunpoint. Her father was fighting off two attackers; her mother was fighting another one as best as she could but wasn't doing well.

Molly called upon the water element to extinguish the flames while Max, Jason, and I split up to help Angie and her family. I rushed to the attacker beating on Deirdre, Angie's mother. Jason went to help her father, Andrew. Deirdre's attacker knocked her out and came for me. He drew a knife and lunged for my throat. I ducked out of its way, but he slashed my arm. The cut wasn't very deep but hurt like hell. "The beast" inside of me surged with anger. I charged him and knocked the knife from his hand. He reached for it again, but I grabbed it instead and hurled it into his chest. He fell to his knees and then onto his face.

I ran to Jason and Andrew's aid. We teamed up on the attackers but still had one helluva fight on our hands. These guys were highly trained and weren't holding any punches. They got in quite a few good hits on us. Andrew was knocked out cold. His attacker left our fight and rushed toward Molly. That was his last mistake. Molly lifted him into the air and hurled him into the trunk of a large oak tree. His head split open, and he sank to the ground.

I looked around for Angie. Max was fighting off her attacker, but she was nowhere to be seen. She must have run to hide. I rejoined Jason and took out his attacker. Then, I helped Max finish off his. Max wasn't even tired. His adrenaline was rushing tenfold. We called the fire and the sheriff's departments. They came out and took charge of the situation once again. We gave them our statements but still did not see Angie. Angie's parents were taken to the kingdom first. Molly returned to help us look for her. Max was the first to notice that Angie's car was missing from the driveway. He ran into the remains of Angie's partially burned home and found a set of keys. He quickly unlocked the vehicle, the keys opened, and jumped inside.

"I have to find her, Chad. I'll call you as soon as I find her. You and Molly should get back to the kingdom where it's safe."

"Are you sure you don't want us to come with you?"

"Yes, I'm sure. You both are far too important to lose. Now, go!"

Max backed out of the driveway and drove off in search of Angie. Molly and I reluctantly headed back to the kingdom to rejoin our families.

Our families and friends back at the kingdom were shaken up, distraught, angry, and saddened for everything that had been lost. We'd tried to reach Max and Angie on their cell phones, but neither had answered. We were all plagued with worry for our friends' safety. It wasn't long before Molly's cell phone rang. It was Max. He'd found Angie, but she was in bad shape. Molly popped to their location and brought them back to the kingdom. Molly and her dad quickly began checking over her and assessing her injuries. Her body should be healing on its own, but it isn't. Something is preventing her body from healing itself. Molly tried to heal her, but it was no use. Nothing seemed to help. Angie was slipping away, and there seemed to be nothing we could do.

Acknowledgments

I would like to thank my husband for supporting me in everything I set out to do. I couldn't have done this without you. You are my rock, my best friend, my everything. Thank you, Mama, for encouraging me to become a writer. You have always been my cheerleader, pushing me to reach for my dreams and make them a reality. Thank you, Daddy, for being my voice of reason, and keeping my feet on the ground while my head was in the clouds. To my stepmom for being my daily dose of silliness to remind me to laugh and not take myself so seriously. Thank you to my sister and sister-in-law, for both being my second and third set of eyes and my advisors. Thank you also to my father-in-law and my mother-in-law for your love and support through thick and thin.

I'd also like to extend my thanks and gratitude to some of my favorite establishments in North Carolina for everything you do for all of your customers, making us all feel welcome. I may not have named them all, but to those mentioned or referenced herein, I thank you for having an impact on my life and the lives of my characters.

About the Author

Larrah Thomas grew up in a small town in North Carolina. She loves spending time with her husband, her family, and two cats. She also enjoys baking, going to a local small arms range to shoot various firearms, and she is also a saltwater hobbyist. Her passion for writing began in her youth, while writing poems, songs, and short stories. She enjoys reading other authors' work as well as writing her own. She loves to travel all over the world, but she is especially enticed by the romanticism of small towns and the people who live there.

If you enjoyed this book, be sure to check out The Liberation Force - A Chosen Novella of the Chosen Saga, coming soon! Follow her on Facebook www.facebook.com/LarrahThomasBooks, on Instagram https://www.instagram.com/larrah_thomas/, Twitter https://twitter.com/LarrahThomas, LinkedIn https://www.linkedin.com/in/larrah-thomas-8a07b41a9, and via https://www.larrahthomas.com for its release, as well as the others to come!

Works by Larrah Thomas:
Chosen Saga
Chosen: Book One of the Chosen Saga
Chad's Choice: Book Two of the Chosen Saga

Coming Soon:
The Liberation Force: A Chosen Novella
Chosen Angel: Book Three of the Chosen Saga

Hope Memorial Saga
Avery's Destiny: Book One of the Hope Memorial Saga

Once Bitten Saga
Once Bitten: Book One of the Once Bitten Saga